I0618705

The Place I Belong

Country Roads Series: Book Five

Grea Warner

The characters and events in this book are fictitious. Any similarity to real persons, living or dead, places, or events is coincidental and not intended by the author.

If you purchase this book without a cover you should be aware that this book may have been stolen property and reported as "unsold and destroyed" to the publisher. In such case the author has not received any payment for this "stripped book."

The Place I Belong
Copyright © 2019 Grea Warner
All rights reserved.

ISBN: (ebook): 978-1-949931-07-5
(print): 978-1-949931-06-8

Inkspell Publishing
5764 Woodbine Ave.
Pinckney, MI 48169

Edited by Jessica Martinez
Cover art by Najla Qamber

This book, or parts thereof, may not be reproduced in any form without permission. The copying, scanning, uploading, and distribution of this book via the internet or via any other means without the permission of the publisher is illegal and punishable by law. Please purchase only authorized electronic or print editions, and do not participate in or encourage piracy of copyrighted materials. Your support of the author's rights is appreciated.

OTHER BOOKS BY GREA WARNER

All My Memories in Can't Buy Me Love
Boxset

Country Roads

Almost Heaven

Take Me Home

Teardrop in My Eye

Every Mile, A Memory (coming soon)

GREA WARNER

DEDICATION

For the Inkspell Publishing team who have helped transform my words on a home computer screen into beautiful books for others to enjoy. A special thanks to Melissa Keir for being a true champion of the COUNTRY ROADS series from the very beginning.

And, for my family. Because of you, I never have to doubt that I have a place where I belong.

GREA WARNER

CHAPTER ONE

A phone call in the wee hours of the morning— before the sun would dare begin to rise or the birds begin to chirp— is never a good thing. Through the darkness of the master bedroom, illuminated only by the bubbling, ebb and flow of our red lava lamp, I tried to adjust my eyes and then my ears to pinpoint whose phone it was. Of course, it was my husband's. Finn's cell seemed to beep more than the rush hour taxis in nearby Manhattan. But the ringtone was the one he had assigned to his parents, and the unusual time, combined with my father-in-law's declining health, was troublesome.

"Finn," I spoke softly in the otherwise stillness of the room. "Finn, baby, wake up…your phone."

On my voice, he opened his natural gray eyes to meet mine. A quick but undeniable glimmer of recognition flitted in them. It was a mixture of a tiny bit of shock and a whole ton of happiness. I knew he was thinking of the night before and the fact that I was not only in bed with him but that we had made love. Despite the tumultuous weeks of pain and mistrust, we had landed back where we belonged. It was because of our core… because of the solid, forever love between us.

Finn leaned over and kissed me quickly, but with adoration, before reaching to his nightstand and his phone. "Hello?" he answered. "Mom, it's all right. What? What's going on?" The silk bedsheet fell a little further down to his waist as he sat up straighter. "Yeah, of course. She's right here with me."

Finn turned his arm slightly and reached for my hand. I took it, thinking how glad I was that his parents had not been wise to our arguing and mini-separation. It was a moot point now and definitely a stressor that my in-laws didn't need, especially since learning of Finn's father's terminal cancer diagnosis. Keeping my one hand entwined with my husband's, I wrapped the other around his body and onto his well-defined abs. As he continued to talk with his mother, I leaned my chest and head onto Finn's bare back. I wanted to cocoon him with me because, undoubtedly, he was going to need my comfort and support.

When he said "love you" as a conversation conclusion to his mother, I pulled away slightly, tapped him on his shoulder, and nodded once. Recognizing my intention, Finn verbally relayed my message. "Lara sends her love, too." After a slight pause, Finn said goodbye to his mom and placed his phone back on his nightstand.

"Everything okay?" I asked.

In lieu of an answer, I saw his eyes openly scan my bare upper body. He then turned and seemed to search for something on the floor. When he sat back up, the green, button-down shirt he had been wearing the night before was in his hands. He paused for another moment and then handed it to me. "Here. Put this on. I can't look at you like that and not want to do something about it. But I should tell you what my mom said first."

I smiled, feeling his love and desire but knowing he needed my listening skills the most right then. "Better?" I asked, after I buttoned his shirt across my bosom.

"No," he admitted. "But thanks."

2

"What's going on?" I placed my hand on his.

"She says Pop is up all hours of the night doing all these little things around the house—fixing things, doing paperwork—and he's always with her. This was the only time she could call without him knowing because he's asleep."

"It's like he's nesting," I said sadly. On Finn's puzzlement, I further explained. "He's getting his things in order." What had been only the faintest of smiles drooped on my husband's face, making me acknowledge his pain. "I'm sorry."

"Yeah." His shoulders slumped before continuing. "So, mom wants to have a surprise birthday party for him and wants to make sure we can come down...and Nola and Will and Kelsea." He spoke of his only sibling, as well as her husband and their nine-year-old daughter.

"You told her yes, right?" I said, grateful that the phone conversation wasn't about anything worse than a surprise party.

"I wanted to make sure it was all right with you." He rubbed my hand with his fingers, which were still slightly calloused from playing the guitar on tour all summer.

"Yeah, sure, it's fine," I replied. "Why wouldn't it be?"

"Well, she knows he'll be against it. He never wants a big fuss for his birthday. So, she was wondering if we could disguise it as Arinn's party since her birthday is only a few days after his—have them both together at their place."

Ah, yes. Our baby daughter would be turning one in just about a month's time. "I know this is probably bad, but I haven't given any thought to Arinn's birthday."

"We've been a little preoccupied," he acknowledged, in a regretful tone.

"Yeah," I admitted, but refused to let either of us think any more about it. "Plus, the CMAs are that week."

"She's more important than an awards ceremony."

"Finn, I know. But the CMAs are important for your

career…for you."

For a country music singer like my husband, the Country Music Awards were the epitome of success and one that Finn had reigned over for many years. "Lara—"

I immediately interrupted. "That's just not a good week to celebrate her birthday. We *could* celebrate it with your dad's, but my mom and brother are going to want to be a part of her birthday, too. And your mom really doesn't want all those people at their house. *And* you're going to need your time to focus."

The burst of air from his lips displayed his frustration even before he said, "Shit, what then?"

It was my turn to rub the top of his hand. "Let me think." Luckily, an idea came quickly. "Why don't we celebrate Arinn's birthday at Thanksgiving? The CMAs will be out of the way, and you might have a little breathing room." As if Finn ever had any down time, I silently thought. "We can have the whole family again at our place."

"But that's not her birthday!"

"It's only a couple weeks or so after," I tried to rationalize. "Plus, she's going to be one. She has no idea when her birthday is. You and Chance and I can do something on the actual day. That way your dad, Arinn, the CMAs…they all get their own moment."

"Chance will absolutely want to do something on the actual day. For a three-year-old, he sure knows his calendar and plans."

I laughed. Our firstborn, who was nearly the spitting image of his daddy, could be Finn's road manager in no time. He had learned a lot of those skills over the summer having countdowns to when Finn would return from tour.

"I guess that's the best solution." Finn broke back into my thoughts. "I'll just tell Mom that we're coming. Pop will have his own party, and he'll just have to deal with a little fuss."

"He deserves it." I spoke honestly.

Zak Murphy was the type of father I had always dreamed of growing up. He was caring, understanding, loving. In essence, he was the polar opposite of the man I had called dad.

Finn reclined his body to a more horizontal position and gently dragged my head down to his chest. After a moment or two of us being lost in our own, but most likely similar, thoughts, he softly called out, "Lar?"

"Yeah?" I replied without moving.

But all he said was, "No, never mind. It's…we're not ready. It's too soon."

I readjusted myself so that I was propped up on my elbow. I wanted to look at him, and I needed him to see me…to understand the truth in my words. "Hey, we're good. What we talked about last night and shared? We're good." I thoroughly believed it, and I needed Finn to, also.

He met my eyes and traced his index finger along my cheek before resting it on the center of my lips. "Being with you and knowing that you have somehow found a way to forgive me, it was one of the best nights of my life."

Feeling like we were more in sync again, I let out a happy sigh and leaned back onto his taut chest. "Then tell me."

He started playing with the long strands of my hair, which was starting to fade back to its natural dark strawberry blonde after I had dyed it platinum over the summer. "I know we talked about this, but it's been a little while, and you might not still think—"

"Yeah. I think we should."

"You don't even know what I was going to say." Had our conversation not been so serious, I'm sure he would have chuckled.

I returned to my partially propped-up position. "You want us to move permanently to Nashville."

"Yeah." He curled his brows at my intuition. "I'll be closer to them." He was obviously referring to his parents, who still resided in their hometown of Louisville, Kentucky. "It'll just be a couple hours' drive or so. I think—"

"Yes, Finn. We should. I think your dad would really like that, especially because he'll know you'll be close by for your mom." I hated talking like that, but it was the reality of the situation. "And it's time," I continued. "You should be in Nashville for your career. You should have always been there. You sacrificed a lot to be here in New York for me."

"It's not a sacrifice." No matter what, he would always maintain that.

"It...okay. I'm not working anymore, and I...I just...I agree. I already agreed before. That hasn't changed. I think it will be a great fresh start."

"I love you. And I will not let you down again, Lara. I won't." His eyes bounced back and forth—our emotions equally on full tilt.

"I know," I declared confidently. "I know you won't let that happen...and neither will I."

It would absolutely destroy both of us if we were to experience the same circumstances we had just recovered from. Without saying it out loud, we both knew there could not be another chance. Our serious tone was flipped when the sounds of Arinn's whimpering gave me the perfect, sarcastic way to respond. "Well, there's your opportunity not to let me down. You be the one to see what's wrong with her."

Finn grumbled at the bedside baby monitor, but I knew he loved our kids more than life itself and would do anything for them. A walk up the stairs, a little pat on the back, and some soothing words were nothing. He pecked me on the lips and started to slide out of bed. I watched as he strung his lean legs into his boxer briefs and began to exit our first-floor master bedroom.

"Finn?" I called out as he approached the doorway.

"Yeah?"

"I love you, too."

He strode back toward me. Kneeling on the bed, he flanked his hands on my cheeks and sucked in a powerful kiss that portrayed his gratitude, passion, and commitment. "Don't move."

"I wouldn't dream of it, Cowboy," I reassured, letting my head flop back down onto the comforts of the silky pillow.

***

"You know," I said, while watching the kids enjoy frozen yogurt much later that day. "There is still one thing we haven't settled."

Sitting next to Arinn's high chair, my husband swiveled around to look at me. Worry was sketched across his face. "What?"

Finn made a point of nodding slowly in the direction of Chance. I knew it was to make sure that what I was about to say was appropriate for our son's always-attentive and knowledge-absorbing ears. Along with Finn's parents, and anyone else for that matter, our children certainly had not been privy to any marital strife between their father and I. We both had made sure of that.

"It's okay," I reassured, while lightly laughing at our son's dairy mustache.

"Okay. What?" Finn raised the baby spoon to Arinn's mouth.

"I believe you owe me a couple massages or so." I grinned widely.

His smile was instantly as relaxed as mine. "You? You've been watching football?"

I shrugged my shoulders. "No, but I know how many times Cincinnati has lost."

Finn redeposited Arinn's bowl onto the kitchen's center island, stood up, and approached me. Luckily, our little girl had her fill and was smacking her lips happily.

Finn bracketed his hands on my shoulders from behind and magically, as only he could, started massaging my back.

"Yeah, I've missed that." His crooner voice spoke of the weeks we had been separated and of the ongoing bet we had since before we were even married. "But they did win a game, too. What was our bet?" he teased, very well knowing that if the Cincinnati Bengals won—the closest home team he had as a native Louisvillian—he got to lick chocolate off my body.

"I believe you get to—"

"Chocolate syrup!" As if on cue, Chance called out for more dessert topping.

Finn and I roared laughing, while Chance looked up at us. It was all so innocent and peaceful. Everything finally seemed to be back to how it was supposed to be.

***

It was two days later, and I was engrossed in all the tedious details of figuring out how to move our family of four across hundreds of miles. While we were lucky that Finn—we—already owned a gorgeous, sprawling, furnished residence in Nashville and we weren't in financial need to have to sell our upstate New York home quickly, there were still many things to consider. On the top of the list was how to get all of our personal belongings to Tennessee in less than a month's time, since we wanted to be there prior to Mr. Murphy's birthday and the CMAs.

Surrounded by a multitude of papers, I was checking items off my list when I heard Finn call out my name. "Yeah?" I replied. When he didn't answer, I looked up from the dining room table. It was the perfect spot to do work and still keep an eye on the kids, who were in the adjacent great room.

"I, uh…" Seeming to hesitate with his words, Finn

stood at the entryway of the dining room, making no effort to walk any closer in my direction. "I have to go out of town for a few days."

"What? Why?" I rose to my feet just as instantly as my blood pressure must have risen.

"It's just for a few days," he offered, as if it were a peacemaking compromise.

"God, Finn."

"You're mad." He said it definitively as a statement because there was no denying my demeanor.

I was most certainly upset. And I wasn't going to lie about it. The fact that Finn had been away on tour most of the summer had hurt us. We had missed and needed one another. And then when he had returned, we didn't get the chance to reconnect because we were thrown into a hailstorm of jealousy, misunderstandings, anger, poor choices, and sadness...before we were finally able to heal. And a few days of reconnecting was not enough time to be secure before he would leave again.

"Yeah. Yeah. You know what? I am."

He finally took a step toward me. "Beauty, listen—"

"Don't 'Beauty' me right now." I denied him one of his favorite nicknames for me. "Where are you going? What could you possibly have to do? We're just—" I broke on my words because I was getting emotional and stressed, especially after seeing Chance grab a toy off of Arinn. "We need time," I semi-begged. "We need time together, not—"

"What if I said," Finn parenthesized his dialogue to me with an authoritative directive to our son. "Chance, give it to your sister." He then continued his original thought. "What if I said that's exactly where I am going...with you. Just us."

My mind tried to rapidly regroup after his last few words. "What?" I asked slowly.

"I want us to go away together— the two of us. Somewhere just for a few days. I know we have a lot going on with the house and Pop...everything. But I think it would be good."

"Yeah? Really? No calls? No business? Just us?"

"I can't guarantee I won't have to text a couple times, but, yeah."

"I'd really like that." My shoulders suddenly seemed tons lighter.

They mimicked my husband's relaxed smile. "Good."

"What about the kids?" I asked, noticing that all was, thankfully, back to being harmonious between Chance and Arinn.

"Nol and Will will take care of them. Kelsea is stoked."

"Is that who you were talking with just now?" I smiled.

"Uh-huh." He mirrored my action.

"I've never left Arinn for more than a couple hours." I spoke, as the realization came to my mind.

"She'll be all right. She's our little Miss Socialite. She likes and goes with anybody."

"That's so true," I agreed, thinking how our son could not be more opposite than his sister. But I also knew that Chance would be perfectly fine with his aunt, uncle, and cousin.

"Baby, you name it, where do you want to go?" Finn was now more animated, knowing that I was one hundred percent on board with his plan.

"I don't know."

He didn't give me a chance to even think before he started rattling off ideas, "Mexico, the Caribbean.... We can throw a dart at a map."

But despite the endless possibilities that Finn's offer produced, there was really only one place I wanted to go. "I want to go back," I said. "Back to campus."

"Really?" he questioned. "We can go anywhere."

"No. I'm sure. That okay?"

"It's...well, that's exactly...."

"That's where you had in mind the whole time?" I asked, but I knew it just by the self-assured, semi-smirk on my husband's face.

"Yeah. But I would have went anywhere you said…Beauty." He exaggerated my nickname, knowing he could get away with using it this time.

I shook my head at the way he knew me so well. "I love you."

"Good to know." His grin was wider than I had seen in such a long time. "You got awfully feisty in the beginning of the conversation."

"I wasn't ready for you to leave yet," I admitted.

"Also good to know," he said, and I knew that meant almost more than the previous three words I had first spoken. Finn seemed infallible to most of the world, but his one crux was being left. It was a deep-seated fear from his childhood. "Me either. Me either."

CHAPTER TWO

Low-powered lights anchored the walls, welcoming us into the empty chapel. It was the time of day when dusk was fading to complete darkness, which just added to the serenity of the setting. Finn took my hand as we quietly and respectfully made our way to the front of the room where we had gotten married. That had been nearly five years before. But it had been fifteen years since we had first met at the chapel's home base—our college alma mater. So much had changed since then. We had only been friends at the very beginning— friends of friends. And then graduation, distance, life, and careers had separated even that, until we were able to reconnect thanks to the strangest of coincidences.

"What are you thinking about?" Finn's melodic voice interrupted the silence.

"Wyatt."

"Huh," he replied with even more tranquility. It was always a little hard for Finn to talk about his nephew, even though he had gotten better with it over the many years since the little boy had tragically passed away.

"I know you and I met on campus," I explained. "But it's because of Wyatt going to his particular elementary school that I got to see you again."

"Who would have thought the technology coordinator would be you? God has mysterious ways." He seemed to twitch his eyes before asking. "Would you do it all again?"

I, undoubtedly, knew the right and only answer to that question. But we all live with regrets. And my life certainly was full of them. *All* again? If I could bypass the past few months starting with Finn going on tour... if I could bypass Wyatt dying...if I could bypass the lonely years that it took for us to reconnect in the first place.... But I couldn't. There are no U-turns in life. There are no smoothly-paved superhighways. There are only long, windy, bumpy country roads. And, in the end, you can only hope to find that proverbial happily-ever-after. Even though I felt more at peace than I had in a while, I prayed that I was nowhere near that end. I knew I had so much more love and happiness to experience with the man in front of me.

So, my answer was, "Absolutely."

"Well, that's good." And then he dropped to one knee in front of me.

"What are you doing?"

"Will you marry me?" He reached into his inside jacket pocket and pulled out an obvious ring box. "Sorry. I don't have a BINGO board and s'mores and—"

"What?" I questioned, simply because I was overwhelmed by what was going on, not because I didn't remember his first proposal at the penthouse—the romantic, unique, personalized way he had proposed.

"Renew our vows." And, with that, he opened up the box, exposing a spectacular, thin band encircled completely with sparkling diamonds.

"Really?"

"Yeah. Whatcha think?"

"I *think* that ring better fit." I smiled at the beauty of the moment, which even outshone the beauty of the ring.

"Who would my girl be without sarcasm?"

"I love you and being your girl. No sarcasm."

"Yeah, then?"

"Yeah. Absolutely." And then I added our personal tagline, "Forever."

Finn finally rose to his feet, flanked his hands on my cheeks, and kissed me softly but solidly—a loving, confirming kind of connection. He removed the ring from the box and explained. "It's identical to your wedding band. You can wear one on each side of your engagement ring. Look carefully." He handed it to me. "There's one tiny difference."

I angled the ring so I could see the inside. Just like my wedding band had our wedding date engraved in it, this one had both Chance and Arinn's birthdays marked. It was perfect.

I looked up and met his glimmering eyes. Equally emotional, I said, "I love it. And I love that you thought of it and the vows. It's…." Before the actual waterworks started, I concluded with, "Yeah."

Finn took the ring from my hand, slid it on my finger, and, emphasizing the last word, said, "I love you."

"I get to wear it now?"

"I want you to have it. Why? Do you want to wait until we renew our vows?"

"No," I admitted. Now that it was on my finger, I never wanted it to leave. "When do you want to make an honest woman out of me again?" I teased.

"I was thinking our anniversary?" he stated in question format.

"Perfect," I agreed, as he took my newly-ringed hand and pulled me to him. "About that 'do it all again' business?" I pointed my chin up so that I could meet his eyes with mine. "I might want to amend some of the dancing parts."

His body bounced in quiet laughter, knowing and accepting my detest of dancing. Finn was the only one who could ever get me to dance, and that was a rarity.

"Lara…" He seemed to lovingly tsk my name. Then he pulled our bodies a little farther apart, clasping both of my hands in his. "Do you still trust me? Do you feel the way you did that night on the bench right before our wedding? Do you know that I will always be there for you?"

"Do you want to get me drunk?" I jested at his memory of one of the only times I had let liquor control my adult life.

It had been the night before our wedding. We had been at a bar—Fat Boys—that was not too far from the chapel. Because I had been feeling happier and freer than I ever had, I had indulged, knowing and trusting that he was always going to be there for me. I had told him exactly that while we had sat on the bench right outside the bar.

Finn answered my "drunk" question seriously, though. "No, I want to know your honest answer."

"Finn, I do. I do as much as I did that night or the next day when I said those exact two little words: 'I do.'" I smiled. "And if you want, I'd be happy to go do some shots with you to prove it." When he didn't respond, I added, "And maybe a quick dance, too."

"Ha!" He was back to his normal self. "I knew if I waited another second, I would get everything I wanted." I looped my hands around his neck. "I thought *I* was everything you wanted."

"Every day…every breathing second."

***

Despite it being a weeknight, Fat Boys was busy enough. But then again, it was a college bar. And school night, weekend, early, or late, there were patrons, legal-aged and otherwise, gathered at the tables, bar, and game area.

Baseball cap securely drawn down toward his eyes, Finn pulled out the only stool at the bar and motioned for me to sit. As I did, he squeezed his body into the space next to me. "So, shot?" He half-asked, half-yelled over the blaring music.

"Fi—" I started and then realized I didn't want to verbalize his name.

Finn was one of the school's most successful alums. And, to top it off, he had a fairly unique name. So, if I said it and any heads turned, ball cap or not, he would surely be recognized, therefore ending our night of ambiguity.

He threw me a wink and used his sexy nickname for me— the one that referenced the classic Police song "Roxanne" and my red lava lamp. "Rox, were you just teasing me before with the shot comment?"

"Can I have a hard cider or lemonade instead?" I just wanted something sweet and easy. Because of my deceased father's past, as well as my own, I was not much of a drinker.

Respecting that, and knowing that he had been conscientious of his own alcohol intake recently, Finn squeezed my hand. "I gotcha." As he leaned further into the bar to get the busy bartender's attention, he nodded in an opposite direction and said to me, "That booth just opened. You wanta grab it for us?"

Grateful that it was far from the dance area, I agreed. I slid into the wooden bench seat and started looking at the flyers tacked haphazardly on the wall. There were ads for local shops, housing availability, and band appearances. I couldn't help but think of Finn's band when we were in college and his pop-up gigs around town. When I turned to glance toward the singer himself, two probable frat boys holding pool sticks were standing at my table's edge.

"You wanta play?" The one in the plain white T-shirt and jeans asked.

I breathed out a half laugh. "No. Not much of a pool player."

"C'mon," the other, wearing sweats that were too big, urged. "We'll teach you. Line that stick up, stroke it a bit, then bam...." His breath smelled of the beer he was holding.

Before I could reply to the stranger's obvious sexual overture, Finn came behind him and firmly clasped him on the shoulder. "First of all, she's a hustler. I'd watch out for her." As Finn slid my open bottle to me, the guy turned toward my husband. "And, second, that is no way to speak to a lady." His tone that time was much more serious. It was the possessive, jealous side of my husband.

"Just having some fun, man," he replied but took a mini-step away. "Keeping her company."

"Well, thanks. But now you're not." My husband punctuated the last three words individually. There was a bit of a macho stand-off between the three, and then the younger two laughed and retreated. Finn slid into the booth, nudging his hips next to mine. "Boys." He shook his head and took a swallow from his beer bottle.

"I'm almost old enough to be their mother!" I proclaimed and then realized, with a flashback to my teenage years, how true that really was.

"You don't look a day over thirty-six." He managed a smile before I smacked him in the bicep for citing my actual age. "I meant twenty-six…twenty-six." He laughed and then kissed me. "You could definitely pass for a co-ed, baby."

"It doesn't seem that long ago, does it?"

"No. It goes fast. All of it."

I could hear the melancholy in his voice. And I knew it was not only about the time we lost initially finding one another again but also about the past month or so. And his career. And… his dad. It did go way too fast.

I leaned my head into his side and felt the familiar fold of his arm around me. When his lips grazed the top of my head, the music blaring from the speakers changed from one song to the next. I shook my head at the irony of Finn's latest tune filling the bar. He tilted his head backward. It was a good thing that his music was being played and held its popularity, but sometimes even the superstar needed a break from himself.

"You wanta leave?" he asked.

"With you." I smiled as he took my hand in one of his and our choice of drinks in the other.

We rotated out the front door with a few patrons who were boisterously coming in. Even though we hadn't been in the bar that long, the October air felt so clean and refreshing. Finn gave me back my black cherry beverage and took a mighty gulp from his own bottle. We walked for a moment or so in silence until we both simultaneously saw the bench. Naturally gravitating to it, we took similar positions to the ones we had five years before.

"Well…" I let out a cleansing sigh. "You may as well tell me what the plan is for the tour this coming summer." I took a swig of the hard lemonade.

"We have to do that now?" Obvious deflation.

"I know it has to be almost set," I countered.

Every year it was like clockwork. No sooner had he wrapped up his tour than the planning for the next one began. There was a final tally of what had and had not been successful and then how to make the necessary changes to the following summer's schedule. That included what opening act/s to bring on, how many shows, where, when, etc. There was a tremendous amount of scheduling, planning, and negotiating. Public announcements were made before the holidays, and tickets started going on sale right around that time, too.

It was mid-October. Of course those things were being done. And, yet, I didn't know a thing about them.

Finn being away on tour from the end of May to the end of August, with only a week-long break to see us, had been the first catalyst in the temporary crumbling of our marriage. And I knew that was the obvious reason he stalled in mentioning the following summer to me. He didn't want to risk another collapse…not when we were only starting on solid ground again.

"There's a lot in place," he admitted with an exhale.

"But I've been putting some of it off. I need to know what you're thinking."

"I'm thinking…" I spoke with pure honesty. "I'm thinking that we can't do what we did this summer."

"I know." After an extended pause, he forged forward. "I have to tour, though. It's expected. And with the new album being released soon, it's gonna be important to get people to keep coming, buying—"

"I get it," I reassured, while resting my hand on his.

I knew the momentum and push and drive it took to keep being on the level that my husband was on in his career. And Finn felt like some of his numbers and accolades had been dropping. So, it was even more important to keep everything running full force.

"I know you love it," I continued. "I know you somehow become more alive up on stage." When I gave him the look of "don't even try to deny that," he closed his prepared open mouth. "I want you to think about this." This time I used my mom voice. "I mean, really stop and think before you answer." And then I asked what I had been tossing around in my mind for a couple of days. "Do you want us to come with you next year?"

Finn was as bad as Chance in the grocery store's candy aisle. He didn't stop and think at all. His response was immediate and direct. "What kind of question is that? Of course I do."

I gave a closed smile at what I knew would be his answer and then spoke slowly. "I think we might be able to pull that off."

"Yeah? I think so, too." His hand was on mine as his smile emerged.

"You have to realize, though, it's going to be chaotic. It was one thing when we just had Chance scooting around the bus. But two of them? Two of them mobile and needing to be entertained?"

"We can look into getting someone to help."

"Well, yeah. I'm not talking about that. I'm talking

about you…what you need to do your job. I know how much energy it takes and all that is expected of you. The kids—"

"You talk about me feeling alive? You. You and the kids. I wouldn't feel that without y'all there. We're gonna do it. We'll make it work," he said, with determination and a whole lot of love.

***

If only we could have frozen time on those few, glorious days that Finn and I managed to escape together. But a life full of obligations brought us back full force. First up was getting everything organized and set for our new family adventure, a.k.a. move to Nashville. Even though our suburban New York abode wasn't officially sold yet, everything was packed, boxed, and shipped either to the ranch in Nashville, or to our penthouse in Manhattan. Even the cars, including my cherished red Jeep, had their own transport.

A few days after we were semi-settled into our now-permanent Nashville address, we drove to Louisville to celebrate my father-in-law's birthday. And, it really was the worst timing. It was the Sunday three days before the CMAs, and Finn was being bombarded with interview requests and confirming the practice schedule—he was singing a short acoustic piece during the show. But there was no way he was going to miss his father's birthday, especially because, without saying it, we all knew it was going to be Mr. Murphy's last.

Finn's dad looked about the same as he did when we had visited just over a month before. He appeared a little more ashen in complexion and was a little leaner. But he was such a tall, broad man that it wasn't really noticeable unless you truly knew him. Besides, he was in good spirits, having been so honored that we all came for his special day. Nola and Kelsea flew in, too, giving Will's apologies for having to work, but promising that he would join all of us for Thanksgiving and Christmas.

We had a delicious, homemade Irish stew dinner followed by cake and the traditional happy birthday song led by Kelsea and Chance. And then we sat down to watch the primetime match-up of the Cincinnati Bengals vs. the Pittsburgh Steelers. From his seat on the sofa behind me, I felt Finn's hands working on the knots in my shoulders and upper back as I sat on the floor in between his legs.

"Hmmm," I murmured. "Already seeing the forgone conclusion, are you, Cowboy?" I teased, knowing the third quarter score of Pittsburgh 28 - Cincy 0 meant an almost sure loss for Cincinnati and a sure massage for Lara.

"It's not over 'til it's over, baby."

"Mmmm-hmmm." I didn't exactly agree. I reached backward to hold his hand for a moment and then stood up. "I think I am, though…over for the night. I'm tired. I'm gonna head up." The move and two wound-up kids—due to family overload and sugar rushes—had me exhausted.

As I kissed him sweetly on the lips, Kelsea, who had been on the floor next to me said, "Ewww."

Finn reached over and ruffled Kelsea's blonde hair, which had not lost one bouncy curl since I met her at the age of two. "Yeah, that's all right that you keep thinking that for a while."

"It's probably your bedtime, too." Nola, whose blonde hair was darker and straighter than her daughter's, chimed in.

"Mom!" Kelsea whined. "I wanta stay up and watch Pop-Pop's team."

"Really?"

The sarcastic doubt in my sister-in-law's voice said it all. She knew, as we all did, that Kelsea had no interest in football. She just wanted to be in the adult group. She may not have been into the kissing scene yet, but she was bordering on it.

"Come on Kels, you can help me check on the little ones upstairs." I winked at Nola while speaking of Chance and Arinn who had already been asleep for a couple hours. "And then, maybe before you go to sleep, your mom will let you read me some of that book I saw you carrying."

"Yeah, Aunt Lara, you'll like it. It's called *Tales of a Fourth Grade Nothing.*"

"I think I may have read that one, but it's been a long time." I fondly recalled the innocence that Judy Blume created momentarily for me in my otherwise dark childhood.

Finn grabbed my hand just to touch it once more before Kelsea and I made our way up the stairs of Finn's childhood home. I felt so at peace there. Its Old-World charm exuded warmth and love as much as the family who had been raised in its midst. And I was happy to look back and see the four of them, donning black and orange jerseys, together again, doing something they all loved.

CHAPTER THREE

"I'm glad that whatever was going on between the two of you last time you were here is better now." I heard my father-in-law's voice as I was approaching the solid-wood pocket doors of their den.

It was the next day, and I was searching for Finn. I knew it was time for us to start heading to Nashville. By the time we got back, it would be the kids' bedtime, and Finn needed a chance to breathe before his day of rehearsals, etc. the following day. I discretely peered in to see the two men sitting in identical dark brown leather chairs facing one another. In some ways, they were mirrors of each other—their height, their noses, and their love for family. But, while Finn had a full set of solid brown hair, Mr. Murphy's hair was now thinning and mostly gray.

I decided not to interrupt. For one thing, I knew the conversation seemed serious. And, for another, I knew it was about me...us. When we had visited last time, Finn and I had tried to hide our marital strife from his family, and I thought we did a pretty good job. Maybe they knew something was off but surely not as bad as it had been. Standing still and off to the side, I listened some more.

"What? There wasn't—" Finn started to deny.

But he was cut off by his father. "Finnegan...."

The name wasn't even my husband's. Finn's name was Finn—nothing more formal. His father just used Finnegan sometimes to grab his attention.

"We're good now," Finn admitted, sounding most definitely like the child to his elder.

"I can see that. I can see it in the ease of her smile and the way you look at one another... the way you touch each other."

My unbeknownst smile faded quickly as I heard Finn say, "I don't deserve her, Pop, and yet she stays."

"From that statement I'm guessing you did something that you know wasn't right."

I lightly flopped against the wall outside of the den and internally sighed. Mr. Murphy's statement was true. We had both been in bad places, but it had been Finn's careless, reckless choices that had really made things go south. The fact that Finn somehow felt like he didn't deserve me was ridiculous, though. It made me hurt for him.

"I...yes. I...." Finn stumbled on his words.

"I don't need to know," Mr. Murphy continued. "That's between you and your wife. But you owned up to it, right? You're the stand-up guy I raised you to be?"

"Yes, sir," he said. And he was.

"Good, because not only will she not put up with it, but you are a better man than that."

"I love her so damn much, Pop. I can't imagine how I could ever love her more, and I do. I see her with Chance and Arinn, and I witness her compassion and the vulnerability she seems to only show me and I—"

Ah, Finn, stop, I silently urged. Otherwise, that vulnerability was going to be on display in the hallway. I wiped a straggling tear and refocused on the conversation.

"Don't ever lose sight of that. That was the best decision you ever made—letting her in—letting her know you and love you. You've climbed your mountains, son, and there have been plenty. I am so proud of who you are. But take it from a dying m—"

"Pop…." Finn pleaded not wanting to hear the words his father was saying about his health. "I'm dying, my boy, and it's going to be okay. Now, that's not what I…. Listen, you have it all. Not just your family but your career. You have managed to succeed in a field that some people only dream of. You can't do any better. Just know that the problem with having it all means that sometimes it feels like the only place is down… that the smallest slide feels like an avalanche."

"Yeah." Finn conceded, and I knew he could relate. It was something he had been trying to deal with for months.

Finn still had thousands and thousands of fans who were there for any event or concert. But he was finding it harder to reach the number ones that had become so much of a regular routine in his career. And since achieving the ultimate accolade of Entertainer of the Year a number of times, the nominations had slowed. It was just how it worked—the business. But it was still hard.

"You can't let it get to you, son." Mr. Murphy continued in his usual wise prose. "You didn't go into this for the money and fame. You did it because it was in you… like the blood flowing through your veins. We saw that early on. And now you don't even have to worry about money. So, forget the other bull. Love the music, and your passion will show. It'll show in your music, but it'll show in your kids and that strong woman by your side. But do not sacrifice yourself or what you have for that mountain. You've climbed it. You've lived it."

"Pop, I wouldn't."

"All that I want is for you to always know that feeling…to know that you deserve to be loved. You are loved for who you are…for you."

I knew my tears were actively flowing then, and if it got much worse, my nose would fill up and I would be a complete mess. I dabbed my wet face and started to quietly turn away. I couldn't handle any more even though it was all the honest, good truth.

As I left, I heard Finn say, "If I could be half the man that you—"

And his dad say, "You're double, son…double."

***

It took approximately three hours to drive back to Nashville. And for the majority of that time, Finn was on the phone catching up with career-related concerns. I didn't mind being ignored because I recognized that my husband had put everything, besides family, on hold over the two days we spent at his parents' place. Although, I think at times Chance didn't understand. His three-and-a-half-year-old self didn't quite have the patience or maturity to wait when he wanted to ask his dad a question, or comment, or sing, and Finn was talking via the handsfree device. Finn tried to do it all—drive, talk on the phone, converse with the kids. But I knew it was taking a toll, especially when Arinn decided, seemingly out of nowhere, to belt out an uncharacteristic cry. I stretched my body the best I could from the front passenger side to stroke her little head, willing her to find a peaceful state. And, miraculously, both kids fell asleep during the last twenty-five minutes of the ride.

When we arrived home, Finn hoisted Chance into his arms while I got Arinn. We silently brought them both up the stairs and into their bedrooms. Skipping the prayers and bed bug routines, we were able to change the kids and get them settled, fortunately, without much of a fuss from either child.

I was just securing Arinn's onesie around her freshly diapered and powdered bottom, when Finn leaned into the nursery doorway and said, "You got them, right? They're settled?"

"Yeah," I answered cautiously.

I knew his tone. I knew the past few days had rattled him— seeing his dad, dealing with the stress of the CMAs, the move. He could juggle singing and touring all week for weeks on end, but, emotionally, this was a whole different scenario.

"I'm going out for a bit." He spoke in a monotone way and started immediately toward the stairs.

"Hold on," I called out with some urgency but being careful not to raise my voice as I closed Arinn's door behind me. After hastily propping the child-proof gate on top of the staircase, I caught up with Finn in the great room as he grabbed his car keys. "Where are you going?"

"I…I don't know. A drive."

I was going to mention that we were just in the car for hours but instead simplified with my hardly-disguised panicked, "Don't."

"I have to."

"Just stay and unwind. It's not going to help."

"Lar…." he almost pleaded, and then I noticed he had never even taken off his coat since we had arrived. He had planned on going all along.

"Please don't. Do whatever you need to here."

"I can't." As our conversation continued, his voice became a little gruffer, stressed, and abrasive.

Whereas mine grew in volume along with my anxiety. "You can! I'm here."

"I know, and that scares me. I'm on fire right now." He turned and started toward the garage.

"I'm scared, too. I'm scared if you leave, it will be like last time." I practically choked on the last few words, but it was the truth.

When things had started piling up on Finn a couple months before, he couldn't handle the pressure. Recognizing it in himself and knowing it would inflame some of his usually dormant PTSD symptoms, he had wanted to back away from me for a couple hours. He was always afraid he would blow up and hurt me. But, ironically, his leaving that night months before had led to drinking and a snowball effect that had hurt us far worse than if he had stayed.

The way he stopped then and slowly turned to awkwardly face me told me he knew exactly what I was referring to. "Damn, Lara, please." It was his turn to beg. "Just... just please."

I didn't know what else to say. There *wasn't* anything else to say. He knew how I felt. I didn't want him to leave. Yet, I knew it had to be his decision.

"I've got it." He wanted me to feel reassured that he was in control. But the fact that he was leaving and the abruptness of his kiss, which *did* feel like fire, told me otherwise.

He wasn't choosing to stay. And I tried hard not to think that he wasn't choosing me. After all, in his mind, he probably thought escaping and regrouping *was* choosing me.

But I ached. I hurt. I worried... from the last glance I had of his back as the door shut to hearing the garage door open and the car starting. And then I tortured myself further by walking to the front door and watching as his car started down the long, trailing driveway surrounded by the sanctuary of tall trees on either side.

I recalled the first time I was on that driveway. Finn's friend and right-hand man, Hawk, who I was meeting for the first time, had picked me up at the airport and brought me through the security gates. It was the day of the CMA awards, almost exactly seven years before. Finn and I had just met up again, and I was being immersed into his wild and wonderful world. Back then, the impressive driveway seemed to go on forever as it made its way to the ranch hidden almost above its reach. But now, that same driveway seemed incredibly short and dark...because he was exiting via it.

No longer able to see the car with my own eyes, I walked over to the security monitor showing both the driveway's edge and the gate that led out to the world. In the matter of seconds, I saw Finn's car approach and then stop. I prepared myself for the inevitable—Finn accessing the gates and departing. Although not perfectly clear, I could see his face via the monitor. He stared straight ahead for a solid minute-plus, and then he pounded the steering wheel and the ceiling of the car a few times. I then watched in wonder and gratitude as he started turning the car around. He was heading back up the hill to our home.

I diverted my eyes from the monitor and walked toward the center of the great room. When I heard the garage door reopen and close, I started to pace, unable to simply stand still. I was overjoyed but also a twinge nervous. And when he came back into the house and stopped in front of me, I released a burst of air I hadn't realized I had been holding in. He silently walked straight over and folded me into his arms, which felt tighter and more stressed than I had been witness to in a long time.

"I'm so glad you turned around." I breathed deeply again—my head still securely tucked into his chest.

He separated our bodies and looked at me sincerely. "I heard what you said. But I'm a mess right now. I—"

"I know," I interrupted. "I know how much you're dealing with. I actually don't know how you're doing it as well as you are. I am so proud of you. You—"

He stepped further away and pierced his eyes. "Don't be condescending."

"What?" I stared at him for a moment, trying to remind myself that his comment was rooted in his desperate need to be the one in charge, even when he should rely on others...most of all me. "I can't be proud of—?" I started.

"No," he confirmed in a definitive tone. "No."

His jittery eyes bounced for a few moments, and then he walked through the double patio doors and out to the magnificent outdoor entertainment area. I wasn't sure if he purposefully left the doors open for me to follow, but I took the bait. I shut the doors behind us and followed him a few more steps, just past the built-in stereo system and before the fire pit area. He glanced up to the closed second-story windows to where our children slumbered. I did, too, silently giving thanks for their existence in our lives.

"Why do you want to see me like this?" he questioned. "You shouldn't have to put up with this."

"Of course I do. I'm your wife. I love you. And Finn…" I paused and then went for it. "Don't ever say that you don't deserve me. If—"

"You heard what I said to Pop." He said it in a matter-of-fact, knowing voice.

"Yeah. I'm sorry. I didn't mean to. I just…I did…a little," I admitted.

"We don't have omissions, remember?"

He earmarked a promise we had made to one another, both in our wedding vows and before that—no lying, amending, or omitting anything from one another. At times, the truth hurt…burned…tore. But it was honest.

"Anything I said to Pop I would tell you."

"If we don't have omissions, why do you push me away? Isn't that omitting?"

"Lara…" With an extreme exhale, he started pacing. "I came back. I'm here. I'm still really unsure about it, though. I still think I need to just drive or something."

"Why?"

"Because I'm so wound…upset. I don't want to take that out on you."

"You never have," I declared. And when he immediately shook his head in doubt, I reiterated. "You haven't." I knew it was one of those relationship moments where you just had to agree to disagree. "We trust each other with everything—our deepest secrets and things we know are going to hurt one another." I paused for a second—that wound was fresh, but we had gotten through it because of our love. "Why? Why won't you let me help you through this? Why won't you let me stand by you when the world gets hard? Finn, I know about the PTSD. I can handle it. Just like you're afraid of hurting me, I'm afraid that if you isolate yourself, it's going to be worse. It's us together... no matter how hard. Baby, we can't...." I stopped ever so slightly, just to get a hold of my own emotions. "How can we have all that we have— the love, the trust—with you feeling like you can't be near me when you are struggling?" My emotional plea didn't seem to change anything, though. I wanted to help, but he was still silent, indicating that he didn't think I should be there. Finally, knowing that he had already compromised by turning around in the drive, I said, "Okay. I understand. I'll leave you be. Thanks for staying." I turned to go back into the house.

"Stop, Lara! Stop!" he yelled, just before I reached the door.

His insistent, forceful, emotional voice literally made me shake. I should have expected it. Finn didn't like conflict, especially between the two of us. He was used to being able to solve everything. And I should have known that somebody leaving was his trigger. So, even if it was just me going inside the adjoining house, it would upset him.

When I slowly turned around to face him, he was shaking his head and starting to look back up at me. "Our love and trust are what gets me through." His wet eyes met mine. "You have no idea how much. And, God, Lara, I want to be near you."

"Will you let me be?" My voice was just a little above a whisper upon witnessing my husband's emotional state.

His pause was a partial sigh. "I don't want to hurt you, but I can see that's what I'm doing anyway."

Exactly, I wanted to say. But, instead, I said, "Let me be here. Let me help you."

Finn took a few strides until he was directly in front of me. He nodded his head up and down and grasped my hands in his. Without warning, he looked to the crystal-clear, star-filled sky and bolted out a deafening, "Ahhh!"

While I did not completely jump in shock, my shoulders squeezed inward causing instant tension all the way down my arms and into my hands which were holding Finn's. He closed his eyes, knowing he had scared me. But it was just the sudden burst of volume that caused my reaction. That, compounded by the fact that I was already tense *and* had survived a childhood filled with seemingly spontaneous outbursts from my father.

I didn't want Finn to think he hurt me physically or emotionally, though. So, I immediately squeezed his hands and let my own lungs loose with a mimicking, "Ahhh!" realizing in that moment how much the action expressed and released.

He looked at me, understanding that I was all right, and then once again yelled, "Ahhh!" with the loud tagline of, "Cancer sucks!"

"It's not fair!" I continued at the same altitude and attitude.

"I love you!" he screamed, but most definitely not in anger.

"Oh, Cowboy, I love you, too." My voice crumbled.

He then took my hand and guided me to the fire pit bench. After stretching out his own strong body, he gently encouraged me to lie on top of him. I rested my head on his graphic T-shirt—exposed from his open jacket—and intertwined my legs with his to find our natural fit. He wrapped his arms around my back and eased his head down to the bench's pillows. We lay there, just like that, in silence. I knew he was trying to emulate the calm and stillness of the crisp, beginning-of-November air. But it wasn't working.

"Baby," I said. "Your chest is beating so fast." I didn't lift my head from it.

"Yeah."

"God, that's not right."

"Yeah."

I had felt the tightness in his arms and in his grip. But now I also knew that his pulse was on overdrive. Everything he was telling me about his body feeling like it was on fire or going to explode was medically true. And, on top of that, it might be even worse because he was trying to mask it for my benefit. For the first time, I wondered if my love was going to be enough to get him through. He needed to legitimately work some of it out.

I slightly rearranged my body and brought my hands to his hips and my mouth to his. We could make love. We were both emotional and needy, and it would be a good energy release.

Finn reciprocated at first. I felt his tongue meet mine and heard the moan come from his mouth. But that sound then turned to one of slight angst. He broke our lock and quietly shook his head. He would not want to make love. He wouldn't want to when he was hurting…not when, although he was letting me in, he was afraid of hurting me. He thought he had done that once before, and, even though I vehemently denied it, he would never get close to ever recreating that again.

"I love you," he said quietly, as if wanting me to understand.

But I knew him, and I loved him, too. "I know," I whispered back. "If you don't want to make love wi—"

He cut me off and lifted my head slightly to see his eyes. "It's not…not that I don't want to."

"All right. I know," I said softly, and then sat up. I rested lightly on his lap and reached out my hand. "Dance with me."

"What?" He propped himself up on his elbows and tilted his head in mock astonishment.

"Don't give me that look. You heard what I said." I used a little bit of my mommy voice, intermixed with a teensy bit of laughter.

"Dance?" He still wanted that confirmation.

"There might be an expiration date on the offer. I

would take me up on it if I were you." I stood up and reached out my hand again.

"I can't just dance it out of my system," he said, but stood up anyway and fit his hand in mine.

"No. But maybe it could distract you, at the very least."

"I'm not going to turn down my wife asking me to dance." Before pulling me into him, he kissed me on the forehead.

Finn started swaying our bodies rhythmically along with the light breeze in the air. At first his grip on my body was tight...so tight I almost had to say something. It wasn't that he was hurting me. It was that the extreme closeness made it a little hard to breathe. But I didn't want to discourage him.

And then, when he started softly singing "Love Letters (to my wife)" — a song he had written for me just prior to giving birth to Chance —I could feel the ease. There was an ease in his grip, there was an ease in his vocals, and there was an ease in the beating of his chest. "You are the best distraction," he said at the conclusion of the song. "This is exactly what I need."

"Remember that." My exhale was cleansing.

We continued to dance under the stars well into the night until everything was better again. I knew I had helped him. But what he didn't know was how much he had helped me. It meant the world that, although he shared and trusted everything else in his life with me, he finally let me get him through when his inner demons raged. He just needed to not have that immediate flight reaction next time.

CHAPTER FOUR

"Finn! ... Finn!" I called out.

"What, baby? I'm right here."

I felt his lips on my bare shoulder, and it made me open my eyes. It had been a dream. I was calling out for him in my dream. Turning around and seeing him lying next to me in bed, I confirmed. "You are. You're here."

"Yeah." He softly touched my face, still adjusting to being awakened in the middle of the night. "What's wrong?"

"Just a dream. Go back to sleep."

"I'm awake. And while I usually love hearing you call out my name in bed...." He trailed his voice off as I playfully hit him. "Tell me."

I paused for a moment, trying to organize the scattered pieces of dreamland in my head. "I couldn't find you," I started. "I was searching and searching. And then your parents came. And they knew what happened." When Finn furrowed his eyebrows, intrigued by my tale, I paused and then told him. "Your grandmother had you."

"Hmmm," he ever-so-quietly acknowledged.

Finn's PTSD stemmed from an incident that occurred when he was a toddler. His grandmother, acting erratically from an unbeknownst brain tumor, had left him in a park. He was alone and confused for hours, feeling abandoned. It was twenty-four plus hours until he was reunited with his family. He had blocked the memory, only to have flashbacked to it in early adulthood when his fiancée, out of the blue, left him for another man. Being left was a huge, traumatic trigger in my husband's world.

"And I heard crying," I continued. "I thought it was you as a little boy, but then it turned into Arinn, or maybe Chance, but I think it was Arinn."

Finn put his hand out to mine. "Did you find me?"

"No. You found me."

"Good. I made it back home?" He was talking to me in a purposefully calm, middle-of-the-night voice.

"No."

"What then? Where were *you*?"

I searched those solid gray eyes, knowing they would grow sad the instant I answered. But I did, nonetheless. "I was under the desk in the bank."

"Oh, baby. Oh, man." He pulled me into him. "You're still dreaming about that?" He didn't let me go.

"No," I denied, shaking my head the best I could while still being enveloped in his embrace. "Really." I gently pushed back. "I haven't. I haven't for a little while now."

The visit with his father had stirred things up for me, too. And it obviously had come out during the only time I allowed myself self-indulgence…while I was asleep. I had stopped Finn from leaving the night before. I had been able to protect him from himself and his anger and hurt. And even though there was nothing that made me feel more loved, cherished, and protected than my husband's arms around me, my subconscious had backtracked to the night before, needing just a twinge more security. In my dream, I chose the one thing that had protected me during a terrifying event that summer—being held hostage during a bank robbery. One desk behind one closed door had kept me safe…that and the encouraging texts from my husband.

"You said, 'I'm right here, baby,'" I noted, realizing it was his real voice that had penetrated into my dreams waking me up.

"I am."

I took a cleansing breath, knowing the dream was already fading. "You didn't hear Arinn crying, did you?"

"Nope."

"Wonder what that part was about?" A yawn partially interrupted my question.

"It's just a dream," he reassured. "Nobody's lost. Everybody's safe."

"Yeah." I kissed him on the lips. "You need your rest. Go back to sleep."

Ignoring me, he said, "Come here," and guided me into our spooning position. Wrapping his arms around my torso, he kissed the back of my head. "Night, Lara. Quit letting those bed bugs bite."

I silently chuckled at our bed bug saying, which dated back to college. "Night back."

***

He kissed me and said something, but it was too hard to hear amid the roar of applause and cheering. Finn's Song of the Year played as he was pulled in the direction of the stage by an onslaught of celebratory back pats and handshakes. At our seats, I received my own hand grasps and smiles from his fellow musicians and their significant others... as if I had anything to do with my husband's success.

He looked so damn dashing in his all-black suit and charcoal-accented button-down as he grasped the trophy and spoke into the microphone. "Thank you," he said, as the crowd quieted and reclaimed their seats. "Not thank you for giving me a trophy to put on my shelf. But thank you for letting me live and love my life the way I always dreamed. Well, better than I even imagined. My pop reminded me the other day of all the treasures I am blessed with. I have fans that support me and my music year after year… song after song. I have the best band of brothers and crew that anyone in any profession could ever wish for. They have climbed these spectacular, breathtaking mountains with me. Thank you. But the mountains would feel terribly cold and desolate if I didn't have my family."

I recalled the mountain reference from his talk with his father just a couple days before. While Finn was usually thoughtful during his acceptance speeches, this one was extra emotional. And since he never let me read what he loosely prepared beforehand—he called it superstition, but I think he liked the element of surprising me—I listened with bated breath.

He made sure to find my eyes in the crowd before continuing. "Lara, I love you and our kids so much. Every road leads to you. You are my home. You are the place I belong forever." I smiled back before he looked toward what I knew was the main live television camera. "Pop, I hope I've made you and Mom proud. This one's for you —the strongest teddy bear I know."

***

There were lots of times during an awards show where, if I attended, I was solo. Sometimes I wondered if it was even worth going. I especially thought that in the beginning of our relationship, when I didn't know anyone in Finn's industry and was introverted enough to not make conversation unless approached. And if I did, I had to be cautious as to what to say, in case things were misconstrued to label companies, the press, etc. But I had gotten better at attending such events over the years, especially because I knew it meant so much to Finn to have me on his arm.

After his acceptance speech, I didn't see my husband

for a very long time. He was swept backstage to pose for pictures and answer inquiring-mind questions. Then he had to prep to go on stage for his performance.

During that time, I managed to send him a text. *CONGRATS! I'm so proud of U.* I figured I could get away with the proud comment since he was in a much better and more settled mood.

He texted me right back. *Wouldn't mean anything w/o U. I love U.*

Right after his acoustic performance, while Finn was still backstage, they presented the Male Vocalist of the Year award. It was the only other award Finn was up for that night. He didn't expect to win, especially after not having won the year before. And he wasn't incorrect with his prediction. I expect that was why he gave his emotional speech for Song of the Year. He knew it was going to be his only chance that night.

Finn then made his way back to our seats. There was a performance happening on stage, so I had to settle for just silently nuzzling into his side. When the break happened for the TV commercials, we got up for a much-needed stretch. Finn and I walked through a throng of people to a slightly less occupied space. I was just about to say something sweet and complimentary to my husband when a woman, maybe in her mid-twenties, approached us. It figured. Award shows were one of the most public, nonprivate settings of my life.

"Finn Murphy." Her wide blue eyes scanned him from top to bottom as if he were an exhibit.

Finn grasped my hand in a very protective way and seemed to stare her down. It gave me a moment to take her in. Her tight black mini-skirt and long black boots displayed how skinny she was. And her red, sleeveless shirt, with the sides cut out, showed that she wasn't afraid to show some skin…maybe a little too much. She wasn't anyone I knew. But it was obvious Finn did, which wasn't really out of the ordinary at an event like the CMAs.

"I was wondering if we would bump into each other." She dangled her black, lacy wrap over her shoulder.

"What are you doing here?" Finn's tone bordered on rude.

"Living here. You know," She glanced over at me while tossing her full set of curly, mousy brown hair. "The label is based here. They're not too keen on my indie rock, though. I think I could do country pretty well."

"Hmmm," was all my husband said, but it was enough to tell me he didn't agree.

"Con-grat-u-la-tions." She drew out the word. "Song of the Year. Maybe the three of us can celebrate with a drink or two." While I was thinking she already had a head start on us, she continued. "This is your wife, right?" She stuck her hand, complete with long red nails, out to me while citing her name. "Briar. Finny and I know each other— Well…yeah, well." She giggled, proving me right regarding the alcohol assumption.

When I went to extend my hand to hers, Finn denied me by squeezing it extra hard with his. "It's time to take our seats." He was right. All the signals—auditory, verbal, and otherwise—were telling us to take our places.

As I let him lead us away and toward our seats, I heard Briar call out, "See you later."

Even on the short path back, Finn was congratulated incessantly. By the time we got to sit, we both needed to be quiet. So, I didn't have a chance to ask the questions that were multiplying in my mind. Having not let go of my hand, he squeezed it and looked over at me. I tried a small smile and let him rest his lips on top of my head.

After the following, final award—Entertainer of the Year— was presented, we were free to go. It wouldn't be a quick and easy escape, however. There were still hordes of people to mix and mingle with before making our way to the car and subsequent after-party. While Finn was talking with some label exec., I decided to call home. Nola and Kelsea had driven from Louisville to Nashville that morning to spend the day and watch the kids while Finn and I went to the awards.

As I concluded the call and returned the phone back to my purse, Finn placed his hand at the small of my back. "God, you're beautiful. Your eyes with that dress are amazing."

"You already told me that!" I stifled a laughing yell while smoothing out the strapless, floor-length blue and green-patterned dress I had purposefully chosen to match my turquoise eyes.

"Not in the last ten minutes," he countered.

"Finn…." I sighed, never able to take a compliment on my appearance well.

"C'mon, let's make a break for the car." He laughed and grabbed my hand.

As we walked in a hurried and determined pace, or for as much as my high heels would allow me, I started filling Finn in on my conversation with his sister. "Nola says congrats."

"I'm sure," he said with mock doubt. He and his older sister had a great relationship full of teasing and admiration.

Things were a little different between me and my only sibling—my older-by-a-year brother, Lane. He had been my protector when we were growing up with a father who let alcohol inflame his temper. Lane and I had remained close, despite living states apart from one another. But things had been a little strained since I learned of his divorce and relationship with another woman.

"You're lucky to have her," I objected, speaking of Finn's sister.

"I know," my husband admitted. "How are things at home?"

"The kids are asleep. Kelsea, I guess, pretty much freaked out when Adam Leone won New Artist. Nola said she was glad we don't have neighbors. There was so much yelling and cheering."

Finn shook his head. "Really? I can't believe that's what the masses like right now."

"Right now, Finn, and…a nine-year-old girl." I acknowledged the finicky pendulum swing of musical styles. "That was very sweet of you to get her his picture and autograph."

"Yeah, well, if she didn't cheer for her uncle when he won, she might not be getting it."

"I'm sure she did." It was my turn to shake my head.

When we reached the awaiting town car, the driver opened up the back door. I scooted across the seat and listened as he asked Finn if he could make a quick call home since the line of cars wasn't moving. Agreeing, Finn slid in next to me and shut the door.

Finally, after many hours, I was in absolute privacy with my husband. "Do we have to go to the after-party?" I asked.

"I should, particularly with the win."

"Is she going to be there?"

"What? Who?"

"Finn…" I sighed. I had to ask. I had to bring it up. It had been wrestling around in my brain since shortly after she had approached us. When he gave me nothing besides a blink of his eyes, still encased with the green contacts his label made him wear to performance events, I cautioned in a casual tone, "Don't make me pull out the no-omissions card, especially when all you need to do is confirm what I pretty much already know."

"I love you," he said, not blinking this time.

"Yes, I know that, too."

"Please, Lara, I had no idea." That was enough of a confirmation.

"So, it is her."

He let out the slightest of sighs. "I was going to tell you once we got home."

"How do these exes always manage to be at—"

"She's not an ex!" Finn exclaimed.

Before I could respond, the driver opened his front door and started to take his seat. Finn, calming down, politely asked him to give us a few more minutes. Viewing us from the rearview mirror, I'm sure he determined the situation accurately because he instantly regained his post somewhere outside the closed car.

"Okay. You're right. It's not Audrey." I spoke of Finn's ex-fiancée, who had shown up unexpectedly at the CMAs a few years back and was, thankfully, living far, far away in California. "What do you want me to call her?"

"Nothing. She meant nothing."

"She wasn't what I expected" was what came out because I just didn't know what else to say.

I wasn't expecting to be thrown into that situation, just as I hadn't expected there to ever be a scenario where Finn had been unfaithful. But it had happened. A series of events had led to the perfect, horrific storm. Finn had just gotten home from a stressful summer tour, thought I was talking with my ex, and found out his father was dying all basically in the same day. When he lashed out at an innocent Chance, it broke us, but most of all him. He totally fell apart—not taking his meds, drinking, ignoring his career, and staying in the city with no contact with us. When he let a wannabe singer give him a blow job at a NYC nightclub, he hit rock bottom and confessed everything to me. It hadn't been an easy decision to forgive him, but I eventually had. I knew he was devastated by everything, and that once he had stopped taking his meds, he was no longer in control. I also knew how much he loved me…how much we loved one another. And I knew, beyond a shadow of a doubt, that there was no relationship with that girl at the nightclub and there never would be. But, now, despite not wanting to, I knew what she looked like, and I knew her name—Briar.

"Lara, please, please, baby."

"This is *our* night," I said about CMA night. "This has always been our night." My very first trip to Nashville had been for the CMAs and was the night that Finn and I had first made love. In addition, it was that night, years later, that our daughter was born. It was always our faux anniversary... our night.

"Let it keep being that way," he pleaded softly.

"You told me she would never have anything to do with our life."

"I know. She shouldn't have been here. It was a complete shock to me. I had no idea she was even in Nashville. I've not seen her since—"

I knew when—*that night*. And I didn't want to think about it anymore. I was getting upset, and I didn't want to be. "I don't want to go to the party," I interrupted, getting back to my original thought. "Just drop me off at the ranch, and you can go."

"Lara," he said immediately and with determination. "I'm not going to that party without you, especially with how you are feeling."

"I don't want to go, Finn."

"Forget whoever else might or might not be there. Let them see us—us, Beauty."

I knew he wanted me to go. It was expected of him, but he also wanted to show our unity. Even more than that, though, he wanted me to be all right.

I tried to explain as best I could, even though I was still trying to formalize it for myself. "Listen, I'm upset, but I'm not mad. I made the decision to forgive you, and I put it in the past. It's done, and we're good. We *are* 'us.' I can forgive, but I can't forget... not when I will be in fear of turning around at any moment and seeing the living proof right in my face." Don't cry. Don't cry, I internally urged myself.

He looked like he wanted to cry for me. "You simply amaze me," he said after a beat and tentatively put his hand up to my face. "You really do."

"Well, I don't really feel amazing right now. I feel little and powerless and—"

He dropped his hand from my face and instead interlocked it with one of mine. "You know I meant every word in that speech, don't you?"

"I do."

Without another word, Finn finalized our plans for the evening by stepping out of the car and finding the driver. I heard spurts of their conversation. But the gist was, Finn wanted him to take us home instead of to the after-party. Finn was going to make sure that the driver was compensated for the entire night, but his services weren't needed after the trip to the house. I wiped one of the damn tears I had urged not to fall just as Finn reentered the car.

"I'm sorry," I offered.

"How are *you* sorry? How has this made *you* be the one who is sorry? Not at all. *I* am sorry."

"I'm sorry for not being stronger."

"What? Two nights ago." He tilted his head at me. "You were so strong, baby. You didn't give up, and you didn't let me combust. You centered me."

I was glad he thought so. The fact that he had let me help him still resonated so soundly in my heart, and I know he felt the same. But that was what marriage was all about. That's what we were all about. It was a given.

"That's not strong," I denied. "That's just me loving you."

"Well…" he said as the driver entered the car and started the engine. "Ditto." Finn raised the corners of his closed mouth and caressed the top of my hand.

I felt the car slowly pull onto the road. I grasped Finn's hand with more conviction and leaned my head onto his shoulder. He wrapped his arm around my torso.

Once we were on the main road, the driver looked at us once again via the rearview mirror. "Mr. Murphy?"

"Yeah?" Finn released his head slightly from the top of mine.

"I'm sorry your night is being cut short, sir, but I have

to tell you that my little boy is sick. You know, just the throwing up stuff. My momma's there right now. That's who I've been talking with. But, I'm a single dad, and he really wants his daddy. So, I'll be able to get there sooner now."

"How old is he?" I questioned, raising my head a bit, too.

"Just turned three, ma'am."

"Ah," I smiled. "We have a three-year-old, too." I felt Finn stroke my hand.

"You should have told me that." Finn spoke to the driver. "We could have taken a cab. You should be with your son."

"Oh, no, sir. No. All's well. I'll get there soon enough. He just has a bug, but it will be good to be there for the little guy," he replied.

"They do admire their daddies," I said, looking in the mirror but squeezing Finn's hand.

"Well, I'm really glad we're skipping that party now. I kinda want to see our little ones, too."

I half-chuckled and laid my head back on Finn's shoulder as the driver said, "I understand you won tonight, sir. Congratulations."

"Yes, I sure did." Finn kissed the top of my head.

***

I went into the house ahead of Finn. He was settling things with the driver, but a lot of it, I think, was "daddy" talk. The ranch was peacefully quiet. Nola had mentioned that she was going to sleep after she got off the phone with me. I was just coming back down the stairs from checking on our slumbering offspring, when Finn entered. He set the security system, shrugged off his suit coat, and walked over to me.

"Hi, baby," he cooed and gave me a hug just like he always did whenever he would first get home, but this time we had only been apart a few minutes.

"Hi." I did a short, breathy laugh back.

"Everyone asleep?"

"Yeah."

"Hmmm." He seemed content standing there in my arms. So much so that when his phone chimed, he looked at it, put it on vibrate, and tossed it on the nearby sofa. During most of our car ride back, he had been sending after-party regrets, with limited explanations, to those in the need-to-know category. "You all right?"

"Yeah."

"Sure?" he asked, while playing with my hair, which I had pulled back on the sides just the way he liked it.

"Yeah."

I knew what he was referring to—her. But he didn't need to worry. He brought me home. He was with me. She was an unfortunate blip in the night that maybe, actually, needed to happen. Maybe I needed to see and face it straight on because, if anything, it freed me even more.

"Finn?"

"Yeah?"

"There is one thing I need, though."

"What?" He pulled away just enough so that he was still holding both of my hands but able to look at me directly.

"It's kinda a big favor...." I let the tail end of my comment purposefully drag.

What doubt was left on his face was completely erased. "Do you want to watch *House Hunters*?" He jested, playing right along with the memory I had sent him back to—our conversation on our very first post-CMA awards night.

"No." I laughed.

"Are you going to ask me?" he teased, while touching his fingertip first to my nose and then to my mouth.

I flashbacked to that insecure, twenty-nine-year-old me seven years before. "Make love to me," I said in a voice that verged on a whisper.

"First of all, just so we have things straight, it's not a favor."

I smiled at his reference of how I misconstrued Finn's intent all those years before. I thought he had really made love to me just because I asked it as a favor. He loved me back then, though, as much as I did him. And, thank God, that never changed. In fact, if anything, our bond grew.

"I love you," he continued. "And it will be greatest thing in the world." He grabbed my hand and gently guided me up the stairs, just as he did our very first night together.

CHAPTER FIVE

"I told you I wanted no part of this!" I lamented while shaking my head and lifting Arinn, still grasping onto the empty shot glass, out of her highchair.

Finn almost doubled over laughing. "What? I was rooting for the rosary beads. I'd be just fine with her becoming a nun."

"No, you wouldn't," I replied. Despite the Murphy family being religious, I could not imagine Finn wanting our daughter to grow up in solitude.

"The shot glass just means she'll be social. And we already know that. She's so easygoing." He started blowing lip bubbles on Arinn's belly, causing her to laugh.

"It's not even an Irish tradition!" I was still on my kick about not having done it in the first place. Having grown up with an alcoholic father, seeing my child, at the tender age of one, pick up a shot glass was not comforting.

"Daddy, me!" Chance chimed in, wanting the belly attention also.

"No, it's not Irish, but it's a family tradition. It's just fun. At least Chance, here, picked the money." He recalled our son picking the final of the three choices— the coin— when laid out in front of him at his first birthday party.

"We'll have something to fall back on with your early retirement." He tousled Chance into his arms and blew bubbles on his stomach.

I laughed at both the money and retirement references. It was true I hadn't been to work in over a year, and I wasn't going back. I had finally made the choice to "retire" from the technology job I had since graduating from college. We certainly didn't need my extra income, and I had plenty to keep me busy as Mrs. Finn Murphy and Mommy. As much as I thought I would miss it, I hadn't. Being able to watch Finn smile and listen to Chance and Arinn exude love and laughter made it even more worth it.

"What did *you* pick as a baby?" I asked my husband as he sat Chance back down.

Finn smirked. "I knocked all three of them down in one swipe."

"Really?"

"Yeah. That's the story."

"Rebel from the beginning." Taking the shot glass from her, I put Arinn down to freely roam.

"Uh-huh." He smiled. "I have a feeling it was Nola, though. I bet she was the one who knocked them away from me. She's like that...never letting me have anything."

A large, exaggerated breath of air left my mouth. "Geez, Finn, give your sister a break! She is one of your biggest fans. Next to me, of course." I amended. "I don't know what we would have done if she hadn't come down here to watch the kids last night."

"I'm teasing!" He wrapped his arm around my shoulder bringing my head to his. "Speaking of, I'm going to check on their flight. They should have gotten in."

Nola and Kelsea had left that morning—the day after the CMAs— to go back to their home in suburban New York. We had gotten up early to see them off but had gone back to sleep for a little while afterward. Luckily, the birthday girl and her brother allowed us that extra time, too.

"I think I'm on diaper duty." I acknowledged the smell that said Arinn's mini-birthday cake must have gone right through her.

"Have fun with that," Finn joshed.

"Hey," I said, lifting Arinn back into my arms. "Can I take that ridiculous red ribbon off her crib now? It's her first birthday."

"Yeah." Finn laughed. "I don't think anyone is going to steal her and replace her with a changeling." He spoke of an actual Irish tradition where, during the baby's first year, mothers use a red ribbon to protect the babies from fairies who want to whisk them off to raise as their own.

"It's a good thing I love you."

"It's a great thing." He enhanced the adjective on purpose and smiled.

***

After the CMAs, we had a little free time to concentrate on what most people would consider mundane things. But I treasured them...the whole, busy lot of them. Especially because they were things we could do together. Finn didn't have as many obligations, or as much consequent stress, since the awards were over.

We started by taking the kids to the farm that Finn had taken me to the first time I visited Nashville. We reenacted the scene by going on a hay ride and buying pumpkins to carve, since Chance and Arinn had essentially missed Halloween due to our partial cross-country move. Their gleeful giggles with every bounce of the cart, as well as our selfie kiss, were well-documented on both of our phones.

We also looked into preschools per recommendations from Finn's friends and colleagues. The kids had been enrolled in one in New York, which, depending on our schedules, they only went to a couple times a week for socialization purposes. It was very important that we found a respectable and ethical establishment to trust our most precious cargo with, especially considering Finn's celebrity status. And, after visiting and interviewing a number of places, we decided on one and planned on starting the kids in the beginning of December.

Finally, we made the kids' bedrooms their own. They had been a guest room and work area before. Now, they took on personality.

When Chance got to pick the color he wanted to paint his walls, he very distinctly said, "Boo."

Of course, Finn couldn't resist teasing him. "You sure? You want us to paint it black with ghosts all over?"

"No!" Chance denied vehemently.

"You said, 'Boo.'"

"Boo, Daddy! Boo!" He tried again to say the color to no avail.

"Yeah, Boo. Ooo!" Finn wiggled around like a ghost in front of our toddler.

"Da—" I could see our son was getting irritated.

"Finn…." I warned.

"Okay, Little Man." Finn conceded, calling Chance a nickname he had given our son since birth. "Blue's one of my favorite colors, too. Good choice. You're going to help me paint, aren't you?"

"Yeah!" His little face brightened up in excitement.

Finn always liked being hands-on when it came to family stuff, and that included the residences. Although we definitely could afford a cleaning service and a decorator, we did those things ourselves. It allowed us the privacy that Finn was so conscientious and protective of. In addition, painting the rooms was fun and relaxing.

For Arinn's room, we selected green for her Irish heritage. We added the accents of shapes and stars and, of course, her two favorite stuffed animals—a spotted dog and a tiny mouse. If she didn't have one or the other with her at all times, her normally pleasant, easygoing personality took a turn for the worse.

Along with installing night lights along the upstairs

hallway, we came up with one more idea for the kids. We painted both Chance and Arinn's hands yellow and carefully had them leave their two handprints on their bedroom door. The yellow was for the brightness they brought into our lives and the small hands to show how much they were going to grow inside their new home.

***

A couple nights after our home decorating day, Finn went into town to meet with his band. It wasn't particularly late when I went to bed, but I had still drifted off before he arrived back home. It was him shutting both of our babies' doors—knowing he kissed them good-night even though they had been asleep way before me—that woke me up. Entering our master suite, he went immediately into the adjoining bathroom where I heard the telltale sign of teeth brushing before the light went back off and he reentered the bedroom area.

"Hey," I said.

"Hi, baby." He softly smiled in my direction. And then, while removing his tan colored T and jeans, said, "Sorry, didn't mean to wake you."

"That's okay. Kinda doing that thing— sleeping and waiting to make sure you got home okay. How'd it go?" I tacked on the question.

"Good." He took a last look at his phone and placed it on his nightstand. "Well, if you really want to know… it was actually exhilarating."

I had to admit, that got my attention a little more. "That's great," I said. "Did you do something different?"

Now just in his boxer briefs, he crawled under the sheet beside me. "No. Nope. It just felt different." He leaned toward me, feathering a few soft kisses on my lips and then circling his fingertips on my cami-covered stomach. "It was like it was normal." He continued his response, "I don't know…at ease."

"It's not usually?"

"Yeah." He paused. "Yeah. Lar, you know what I was thinking about driving home?" He didn't wait for my response. "How incredible you are."

"Mmmm. Well, yeah, of course. Just figuring that out now, are you?" My sarcasm covered the truth of how unbelievably un-incredible I really felt.

"No, listen." He didn't even bother to shake his head, but I knew he was thinking it. Instead, he propped himself up on one elbow and turned a little more directly to me. "I love free jammin' and talking music with the guys. But knowing that I could do that and be right back here with you? It opens everything up. When I was here and you and the kids were in New York, I made the best of it. At least I thought I did. Until I realized tonight how much it means always knowing you're near. *You* made that possible."

Some time while he was talking, I had sat up to meet him. Now, running my fingers along the back of his head, I spoke my side. "I know exactly what you mean. I'm not worrying about flight departures and arrivals." Although, I knew he was going to have to go places without us sometimes. "I don't have to think as much about, you know, will this be something when Finn is in town or am I doing this alone." Seeing his eyes go instantly sad, I continued quickly. "I didn't even realize I did that until we've been down here, and now I don't have to. It's just that we never knew any other way. We've been living like that since before we were even engaged. I may say this has been best for the kids, and it is, but I feel more at peace, too." I thought about it being a fresh start as I moved my hand onto his hip. "Closet space and toys and juice boxes—we really changed your world, huh, Cowboy? This is far from the bachelor pad I first visited years ago."

"Thank God," he sweetly replied, pushing his hand through my hair.

"You really changed mine, too," I offered.

"Some of it has been for the better, right?" he asked,

but I knew he was confident enough of my answer.

"Quit fishing for compliments." I poked him in the side and then rolled my body onto his. Straddling his muscular legs, I kissed him. "I'm glad we're here."

"Yeah?" His serene smile was just mere inches away from my similar expression. "You have no idea how happy that makes me."

I kissed him with a little more intensity, and he scooted me more snugly onto his lap. "Maybe I do." I teased, feeling his manliness through his gray boxer briefs. I pulled at the waist band and reached my hands under the fabric.

"God," he partially groaned when I practically swallowed his tongue with mine, all the while not moving my hands from his briefs. "Roxy…" Bringing my hands up to his lips, he said "Now" and flipped me onto my back. As we dismantled the rest of each other's clothing, Finn said, "I want to make love to you all night. I don't want us to be even an inch apart."

"I wouldn't want it any other way." I wrapped my legs more definitively around him, and we began to rub and rock, both calling out each other's names as happiness mixed with pleasure and with love.

***

And then it was Thanksgiving. The wholesome holiday went as well as could be expected, considering the number of relatives who bombarded our abode. We had arranged for everyone to board at a nearby hotel with the exception of Finn's parents, who we had stay with us. Nola and Kelsea returned with Will. Will's parents, who lived in Boston, also joined us, as they had since before I even became a member of the family. They always seemed a little distant to me, but it was probably my imagination, since, before me, they had been determined to set Finn up with one of their friends' daughters. My mother also joined us from Pittsburgh, bringing her famous chocolate chip cookies.

But my brother wasn't there. He remained in his North Carolina home to spend the holiday with his girlfriend, Piper. I had mixed feelings about his absence. I hadn't seen him in nearly ten months—since the surprising big divorce and girlfriend reveal. And I had never met the infamous Piper. I tried not to, but I resented her, even though Lane insisted she had nothing to do with his divorce. So, I was glad for another reprieve of meeting her. But, at the same time, I missed my brother, and I was sad that I would have to wait until our vow renewal to finally see him again.

And although there were things we wished we could change and diseases we wished we could cure, we still found thankfulness and took turns sharing our gratitude with one another. We were thankful for pumpkin cake. We were thankful for little girls celebrating their first year on Earth. We were thankful for climbing mountains. We were thankful for family. We were thankful for love.

***

It was the Friday a week after Thanksgiving—a few days since everyone had gone back to their lives in their respective states. Our family of four was resettling into our routine…what little we had established since moving to Nashville. Finn had gone to the studio in town and, having just finished lunch, I was getting Chance and Arinn ready to go to a local park for a children's theater production.

Knowing I had a little time to spare and craving some adult conversation, even if it was via a technology format, I texted my husband. *The new Ben Winthrop romcom premieres next week & we ARE going 2 see it.* I didn't expect an immediate response. So, I went on my way making sure everything was secure in our house before we left.

When I came back to my phone, however, there was a text back from my husband. *Really???*

Yes! I typed back, laughing.

I could just picture his face. He detested going to movies because they were such a public thing. And, to top it off, he knew Ben Winthrop was my "celebrity crush." But he also knew he had nothing to be concerned about because Finn was my real and only love. Plus, we had met Ben months before and became instant friends.

No excuses. I added.

Okay, boss. What do I get in return? He typed back.

I laughed even louder, making Chance question what was so funny. "Your dad," I answered generically.

"He is funny," Chance agreed. When I stuck my tongue out and crossed my eyes at my son, he added while laughing, "You funny, too, Mommy."

"Thanks, Chance." I chuckled, in a beautifully light mood.

"Even Arinn funny." Picking up on the good humor in the room, he wanted to keep it going.

"I'm glad you think so," I said.

"I wuv Arinn."

I laughed, recognizing the schmoozing part of my son. He did love his sister. But I knew he had said that for my benefit.

"Go get your orange coat. We'll be ready to go in a couple minutes."

"The one with no arms?"

"Yes, Chance. The vest."

His three-year-old description amused me. But, responding to my husband dictated comedic concentration. So, I sent my little boy on his way to get the in-between seasons attire and gave myself a moment before creatively responding.

Your choice. I finally settled on the text to send.

Hmmm… already planning. Def. involves U tearing my clothes off.

"Oh, God!" I verbalized, while laughing and smiling at his accompanying wink icon.

Before I could think of a response, he sent another text. *What's the plan 4 dinner?*

Our sexting seemingly momentarily halted, I wondered if he had an audience or if he was legitimately hungry. Watching Chance struggle with putting his little vest on, I answered, *Leftovers or I'll try to pick up something after the play. Gotta run. Love U.*

I must love U, too, if I am going to this movie.

U do. Forever.

***

And then the bottom dropped out. It came crashing violently to the ground and fractured into so many millions of pieces, I didn't know how it could ever be repaired. I didn't know how I was even standing, nonetheless breathing.

"Finn! Finn!" I was screaming, and this time it wasn't a dream. I was in a real, awake, live nightmare.

"All ready?" My husband's voice came from across the phone line, obviously completely oblivious to the terror in my voice.

"What?" What was he talking about?

"For tearing my clothe—"

"Finn? Finn, do you have Arinn?" I interrupted with a pleading, praying query.

"What? No. Why would I have Arinn?"

My already nauseous stomach felt like it was going to unload itself. "You don't have her? You didn't ask someone to get her and bring her—"

It was his turn to interrupt me, and I could hear the panic start to register. "No. Why? What are you talking about?"

"Oh, my God," was what I managed verbally. I had been hoping beyond hope that maybe, just maybe, that was the case. But, deep inside, I knew Finn wouldn't have someone get Arinn, especially without telling me. "He doesn't…" I turned to speak to the theater personnel. "He has no idea."

"Lara?" Finn's voice was trying to draw me back in from across the line. "Lara, what's going on? Where are you? What's going on with Arinn?"

As I watched the childcare workers scramble once again and get on phones, etc., I answered my husband. "Finn, she's gone! She's…I don't know…missing." I had been too caught up in the moment and flurry and hope before then to even cry. But now, verbalizing the truth, tears began to invade my cheeks.

"What are you talking about?" His voice was now beyond panicked. As the theater's childcare supervisor told me the suspect's—God, suspect! —phone was just going to voice mail, my husband was belting out my name. "Lara, tell me what's going on!"

I swiped at the tears and tried to breathe. "I'm at the park. It was that kids' musical theater thing. She's…she's gone. Somebody took her. Oh, my God. It was one of their people. They said I asked her to bring Arinn to me. I didn't! They… they think maybe she just walked out with her. She's not answering her phone. She took her. She took our baby."

"Call the police," came my husband's directive. "Call the police right now."

"They did. The cops are already on their way."

"Lara, where's Chance?"

"He's here. He's with me."

I looked down at our son, whose hand I had not let go of since the moment I heard the news. He was being remarkably still and quiet. If he couldn't quite make out what was going on around him, he at least knew it wasn't a good thing.

"Okay." There was the tiniest sigh of relief from Finn.

"We were watching the play," I tried to explain, but I knew it was coming across in splintered spurts. "Arinn was with the show's child care service. Oh my God, Finn."

"Baby, I'm on my way, okay?" He was pushing aside some of the fear I knew was metastasizing in him and was taking charge, just like he always wanted to take care of all of us. "What? What park?"

I was hearing rumblings from his end of the phone conversation and, of course, there was chaos happening right in front of me. I needed him there right away. But I couldn't think. I was so rattled and distraught, nothing was coming. "I...I...uh...uh, the park... the park near where you took me the very first time I came down here. The takeout..." I flashed back to that peaceful, loving memory of Finn first introducing me to Nashville all those years before. I was there. I was standing there, and I still couldn't remember the damn name. "Finn...." I cried.

"Centennial. Centennial Park. Okay. Okay. We're good." I admired his attempt at calming, choice words even if I knew we were far from being good or calm. "I'm close by. You'll stay there?"

"Yeah. Yeah." I was distracted, not only by my own cycling brain, but also one of the performers telling me our exact location. I relayed it to Finn. "Uh, yeah. Near the parth—"

"Parthenon. I got it," he said.

"The police are here."

"Good. I'll be there."

"Finn, God...."

"Hey, it's...." I knew he was trying to say the right thing—something reassuring, but I also knew he was as terrified as I was. "I'm on my way. Seriously, five minutes."

"Hurry," I encouraged. But then in my manic, pessimistic mind, I thought of what hurrying could lead to. "I mean, get here, but be careful."

"I will. Christ!" he shouted, and I knew he had been reacting on instinct up to that point, and now it was really setting in. "Okay," he tried again. "I'm gonna make some calls. I'll be there soon. Call me if you hear anything."

"Yeah."

There was a pause before he offered, "She'll be all right."

"You don't know that," I replied, wondering if I was still being pessimistic or just realistic.

"She will. You believe that, Lara," he said with an authoritative tone.

I closed my eyes and tried to imagine what he wanted me to. But when I reopened them, there were serious looking police officers, frantic park personnel, and a terrified little boy grasping my hand. It was hard to believe… no matter how much I wanted to.

CHAPTER SIX

After telling us they had patrol cars circulating throughout the park, the initial two officers on the scene were asking the childcare workers and I questions when Finn arrived. I saw his shiny roadster pull up via the windows of the part of the building they had us sequestered in. If the cops didn't have more serious things on their minds, I'm pretty sure they could have ticketed my husband for his fast and erratic driving. Leaping out of the car just as quickly, he beelined through the doors and over to me. Scooping up Chance, Finn buried our son to his chest and then tugged me into his body kissing the top of my head.

"You okay?" he asked, with me still secure into his side. "Lar?"

Of course I wasn't okay—nothing was okay. "I'm sorry. I'm sorry," I lamented, still trying to accept what had happened. "I left her with the theater's sitting service."

Parting our bodies so he could place Chance back down, Finn then grasped onto my hand before letting loose on the staff and the police. "What the hell happened? What the hell did you let happen to my daughter?"

"Mr. Murphy?" The police officer who had been questioning me extended his hand to my husband, but Finn rebutted the offer. "I'm Officer Rivers." The bald forty-something introduced himself anyway. "We're investigating what happened. The facts as we know it are: your daughter was with the child care service right here while—"

"You don't lose a kid in a park!" Finn screamed. "You don't...Jesus! Not in the fucking park."

Even though I obviously knew he was upset, his outburst startled me. And then I thought more carefully about his words. The park. Shit! Finn had been lost in the park as a child with his grandmother. Oh, God. As messed up emotionally as I was, I needed to comfort him. I rubbed circles on his back accentuated by his black and gray Under Armour sweater.

His voice was still abrasive but, perhaps, a notch less as he started again, "You don't leave a kid alone to—"

"Let me reassure you," inserted Teddi, the childcare supervisor who looked as nervous as hell around an irate Finn. "She wasn't alone. We just need to find—"

"Who? Who is it? Who took her? How?" He was asking some of the same questions the police had asked, just in a completely different manner.

"Her name is Brianna," Teddi answered.

"This Brianna was the last person seen with your daughter," Officer Rivers explained the facts that I already knew but Finn did not.

"Who is she?" Finn still wasn't calm.

"She's one of the performers in the first half of the show." Teddi fidgeted from one foot to the other.

"And? How did she get my daughter?" As Finn asked, I gathered Chance back into my arms.

"She said she knew you...you and your wife," offered the even more distraught childcare worker who actually gave Arinn to this Brianna person. "She mentioned her by name. She said she was just going to walk her over to Mrs.

Murphy." Guilt stricken, she looked over at me—no one had brought Arinn over or even approached me until I went to pick her up after the performance and she was…she was…she was gone.

"And you just let her?" Finn looked from one worker to the next.

"I'm sorry," the second one said. "She's our employee, and she said Mrs. Murphy wanted her to."

Finn turned to me, a glimmer of hope possibly in his eyes. "Did you know someone in the show? Maybe—"

But I hadn't. "No," I answered teary-eyed once more. We were getting nowhere, and whoever had Arinn was getting further and further away. "You know I don't know anyone in Nashville. Plus, a lot of the performers had costumes and masks on. Finn, who knows who I am? Who knows who I am and wants to take our baby?"

Because that was the truth of it. Finn had always maintained a very private, personal life, even before me. He liked his privacy. It kept him grounded, and it allowed all of us— the children, myself, and him—some freedom. Besides a few very select social media postings and big-event spottings, the only thing that was out there about Finn was his music.

"Fuck! Fuck!" He turned around once and then again—a classic, sure sign of Finn's frustration.

"Mr. Murphy, I know this is extremely hard, sir, but we need you to calm down." Officer Rivers, if anyone, was the rational one. "We are waiting for the video feed," he spoke of the security camera footage I knew they were pulling up. "In the meantime, can you give me a description of your daughter? Height? Weight? Hair and eye color? What she was wearing? Any recent photos or video would be a huge help." He looked from Finn to me.

I was the doctor check-up parent. I went to those things. I knew those things. "She's, uh… She was thirty inches last time. She's probably thirty-one now. Weight? Twenty pounds. She was wearing a sparkly tutu-like skirt, red and white tights, gold shoes, and a white onesie with the words 'future rock star' written in gold and red."

I could picture her so clearly. She had looked like a shining star when we had arrived. Her smile had matched her sparkling outfit. She had been so happy. Everyone there had said so. The thought of that made the true deluge of tears start. Finn put his strong, large hand on the back of my head to help settle me as I put Chance back down.

Wiping my self-indulgent tears, I said, "I'm sorry. What else did you ask?"

Finn took over, though, while I tried to regulate my breathing. "Her hair? It's like a brown with some red in it, and her eyes are identical to my wife's."

Officer Rivers looked at me, presumably identifying my eye color, wrote some things down, and said, "Anything else? Allergies? Birthmarks?"

"No. She's perfect." Finn answered as a biased father, but it was true…our daughter really was perfect.

"I had one of those headbands in her hair. It was red and gold." I kept getting flashes of my smiling girl all decked out. "And she had a pink fleece coat and hat. Did she have that? You don't think she's cold do you?" The thought just made me shiver.

"We gave Brianna her coat, yeah," the second worker said with confidence, which only made me feel slightly better. "But she didn't take the—"

"Mousey!" Chance yelled out when the woman turned toward the table behind her where Arinn's favorite stuffed animal sat.

I went over and grabbed the soft toy. "Oh…oh, no. Arinn…." I cried out for my daughter who, despite her bubbly and friendly personality, had to be scared without any of her family or her comforting mouse.

"Lara…" Finn, seeing that I was going to break, took the toy and handed it to Chance. He then drew his arms around me. "It's all right. Here," Finn was at least sounding a little more rational, but I'm sure it was for my benefit. He showed his phone to the police officer. "I have photos from her birthday just a few weeks ago and there's also a video."

"You do?" Officer Rivers asked, trying unsuccessfully to mask his surprise.

If the circumstances were different, I would have been all up in arms over his question. There was a general presumption that anyone with any kind of celebrity status showed no interest in their children—having them raised essentially by nannies and boarding schools, etc. And the wives or girlfriends just had the kids to hold onto their man. It disgusted me, and it couldn't be more wrong.

While Finn and Officer Rivers transferred the pics over to the police, I tried to fake play with Chance and Mousey. Chance was being good, but you could tell his patience was growing thin. He had enjoyed the show, but it had been long, and he needed to move around a little. Keeping the closest of eyes on him, I let him literally run around the room while some of the patrols came in to update us on the search. They had looked in any places Arinn could have been trapped in and searched all the parked vehicles, but, unfortunately, there was not any sign of our precious baby girl.

When they left to resume their search, Officer Rivers asked another question. "She is your biological child, correct? Both of yours?" On our immediate and joint affirmative response, he explained. "We just need to make sure it's not a custody situation."

"Absolutely not." Finn looked and sounded offended. I'm not sure if it was because he thought they were once again generalizing his profession or simply doubting his manhood. "She's our child, and she has a very loving and stable home." He grabbed my hand once again to show our bond.

"Okay, sir. I'm sorry. I need to ask. It can eliminate things and make it easier to help us find your daughter."

"We got the video pulled up!" yelled out another police officer in the back of the room. All of us, including the childcare workers and me toting Chance, scurried over to the monitor.

"That's her." Teddi was the first to speak and confirm. "That's Brianna."

I let myself look then. This was going to be the real proof. The real proof that my child was gone and that someone took her...on purpose. But why?

As I was still adjusting my eyes to the monitor which confirmed Arinn was in the woman's arms, obviously leaving the facility, Officer Rivers asked, "Do you know her, Mr. and Mrs. Murphy? Family? Friend? Play group parent?" He offered positive, hopeful suggestions as to the culprit.

I swallowed the vomit that had made its way up to my esophagus. I did know that woman. I had met her. It had been once, and it was far from positive.

"Oh, my God. Finn, is that?"

His words were coming out at the same time as mine. "Shhiiit. Shit." And, once again, that's all he needed to say to confirm.

"Oh. Oh, my God." I gasped, bringing my hands up to my teary face.

"Do you know—"

Finn didn't let the officer finish. "Briar," he admitted. "Briar is her stage name. Brianna—"

Finn looked over at me. I had my hands to my knees. I wasn't breathing, was I? I know for sure if I stood straight, I would pass out. I could see the guilt in Finn's eyes. I could see the guilt and the worry not only over our daughter but over me. He softly rubbed his hand on my shoulder.

"And you know her how?" the officer asked slowly.

"She's in the music business, too. I helped get her on a label." Finn spoke the truth. Immediately regretting that night a couple months before, Finn had arranged for Briar to be on a label—not his—in exchange for her silence with the press. "But we've only met twice. What the hell?" he spit out the last part, angry again.

"Just to confirm, that is who you handed Arinn Murphy off to?" Officer Rivers asked the younger childcare employee.

"Yes," she admitted. "I'm so, so sorry." She met my eyes that time as I was slowly trying to stand erect again. "I had no idea. She said she knew her. I thought she was all right."

"Her full name?" he continued his questioning.

"Brianna Yorwood," Teddi cited. "She was part of the performance crew."

"I didn't recognize her." I was looking at Finn now. "They all had elaborate costumes and masks."

"Okay, baby." He met my eyes. "Why would you? And why would you think she would— God!" He did his turn-around thing again with Chance looking up, fearful of the scene.

"What reason would she have to take your daughter?" Officer Rivers inquired.

"I don't know!" Finn bellowed.

"Do you think it's a ransom thing?" He continued his questioning.

"No," my husband answered back. "Do people really do that?"

"People take kids for all different kinds of reasons. No idea?" the officer asked one more time.

"No!" Finn had answered the question enough. His frustration was apparent even to my spinning, spinning brain.

Officer Rivers decided on a different path. "Do you happen to know what type of vehicle she drives?"

I heard Teddi say something about a smaller red car but not candy apple red. But I wasn't concentrating fully. I was picturing Briar or Brianna—whatever the hell her name was— at the CMAs, having the audacity to approach

Finn…to approach me… to approach us. I was imagining the two of them behind that Manhattan nightclub. She was a two-bit slut. She was someone who wanted to get things without working for them or earning them. What did she want with my baby?

"Okay, I'm going to update all our personnel on the facts and descriptions." I tuned back into Officer Rivers voice. "And we're trying to get contacts for Miss Yorwood's family and friends. We've got to talk with them and get a clear photo of Miss Yorwood. I'm going to have to ask you all to stay put and calm for a bit."

"Find my baby. She has to be so scared," I pleaded, looking at my other scared child clutching his sister's mouse.

"Ma'am, we're doing everything we can. We have eyes on the airport and all the train and bus stations. And we have everything in the park shut down."

"We know." Thank God Finn calmed down for that second to be the rational one. We were a team, even to the point of knowing when to switch roles of falling apart and appearing to have it all together.

Officer Rivers asked for everyone to clear the room to give Finn, Chance, and I the opportunity to be alone together. After a few pitiful glances, everyone did as instructed. While I had thought I had lost it before, I completely fell apart then. My energy level kicked up about five thousand notches. I started circling around the room as if I were on skates in the Stanley Cup final and my team was down.

Even though tears were hindering my vision, I was able to look out the window and see all the yellow crime scene tape. When had that happened? Crime scene…crime scene…crime scene…It all seemed so surreal.

And Finn was lost in his own world. I heard him mumbling on and on about how he was never going to set foot in a park ever again. I saw him looking at his phone screen, and I wondered if he was waiting for some miraculous call or if he still had her photo up...that silly one-year-old grin.

When I heard sweet little Chance's voice telling his dad that he was hungry, I slowed my "skating" pattern down and wiped the tears to look over at my two boys. They were so similar in appearance—brown hair, gray eyes—and so similar in persona—caring, strong, determined. They were both miracles in my life— them and Arinn.

"I know, bud. I'm sorry." Finn spoke to our son while sitting down on the worn patterned sofa. "Come here, sit on my lap. You're being so good."

Surprisingly, I was able to calm my jittery body enough to be able to sit down next to them. I searched through my purse until I found what I knew I always tried to keep in it—a snack for the kids. After all, it was just about that time when I should have been starting to think about picking up dinner. I unwrapped and handed a granola bar to Chance instead.

"Thanks, Mommy," he said without being prompted, and that alone almost broke my heart. His sweetness and understanding was a blessing to be cherished.

"You're welcome, Little Man." I kissed the top of his head through my tears and then looked up at my husband, who was slowly shaking his head. I didn't know if it meant anything in particular, but I suspect it summed up the entire afternoon. "She won't hurt her, will she?" I practically whispered just in the fear of saying the words out loud.

"No," he started. "No. I don't even know why she...Damn it!" He swore, making a startled Chance look up mid-munch. "Sorry, Little Man," Finn apologized. "Lar?" It was a generic query into what I was thinking.

But I didn't know. I had no idea how to cope or even think. I was trying to be brave and quiet for our son, but all I wanted to do was break down or scream. No. All I wanted was for the nightmare to end and my daughter to be back.

I leaned into Finn's side, or we leaned into each other, for a little while before Officer Rivers returned with a couple other officers. They reassured us that they were actively out searching the park. They also had highway patrol looking for Brianna's car and were on route to her apartment.

"Why would she still be using that car, though?" I asked. "And going to her apartment? Do you think it will be that easy? I mean if she really wanted to get away with—" I stopped myself, looking at Chance. No one had used the word "kidnapped" in front of him, and I wanted to keep it that way. And as much as I would have loved for it to be that easy as to track down her car or knock on her door, I knew better.

Finn must have been thinking the same thing because he was still concentrating on closer locations. "And you have checked everywhere in the park? I mean, bathrooms, vacant areas…?"

"Yes, sir, and we will do it again." When Finn didn't rebut, Officer Rivers continued with what would come next. "I'd like at least one of you to take me home to your residence. We'll set up a post there to keep watch out for the perp and keep you safe. We'd also like to get a sample of your child's DNA. We can use maybe her hair brush or a sippy cup. And if you have a piece of clothing or something for her scent." He started looking at Arinn's stuffed mouse in my hands.

"What?" I know I screeched out the word. "DNA? Scent? Oh, God. No." I tugged onto Mousey harder.

"Hey," Finn said in an authoritative way to the cops. "Take it easy with what you're saying."

"I'm sorry, Mr. Murphy. But we need to implement everything we can in order to get your daughter back."

Although not my favorite, I had watched enough crime shows to know what they were asking for didn't necessarily mean they would get her back alive. Finn knew what I thought, and I'm sure he feared it, too, with the police request. It was something neither of us wanted even remotely in the back of our minds.

Bracketing his hands on my face, Finn got me to look at him and, in as much as a reassuring voice as he could manage, said, "Lara, you go. Get them what they need there. It's all right. It will help. And take Chance. He needs to be home."

Before I could reply, one of the other officers, obviously reading something sent on his phone, asked, "Mr. Murphy, do you know of any e-mails or social media for Miss Yorwood that we can try to contact her on? Or another phone line? If you—"

Finn dropped his hands from my face. "No! I don't have her number, and she shouldn't have mine." Everyone in that room knew he meant business from the force of his denial.

"Okay." The officer took it in stride, though, surely having to deal with emotional and angry people on a daily basis. "What about you Mrs. Murphy?" He turned to me. "Has she ever contacted you?"

"No. I just met her at the CMAs." I glanced at Finn. "I don't even know her."

"Well, she knows you and your kids apparently." Officer Rivers' comment made me physically shiver, thinking about how much Briar/Brianna knew about our lives. "Let me just send this text out, and then I will personally go home with you, Mrs. Murphy," he said. "Mr. Murphy, you're staying here to continue with our team?"

"Yes. Absolutely."

"Finn, I can't leave. Don't they want us to search? I need to be out there," I pleaded, looking directly into my husband's eyes. "I can't leave her." It was just like when I miscarried a few years before. I didn't want to leave the hospital. It was the last place I still had that baby with me. The park was the last place I had Arinn with me. I could not leave her.

Finn took a deep breath, closed his eyes for a second,

and tried to radiate whatever strength he was managing onto me. And I knew there wasn't much because if anyone understood the fear of leaving, it was my husband. "I'm here. I'll do whatever they need. I'm not leaving," he stated. "The police aren't leaving. We need you to, though. *I* need you to. Chance needs you to. Arinn…" He said her name slower than the others. "Arinn needs you to. You need to be there to help the police. Lara, please, baby. I know. I know, it's hard. God, I know. Come here." He pulled me into his chest and fiercely, protectively, held on.

When he eventually threatened to break our embrace, however, I wouldn't let him. If I could manage to leave the park, I couldn't do it alone. I didn't want to be at the house with just strangers, even if they were police officers. I needed him.

But he thought I was strong. And he needed me to be strong. "Okay," he said, lightly forcing us apart. "You can do this."

It was, ironically, witnessing the tears pooling in Finn's eyes that gave me the strength. I took a couple big, big breaths and nodded my head up and down. "Okay," I finally managed.

"Okay," he echoed, touching my face before picking Chance up and saying, "I love you. You know that, right?" When our little boy, as tradition, stretched out his arms extra wide to show how much, Finn choked on his first words, "Yeah, buddy, and more. Go home with Mommy. I'll see you soon."

"Daddy?" Chance said when Finn eventually released him. "Where Arinn?"

Finn glanced at me before answering. "She's…she'll be home later." And then to me, "Lara? Are you all right to drive?" On my slightest of hesitations, Finn looked at Officer Rivers. "You'll drive our car, yes?"

"I'll follow her. It'll—" The police officer started to reply.

But Finn cut him short with his firm clarification.

"You'll drive them home in our car."

"Yes, sir. I can do that."

Finn brought me back into his arms. "I love you." He held his lips to the top of my head for an extended moment.

Moving my head up and down in agreement, I managed an "I love you, too." But it was in that high-pitched, squeaky, fearful kind of way. And then I took Chance's hand and led the policeman to my car.

***

Finn and I were either texting or talking on the phone with one another pretty much nonstop from the moment I left to the moment he eventually made it back home later that evening. There were additional police personnel, including specialized units, brought in both to the ranch and to the scene of the crime to continue the investigation. We both had police stationed with us, and we shared with each other what we knew. They had personnel watching Brianna's apartment, tracking her credit card and phone, and monitoring social media. But, essentially, it came down to nothing. There was nothing to report. Our daughter was still missing, and there weren't any significant leads.

I tried to play hostess for a while—preparing coffee, showing everyone around the grounds and house, and offering food when I knew I needed to make something for Chance, if not myself, to eat. It helped ever so slightly to keep my mind occupied, as did playing with Chance. But the thought that there should be another little being joining us often overtook my fake smile. And the laptops, walkie-talkies, and uniforms monopolizing our dining room brought me to downright tears.

I eventually needed time alone. After getting Chance to bed, which was later than usual, I let the remaining officers know I was going to be upstairs if there were any new developments. The number of police had diminished, with one staying in the dining room and one at the driveway's gate. And, I couldn't help but wonder if we would have even had that if it weren't for Finn's fame. I guessed, in that case, it was a good thing.

I sat in Arinn's nursery for a while. I rocked Mousey and Spot the dog in the glider chair, as if they could even remotely be a replacement for my precious little girl. I opened the music box that Nola and family had given her for her christening. White with pink hearts, it was custom-made to play a couple of Finn's softer ballads. I looked at the framed photograph of Chance, who was ever-so-gently, with just his fingertips, touching the top of Arinn's head right after she was born. He had been so gentle with her, as if she were going to break. I wondered if he had subconsciously gotten that fear from me. After all, I had two babies taken away before Arinn—one I gave up for adoption, and one, who Finn and I had named Chloe, I had miscarried. Was it happening again?

As if on instinct, Finn texted me at that moment of lowest despair, telling me he was on his way home. There wasn't anything else he could do at the park. And, selfishly, I was glad he was coming home. I needed him more than ever.

After some pacing, checking on a sleeping Chance, and getting no new information from the officer downstairs, I went to our master bedroom. I was curled in a fetal position on top of the bedspread when I heard the garage door open and close, then Finn's muffled voice mixing with the police officer's downstairs, and then his feet sluggishly making their way up the steps. My heart almost broke hearing him open and close both kids' bedroom doors, surely only seeing half of what he wanted to.

And then I saw him. Despite it being late and very dark outside, the light from the sitting room just before our master bedroom illuminated his figure at our doorway. Holding my breath, I looked up at him, hoping that by some miracle he would have Arinn in his arms. But, of course, he didn't. And it broke that tiniest little string of hope I had been holding onto. And I bawled. Looking as defeated as I felt, Finn hung his head, put his phone on his nightstand, and silently climbed onto the bed next to me. We held each other as if we were standing and hugging, not our normal spooning position.

When my sobs eventually subsided into a few straggling tears, I slightly retracted and dared to ask, "Anything?" Even though, because of our constant correspondence, I already knew the unwelcomed answer.

After a beat, he shook his head negatively but offered, "I told the police everything."

I knew what he meant. And I appreciated it. But it really didn't make any difference. Whether Briar considered herself a jilted musician or a jilted lover, the end result was still the same. She took our baby with some sort of malice, and the police were acting accordingly.

"She's so little." I concentrated on Arinn. "She doesn't know. What if she's cold or hungry?"

"Lara, we have to believe that Briar—" He went for my hand.

But I cut both his words and actions off. "Don't say her name!"

His sigh was quite audible, and he amended his word carefully. "We have to believe that *she* is taking care of her." When he got no reaction from me that time, he brought his hand to my face. "Can you try to sleep, please?"

"Can you?" I countered.

He shrugged his shoulders. "No."

"Mmmm-hmmm."

He widened his legs and encouraged me in between them. When I did, he wrapped his arms around me from behind and dipped his chin onto my shoulder. We didn't say a word. We didn't sleep. We just held each other and prayed.

CHAPTER SEVEN

A sleepless, quiet, no-news night meant an even harsher, crueler, facing-reality morning. A sergeant and one of his officers emerged onto our residence early that next day. After they set up post once again in the dining room, the sergeant spoke with Finn and I regarding what little activity they were able to get from any credit cards listed under Brianna or Briar Yorwood. There was one purchase at a convenience/drug store.

"A drug store?" I immediately panicked at the word. "She was getting some kind of drug?"

Finn securely laced his hand on top of mine which was resting on the table. "Do you know what—"

The police immediately answered with, "Hair dye, diapers, bottles, onesies."

The breath of air that escaped me was one of pure relief. She was taking care of her. That's what those items had to mean.

But that slightest reprieve was countered by so many other thoughts and fears. "There's more to taking care of a one-year-old than diapers and bottles," I said. "Does she know what they are allowed to eat? What about a car seat? God, will she be able to keep her safe?"

"But we know she's making an attempt. That's good, right?" Finn tried to bring us back to the positive.

"Well, of course, we don't know this for sure, but it looks like it wasn't premeditated. She didn't have any of the necessary items to take care of a child. But..." This sergeant was pure business. "There has been absolutely no activity since then, and it does not appear that she has any intention of returning the child. The hair dye—" he started, only then making me realize the implications of a disguise.

"Not having her return is not an option." Finn's grip on my hand became fiercer.

"For us, either, sir."

"Okay," Finn continued. "So now what?"

"Well, we were hoping to have had all of this resolved by now."

"Obviously the knocking on her door tactic didn't work." My sarcasm, which was usually sweet, this time bordered on vengeful.

"No, ma'am, it did not." He let my snide comment slide as Finn's hand stroked mine. "I think it's time to put it out there. I think it is time to inform the media. We've known who the perpetrator was from the beginning. So, at first, we didn't want to tip her off by announcing things in the press. And then, of course, there's Mr. Murphy's celebrity status. This could be a three-ring-circus of hoaxes and media taking up valuable resources, but, ultimately, we need people to know. We need those pictures of your daughter and Miss Yorwood out there. We need them in the press and not just in police officers' hands. What do you think?"

"Finn?" My head was spinning. I couldn't make a decision to save my life...or maybe my daughter's.

Finn looked at me and then said to the sergeant, "Immediately. Do it."

"Yeah." I made it to the powder room before throwing up.

***

Finn found me in our master bathroom having just finished brushing my teeth. Not seeing or hearing him approach, I both jumped and screamed when he said my name. While a slight shake would have been my norm, my nerves were on full tilt, and my reaction showed it.

"Hey," he cooed in an apologetic way while wrapping his arms around me. "Sorry I scared you. You all right? Did you throw up?"

"Yeah," I acknowledged. "I didn't know I even had anything in my stomach to let go." When I tried to remember the last time I had eaten, I realized it had been pizza for lunch before the theater…before everything changed. I shook my head as if I were clearing cobwebs and refocused on what had set my stomach in a lurch. "Putting the pictures out there," I stretched my arms slightly so I could look in his eyes. "That's a good thing, right? I just…I can't seem to trust my decision making."

"We're going to get her back," he replied, with what I hoped was true confidence. He held me tightly again for a few more seconds before stepping away to take my hands. "Okay?" When I didn't respond, he continued. "I think we need to call our families. They need to know before all of this breaks." I stared at him, surely doe-eyed, as he trudged on. "It's going to hit nationally." He didn't have to say it. It was because of him. It was because of his career. "I don't know if that's good or bad," Finn said as if reading my mind. "But we need to tell my family and yours. They need to be prepared, especially if the press contacts them. They need to know."

"Yeah." I was slowly tuning back in. "All right. I'll call Lane. Maybe he can call my mom." The last thing I needed was to deal with my hysterical mother.

"I'll be out back. I need some air. I need to figure out exactly what I'm gonna tell Mom and Pop." He gave me a sad face and said, "I think I'll start with Nola."

I released some stressed air from my lungs. "I'll be down in a little bit."

As my luck would have it, it was Piper who answered Lane's phone—she and her over-the-top bubbly "I'm so excited to be coming for the vows" voice. But I couldn't be bothered. Not just because my only priority was Arinn, but because it was due to some homewrecker like her that Arinn was in this mess. Piper was the other woman in Lane and his ex-wife's relationship, and Briar—

"Ahhh!" I literally screamed into the phone. "Get Lane. It's an emergency."

By the time my brother got on the phone, what little patience I had was gone. I quickly explained what was going on, omitting, of course, how Finn had first met Briar. After the initial disbelief, Lane offered to come to Nashville and help.

"There's nothing you can do, Lane. I just needed you to know in case...damn, *when* it goes viral."

"I want to help."

He had always helped and protected me when we were young. But being hit a few times was nothing compared to this. This was worse than third-world torture techniques. This was a beast tearing my heart out. And my brother could do nothing to help that.

"Call mom," I said and then added, "Please. I can't deal with her right now." Our mother was a natural, eternal worrier and something I certainly didn't need on top of my own stress.

"She's gonna want to talk with you."

"I know. Keep her at bay." Mid-conversation, I had stepped out to our master bedroom's balcony. Now, looking down into our backyard, I spotted Finn walking around with his phone to his drooped head. I needed to be there to support him —that phone call to his folks was going to be particularly rough. "I need to go," I said to my brother. "I'll...I'll fill you in when I can."

I noted Chance in his bedroom—earphones up to his little head and innocently playing a video game—before I made my way down the stairs, past the police officers, and out to the backyard. Finn was down the wooden path near the closed hot tub. As I approached, I could hear a little more of his phone conversation.

"What?" he said into the phone, but to whom he was speaking was still unclear. "Oh, oh, crap, yeah, it's on tonight." "Hey" he mouthed a greeting to me as my mind circled trying to think about what was on that night—a news program? "No, we didn't forget," he continued into the phone. "Of course. Mom…" With that word, I now knew who was on the other line. "Mom, where is he?" After a moment for her response, Finn said, "Good. Listen, I need to tell you something, and you have to remain calm, and you have to promise me something." He emphasized the word again. "*Promise* not to tell Pop."

I knitted my eyebrows at my husband. Was that the strategy he was going to use? He was going to keep his father in the dark about what was going on? I knew Finn was, with due cause, concerned about his dad's health, but what would happen if Mr. Murphy found out from someone other than us?

Finn's eyes had that look in them that made me know he wanted my support. I grabbed his hand as he said to his mother, "No. I know." And then, after another beat, he said, "No, I don't keep anything from Lara." I leaned into him then as much as a support for him as for myself. "But, listen, I wouldn't be telling you this, but it's going to be all over the news feed."

I blocked out most of what he said next. I couldn't take reliving it one more time. I had just done it with my brother, and I was living and breathing it every torturous second that my child wasn't with me.

"I don't want him to know. God, Mom, tell me you won't tell him. That's the last thing I want on his mind. I don't want him stressed because his—" Finn was getting more agitated. The animation and friction in his body naturally drew us apart from one another. "Make sure he doesn't hear it from anywhere else."

As he said his goodbye to his mom, he started walking in circles. I watched, feeling helpless. I knew I should comfort him, but we were both a mess. We were both at our breaking points.

"Oh, God! God! God!" Off the phone now, he flung it onto the nearby chaise lounge. He then turned to me. "Why did you give her to strangers in the first place?"

"What? What!" I reacted without a second to breathe and think. "It wasn't strangers! It was a child care service so many feet away from me."

"You didn't know them." He put his hands up to the back of his head. "We could have had someone come to the house."

"Who? Summer? Nola?" I spoke of his cousin and sister who both lived in New York. Even though he wasn't downright yelling, I felt like I was being interrogated. "We're far away from anyone I know." My statement only made me sadder because I really did need that support of family and friends more than ever.

"I…why didn't you just keep Arinn with you?"

"Finn! Just like Reese's wedding, she wouldn't sit still. She's too young. Chance could enjoy the play better, too."

"Why—"

My sleep-deprived, worried soul couldn't handle any more. I went on attack. "Why? Why? Why? Why did you fuck her?"

My crassness and abruptness stunned him as it did me. He looked me solidly in the eyes. "You get to say that one time. One…time!" he reiterated. "Because I know you're upset, I'm not going to play word games with you. But, Lara, I did not fuck her." He spoke about the evil temptress who had our daughter. "And you know that."

"Call it what you like," I said more calmly but still feeling the pressure of being accused. "It was your association"— I tried a new word — "that brought a stranger into our lives. You said she wanted more, and you rejected her. You," I punctuated. "This is your fault."

Finn was still on the defensive. "I—" So when I started to walk away and toward the glass doors that led into the house, he only got more upset. "Lara, don't. We need to finish this."

My body felt like it was squeezing into itself. I was feeling pressure from all around. I needed to preserve what little sanity I had left. So, my infamous "Lara walls" were being built to protect me, and they seemed to be going up in record speed. This time I think I was building a skyscraper.

"Lara! Damn it! God damn it!"

I couldn't turn around this time. I couldn't stay and help him. I was too fragile. I was too hurt. I really, truly, this time wasn't strong enough. Plus, I didn't want to be blamed. I had already burdened myself with those same "what if" questions nearly every minute since she had gone missing. Ultimately, it was me. I had left our daughter. And, now, she was gone.

***

Finn and I remained in our proverbial corners throughout the morning and into the afternoon. It was fine. He was dealing with the police, and, despite our blow up, I knew he would tell me if there was anything noteworthy. Plus, he needed to be in contact with his own team. He had already spoken with Reese, who was flying in from New York so she could be on top of the media circus. Since he had the police and media covered, I was able to concentrate on the child that remained safe and sound at home. I stayed holed up with Chance in his room reading books, playing games, and trying to divert the "why are the policemen here" and "where is Arinn" questions.

"Hi, Daddy," Chance belted out, and I looked up to see Finn leaning in our son's doorway.

"Hi, Little Man," Finn said, looking weary and worn.

"You play, too?" Chance asked, regarding the video game he was crushing me in.

"No. You know what? I need to talk with Mommy for a little bit."

I stood up. My empty stomach rumbled again. Was there news? Or did he want to talk about our disagreement earlier? Suddenly, I felt like I was better off just sitting playing a game with my child. Sometimes the unknown was better than reality.

"What is it?" I whispered.

"There's someone downstairs they want us to talk to." When I must have given as puzzled of a look as I was feeling, he further explained. "It's a police liaison. The sergeant and detective left. Besides the patrol at the gate, we'll deal with her. Everyone else needs to be out in the field doing what they can to find—"

He stopped himself and looked at Chance. Our little boy had already heard way too much. And both of us wanted to protect him from further pain or worry.

"All right," I complied. "Let me just get Chance settled for a nap."

"Mommy!" he whined.

"Chance," I countered immediately. "You need a nap. Just a short one. It's late anyway. We don't want you cranky."

"But, Mo—"

"Chance, in bed... now."

Stressed from everything, Finn used a firmer voice than our son was used to. But it did the trick. Chance scurried into his big boy, queen-sized bed, and Finn went right over to him in an apologetic kind of way.

"I love you, Little Man." He kissed him on the forehead. "Try to nap."

I walked ahead of Finn and down the stairs to meet

Cayla, the police/family liaison. She was petite, wore her black hair in a bun, and seemed like she was fresh out of college. But she knew her job, and she did it well. One of the first things she talked with us about was the tremendous amount of stress that Finn and I were facing as a couple. She came straight out and noted how we were sitting on opposite ends of the sofa while talking with her. She told us that we needed to talk through everything and not take anything personally...that these were extreme circumstances. Finn and I both looked at each other but did not offer anything in response.

"Thanks, Cayla," Finn finally said. "But we don't need a marriage counselor. Everything is fine. We just need our daughter back." What he said was true. But, even if it wasn't, he would never let anyone inside our personal relationship, especially a stranger.

My response was a sneeze. My nose was clogged up. I wondered if it was because of the deluge of trauma my sinus system was harboring with the tears or if my immune system was weakened from the same trauma. I blew my nose and smelled Cayla's perfume. With my highly sensitive allergies, that could have definitely been the culprit, too.

I could have sworn Cayla looked at me with sympathetic eyes while changing to more skeptical ones when directed at Finn. It made me wonder if she knew the true connection between Finn and Briar. I suspected that she did. She was, after all, part of the police team. It was nice for a change, though, not to see a younger woman goggle over my husband.

I brought a tissue up to my face. "What can we do? What can we do to get Arinn back?"

"Keep positive thoughts. Keep your son happy. Because of this particular, unique situation, where we know who took your daughter, plus Finn's celebrity status, we just want you to stay put. We want to know where all three of you are. Let the police do their job. A lot of times families want to call for updates nonstop. That's what I am here for. And, let me tell you, they're a good group. Every single one of those officers is a parent, and they are working triple time to get your daughter back home to you."

"Yeah," was all I could offer.

"Until then, I can answer any questions you might have. If I don't know it, I'll find out," she added.

"The media has everything then?" I asked. "Yeah, alerts went out. They're flashing on television screens and phones. It's on the news. I will be handling any media from the police standpoint."

"My publicist is on her way," Finn said about Reese. "She'll want to coordinate with you."

"That's fine," Cayla replied.

That made me wonder if Finn had told Reese everything, too. Reese was a long time employee of Finn's…long before we had even started dating. They had gone through a lot together. And Reese didn't let Finn get away with much, which was good because he was used to it. They were also good friends, though, and I know Finn wouldn't want to disappoint Reese with his admission. But, in reality, it didn't matter to me. He had told *me* straight away, and that's what mattered…his honesty.

"Speaking of, that's Reese now." Finn said, looking at a text on his phone. "She's nearing the gate. I'll tell the patrol to let her in."

Finn got off the sofa and patted my right thigh in the process. I tried a smile, but I couldn't manage much. It was hard to imagine that I would ever smile again.

I excused myself, allowing Finn, Reese, and Cayla the opportunity to coordinate whatever they needed to. I didn't want to be a part of it. It wasn't my expertise, and it just depressed me further to think about the purpose of the meeting. In lieu of calling back, I texted my mother and then found solace in the master bedroom shower. I was hoping the pulsating water beads would drown out the sound of my sobs.

And then I did what I knew I shouldn't. I looked online. There wasn't much yet, but there was Arinn's picture—her darling little picture. It had been taken on her birthday. She had a toothy smile, and we had managed to get her index finger propped up next to a number one sign.

My precious baby girl's photo was adjoined with the other picture—the one of "her." Underneath it, both names—Brianna and Briar—were listed. It was obviously a posed, industry cover shot. She had dangling earrings and her hand was up to her face, sporting a white pinky ring. The description said she had a butterfly tattoo on the back of her neck and scars on her arm. Arinn and Briar could not be more opposite. But, the two of them were, inevitably, connected.

"Hey, don't look at that stuff." Reese entered Arinn's nursery where I was sitting on the glider with my laptop.

"I needed to see it," I explained as she bent down next to me, gently closed the computer, and gave me a side hug. "It's like the time when Chance wanted a mirror to see his bloody nose. He was hysterical, imagining the worse until he actually saw it."

"And is it as bad as you imagined?"

"Half of it is." I was referring to Briar/Brianna's half, and Reese knew it. "Nothing makes reference to Arinn being our...Finn's daughter," I stated the fact.

"Not yet. That's good for now. People will want to help a missing child, regardless. It's the nutcases who come out once they find out about Finn's connection that we have to be concerned about."

"Tell me about it." The number one nutcase actually had our daughter, I thought.

"It's only a matter of time. With all those people at the play when Finn showed up, I'm surprised it's not out there yet."

"Look after him, Reese."

"He doesn't make it easy," she lamented.

"I know."

"You know, he sent me up here to check on you."

The tear came instantly down my face. In the midst of all the cruelty we had unloaded on one another in the backyard, it was undeniable how much we cared for and loved each other. That was forever.

Reese proceeded on filling me in on what news the liaison was getting from the police department. Through searches and the help of other departments and organizations, the detectives had talked with Brianna's neighbors, label company, friends, former bandmates, and family members. It provided invaluable insight. Brianna was estranged from her family. Her mother said she was doing drugs when she found out she was pregnant —a little more than a year before she threw havoc into our lives. The baby daddy wanted no part of her or the child. And when the baby was born premature and died within hours of her giving birth, Brianna basically lost touch with her family. But her mother swore that being pregnant was what calmed Brianna. In addition, one of her ex-bandmates said she had just texted him to say that things weren't going well with the label. And, a neighbor hadn't seen her for about a week, but that didn't mean anything because people in that neighborhood kind of kept to themselves.

"Mommy?" Chance's voice made Reese and I look up to where he was groggily standing at his sister's door.

"Come here, bud," I said. "Why don't you give Reese a hug? She's missed you."

"My favorite little ring bearer," Reese said of Chance's job at her early September wedding.

"I did a good job." Chance boasted, while wrapping his arms around Reese, who was like a second aunt to him.

"You sure di—" she started.

"What happened to your hair?"

Chance's words, although not the most politically

correct, made me look at Reese more closely. Normally caramel colored, her chin-to-shoulder-length hair was now a brilliant natural-looking red. It accentuated her light eyes beautifully. It was a big change, and I hadn't even noticed.

"I'm getting old, Chance. And your dad gives me gray hairs," she teased.

"It looks nice," I noted. "Sorry I didn't—"

"You have much more important things on your mind," she consoled.

"I hungry. I want Daddy." The preschooler, with limited attention span, was on to the next subject already.

"I bet we can do something about both of those things," I answered.

"Do you want me to take him?" Reese offered. "You know, do you need a minute to take in everything I just told you?"

I probably should have. Some of Briar's motives or reasoning might have made more sense. But, in the end, it didn't matter. I didn't care why she took my baby. I just wanted to know how I was going to get her back.

"No, let's go together. I probably shouldn't sit in here any longer." The formerly happy, green painted room was only depressing me more.

I took Chance by the hand and he, Reese, and I made our way downstairs. The television news broadcast greeted us in the great room. Cayla and Finn stood gathered around its screen. On it were the same two pictures I had seen on my laptop just moments before. It stopped me in my tracks.

"There Arinn!" Chance gleefully pointed to his sister's picture.

"Shi—" Finn partially swore and fumbled with the remote to eliminate the image from our son's vision.

"She on TV like you sometimes Daddy."

Finn glared over at me. But how was I supposed to know they were going to be watching the news? I hadn't even known what time it was. Everything had been a blur since Arinn had disappeared.

"I'm going to make him something to eat." I ignored the implied accusation and plowed on. "Turkey sandwiches and chips all around, okay?" Keeping it simple, I asked the three adults standing before me.

Finn scooped up Chance. "Yeah. You need help?" His query was surely automatic because it was always his natural inclination to help me.

"Chance can be my assistant. You all do what needs to be done."

"I a big helper." Chance scrambled down from his father's embrace.

"Might be a piece of pie for helpers," I said, hoping there was still some left to defrost in the freezer. "I'll let you know when it's ready," I said to the others. I glanced back to the television set—even off, its disturbing image was still embedded in my brain.

CHAPTER EIGHT

Dinner among the five of us was awkward. Cayla had practically insisted that we all sit at the table and eat together—that everyone needed a break. But it really wasn't one. None of our minds—besides maybe Chance's—were on food. We ate in practical silence... each of us giving into our own damning internal thoughts.

It was only the rings and vibrations of our phones that kept us actively involved. And no one dared ignore their cellular devices. All rules of table etiquette go out the window when your daughter has been kidnapped. But, unfortunately, none of the interruptions led to anything credible.

When both my phone and Finn's went off simultaneously, signifying an incoming joint text from Nola, I read it silently. *We love U & R praying 4 Arinn. Stay strong. Call when U can.*

I looked past Chance—who was sitting next to me—to Finn, who was at the head of the table. Having just finished reading the same message, he gave me a mirroring sad smile and placed his phone back on the table. Then Chance started to ask something, and Finn's phone rang, and he asked me to text Nola back, and he picked up his phone, and…and… and…and I was just spinning.

"Daddy?" Chance asked.

"Chance, I'm on the phone!" Finn I know tried to keep his voice sane, but it did rise.

Hoping that it was enough to calm and reassure him, I reached my hand to our son before I started to text Nola back our appreciation. Immediately afterward, a text came in from Vanessa, telling me that Carter had just called and told her the news. She didn't want to interrupt, but she wanted to know what she could do. I decided to let that one go until later because I was noticing how, in the matter of mere minutes, Chance was rapidly changing personas. At first, he was squirming. But, after all, he was a three-and-a-half-year-old. Then he went statue-like still. And then his whimpering very quickly turned into hysterical crying.

"Mommy!" he said before I could even react.

"What?" I asked, trying to downplay the fear of the unknown that had catapulted into me.

"Chance?" Finn's voice was rough, but it was out of concern. He hung up his phone and started to rise out of his seat.

"Mommy!" Chance glared at both Cayla and Reese, sitting directly across from us, and then practically buried into himself.

"Chance, what's wrong?" I pleaded, holding his little hand.

"I sorry."

"Chance, what? What are you sorry about?" Finn was now crouching on the other side of our son.

"I sorry." Crying still, he turned his eyes away from Cayla and Reese as if he was embarrassed.

I looked at Finn, not understanding. I could see the worry in his eyes, too…as if it hadn't already been embedded there since the day before. "You need to tell us what's wrong, bud," I tried again.

"I peed." And our little boy bawled even harder.

"Oh." I could feel my shoulders sag in relief as I exhaled.

Finn brought his hands up to the back of his head and walked off doing a calming down pacing move. "Geez."

"It's okay," I said to our son. "That happens."

But it never had for Chance, besides a few times at night. Our little boy had been a joy to potty train. It was like some kind of magical wand hit him a few months before he turned three, and he was good to go. It happened just around the same time that Arinn was born. He seemed to take pride in the fact that he was going to be the big boy and give up those silly diapers to the baby.

"I sorry," he repeated again.

"Chance, it's all right. Come here." I pulled him into my arms, felt his wet bottom, and noted the puddle on the seat that dripped onto the floor. "We'll get you changed, and everything will be all right." I stood up with him clinging to me.

He was starting to calm down when he asked, "Mommy, where Arinn?"

I swear I would have dropped him if my motherly instincts hadn't taken over. But I readjusted my grip and held on tighter. I needed to feel the love of his precious little innocent body as much as he needed to know that he was safe. Because it didn't take a psychologist to understand why our son was acting this way. We had tried, but we couldn't shield him completely.

I looked over to Finn who was harshly rubbing his temples. "Ah, shit," he said plainly.

Between both of their comments, I wanted to cry, too. "Finn?" I said but didn't really even understand myself what I wanted. Was I wondering if he was all right? Or was I asking him to answer our son?

He took all of it on, though. Walking over to the two of us, he stroked the back of Chance's hair and said, "Everything's all right, Little Man. Give me your hand, and we'll go up and get you changed."

Swinging his head around to look at his dad, Chance said, "I sorry, Daddy."

I knelt down and let Chance go to Finn. "It's okay." Taking his hand, Finn reassured our son with a kiss on the top of his head.

"Finn?" I said just as they were turning to exit the room. "He needs time with you."

"I know." My husband sighed.

We both knew. When Finn had gone away on tour during the summer, it was the longest time he had ever been separated from the kids. Arinn was too young to really comprehend. But Chance? Chance had not liked it. He developed fears and tantrums. Now it was obvious that Chance knew something bad had entered our hemisphere. This time, though, it wasn't his dad who had left. It was his sister. And this time he wasn't throwing any tantrums, but he was afraid and needed to feel safe.

"Can you take him outside for a little bit, too?" I asked, knowing it would benefit both of them—a toddler needed the movement and time with his remote dad, and Finn needed to decompress as best he could.

He blinked at me as an answer and walked with our son up the stairs. I took a second or two to breathe myself and then turned to get on with the task of cleaning up the mess. But Cayla and Reese were already on it. Their help alone made me want to burst into tears.

"Don't worry," the newly hued red-head said. "We got this."

"Oh, God." I was mortified. "You shouldn't have to clean that up."

"Seen much worse," Cayla chimed in, having found a rag and using it to absorb. "You need to debrief, too. You've been with your little boy all day, trying to keep up a good front. You need a moment to yourself."

"I...I..." I didn't even know what that would look like. "I need to be doing something."

If not, I was going to cry and maybe not ever stop.

"Take care of yourself. Arinn needs a strong mom for when she comes home," Cayla said.

"I know. It's…I just feel like if I take a break, I'm letting her down. It's been too long. We need to find her."

"We will," Cayla spoke confidently.

"That little girl is so loved." Reese touched my hand. "She can feel your love and Finn's love wherever she is."

"I'm serious," Cayla continued. "You need to take care of yourself. You threw up and now it seems like a cold?"

"I…I think it's just my allergies." I swiped at my nose and realized police and liaisons really must share everything—I hadn't even met Cayla when I threw up that morning.

"Allergic to what?" I could tell Cayla was instantly skeptical.

"I think it's your perfume." I laid it out. "I can't handle strong scents of any kind."

"Huh," Reese said as Cayla lifted her wrist to her nose. "I didn't even know she was wearing anything."

"Sorry," Cayla offered. "It's just a dab of lotion. I can wash it off. I really don't even smell it."

"Sensitive nose 1-0-1," I tried to joke. "I'll be fine."

"Still. You need to rest and relax. Is there someone you can call and just talk to?" Cayla asked. "Maybe your mom?"

"God, no." I almost laughed.

Finn was always the number one person I would turn to talk to. But that just wasn't going to happen…for a number of reasons. Most of all because our son took priority.

"Vanessa," I decided out loud.

"Yeah. Call Vanessa," Reese agreed.

"Who's Vanessa?" It was the cop part of Cayla.

"My best friend. She lives in New York," I replied, feeling like I was in a semi-catatonic state. "She knows. Carter told her."

"Yeah. We just told the band before you came down."

Reese spoke of Finn's crew, which included the dark-haired drummer, Carter, who was dating Vanessa, albeit long distance.

"Vanessa," Cayla concurred. "That sounds good. In the meantime, I'll go wash my hands."

As Cayla walked toward the powder room, I picked up my phone to call Vanessa. At the same time, Chance, still a little shy, was coming down the stairs with Finn. They went straight out the patio doors. I was going to say something about needing a jacket, but I decided to let it go. Finn was an adult. He was a parent. He would know if it was too cold. The important part was that Chance got to run around and feel better.

I escaped to the main floor guest suite to talk with my best friend. It was neutral ground. It didn't have any reminders of Arinn or Finn in it, and that was kind of what I needed at that moment.

As I tightened my body into a ball against the headrest of the bed, Vanessa talked to me for endless minutes, trying to understand what had happened. And then she talked with me some more about pointless, mundane things like the weather and traffic just so I could try to clear my mind. It didn't work. But neither of us had truly expected it to.

We were still talking when Finn took a couple tenuous steps into the room. "Lara?" he said in an even tone.

"Yeah?"

"It's out. The media is broadcasting that she's my daughter. It's blowing up."

I nodded my head and sighed. "Vanessa?" I spoke into the phone.

"Tell Finn…tell him Carter is ready to help. And that we love you guys." She knew just by my tone that I needed to go.

"I will. Thanks," I replied.

"You let me know if you hear anything. Got it?" she said before hanging up.

I stood up to meet my husband. "They need to keep the focus on Arinn, Finn." I had my directive tone with him because I couldn't let my guard down one ounce or I would not survive the flood from my eyes.

"That's what Reese and Cayla are doing right now. I'm gonna make some calls, too." He touched my arm as I neared him and said, "Lara…." in the way that I knew he wanted to clear up some of the crap that was heavily hanging between us since the fight on the patio.

But I couldn't. The dam that was containing my tears was threatening to break right behind the surface of my eyes. And our son didn't need that. He needed a confident mother. And I knew it was my time to play that role again and spare him of knowing any more than he already did.

"I'll get Chance. We'll be upstairs."

His eyes shifted around, searching mine before he relented with, "Okay."

***

After giving Chance a bath and putting him in his superhero pajamas, I had him come and snuggle with me in our master bedroom. I thought we could find some fun kid movie on television to watch together. But almost as cruel as seeing my daughter's "missing" photograph on the screen, was the movie that was on that night. *It's a Wonderful Life* was playing in all its black and white glory. It slammed me straight in the gut. That was what Finn had been talking to his mother about earlier on the phone. It was a Murphy family tradition to watch that movie on the night it was broadcast each year. No matter how many miles apart they were, the family felt a little closer, knowing that everyone at that moment was doing the same uplifting thing. The irony of the title made me cry out a messy laugh. It was far from a wonderful life when your daughter had been missing for over twenty-four hours and you are going on the second, long night without her.

***

It was much later, toward the tail end of *It's a Wonderful Life*, when Finn entered our bedroom. I had long since put Chance in his own room down the hall. The lights were off, with the exception of the adjacent sitting room lamp. Using the remote, I muted the movie and looked at my husband.

Not knowing his exact demeanor, I cautiously asked, "What's going on?"

"Everyone left," he answered. "All except the rotating patrol at the gate. I brought him out some coffee."

I knew that. When I had heard the security system say for the third time that someone was leaving, I had worried. Reese and Cayla could be two departures, but Finn would have had to be the third. I really didn't want him taking off—not only for his own state of mind but also for mine. So, I had watched the monitors in our bedroom to witness Finn's coffee offering. I didn't let him know that, though. I didn't want him to think I didn't trust him.

I looked to the screen. Jimmy Stewart was hoisting his family up into his arms. Everyone was glad to be together. It was the proverbial happy ending.

Finn saw it, too. Taking his hands, he brought them up to his head and wrung them through his unruly hair. He then rubbed them, almost violently so, on his face as if he was trying to peel away the pain scribbled all over it.

"Are you all r—?"

"Yes!" he interrupted with abrupt verbal force before walking directly into the master bath.

I heard the sink turn on and off and then watched as he returned into the bedroom, tossing his white T-shirt haphazardly onto the armoire. He then sat down on the bed to remove his socks. I noted how he left his jeans on, just as I was still adorning a simple bra, pink tank top, and coordinating sweats. We both remained dressed enough, as we had the night before, to be able to get up and go if we needed to in a split second.

When I turned off the television, Finn immediately filled the silence. "You don't think I know the reason we're in this situation. You don't think I know the part I played in it?"

He was obviously picking up right where we had left off in the backyard. I knew he wanted to before in the guest room, and it was inevitable and necessary. But it was still going to be tension-filled.

"You don't think I blame myself?" he continued. "I know what I did. But you throwing it in my face and refus—"

"I'm sorry," I said straight away. "I don't blame you." And I reiterated it because it was the truth. "I don't. I feel horrible that I said that. But you were so mad, and it felt like you were accusing me. And it's true. I was the one that left her, and I knew you knew that, and you were angry, and I couldn't handle it."

"I... no." He was at least a little calmer. "I wasn't accusing you, Lara. God, if anyone knows what it feels like to be in charge of a kid and they get hurt or—" He stopped himself. We both knew he was thinking not only of our daughter but the fact that he had been the one with Wyatt when he had been struck by a car and killed. "I would never do that to you. I just needed to wrap my brain around what happened... how it ...how our baby...how our little girl.... You know I lose my shit when it comes to the safety of you and the kids ...of losing—"

"I know." God, did I know that. And I should have been more cognizant of it, but both of us were too emotionally frail.

"Christ." He exhaled but there was an escalation developing in his voice again. "We need each other for this, and you just walked away. That didn't help anything. You can't build up your damn walls... not now!"

"I'm sorry," I tried again, silently acknowledging both

of our weaknesses and knowing that the combination was not good for either one of us. "I know I did. I shouldn't have. I was just at my breaking point. You know I love you." I reached out my hand, but he didn't take it, which literally made my stomach surge in pain. "Finn…" My voice sounded younger and more desperate than I ever remembered. "Please don't punish me by doing the same thing…by pushing me away. Can you just…please…please just touch my hand. I need to know you're with me." When he didn't make any motion to honor my request, I resigned myself to a solitary, sleepless night and turned over so that I wasn't facing him any longer.

In another moment, I heard him sigh and then felt his arms spoon around my body. "It's been a long day. Let's let it go." As I nodded my head up and down in agreement, I felt his wet lips resting on my bare shoulder. "And, Lara, I love you, too."

I let his words and touch settle me for a minute before I gave him a receptive, thankful squeeze. It calmed me, but I knew it calmed him, also. I knew it from the relaxing breath he took and how he rested his head near mine. And by some kind of miracle or pure exhaustion, I was able to fall asleep.

***

However, when I woke up about an hour and a half later, Finn was not in bed with me. Adjusting my eyes, I got up and looked out the bedroom balcony first. All seemed quiet in the darkness, but, of course, all wasn't well. There was still a patrol officer standing guard just beyond my line of vision, and there was still a little girl lost.

I found Finn in one of the chairs in the sitting room. He was asleep, but I knew from years of being with him that it wasn't a deep slumber. Standing there, I watched him for a while until his phone vibrated in his hand. As I had assumed, he was instantly awake and focusing on his phone. With a sigh, he did not react to the text that came through and instead put in back down on the table next to him. That's when he spotted me. He closed his eyes again but this time as if he was in pain, and it told me what I already knew—the text meant nothing. I sagged on the door frame and then walked over to the other oversized chair. Sitting on it, I peered aimlessly out the window. Silence took over the two of us in that room until about a half hour later when, once again, Finn's phone vibrated. But, once again, it was nothing. It was my turn to sigh and return to bed alone.

I was not able to get back to sleep, though. While Finn remained glued to the chair in the sitting room, I roamed the house like the lost soul I felt I was. Nighttime was definitely the worst. It was too quiet. It gave me too much time to think. During the day, when there was natural light, I could at least throw in some waves of hope among the crevices of despair. But at night, my thoughts were as dark as the sky above.

***

After finally falling asleep around six a.m., it was after eight when I awoke next. Finn, who had dozed on and off the entire night, was not in our bedroom or sitting room. In my own lack-of-sleep, groggy state, I wondered how he was managing. He was getting even less sleep than I was.

I made my way downstairs to discover both he and Chance, fully dressed, in the kitchen. Finn was drinking coffee and Chance was sloshing some kind of tan colored circular cereal with a spoon. I kissed the top of Chance's head as Finn poured coffee into one of my travel mugs. I preferred them over a regular cup... that and a teaspoon of honey, which I noted Finn adding. He put it in my hand while encouraging me into the nearby great room.

"Before Cayla comes, I'm taking Chance to Carter's."

He bent down ever so slightly to meet my eyes.

"What?" I brought the coffee back down from my lips.

"Carter can watch him today." Finn's friend and bandmate lived nearby.

I was more awake now, and I didn't think it was the caffeine. It was the fear of letting another child go. "What? Why? No!" I grasped onto the mug tighter.

"I don't want him around this." He was using a calm voice and glancing over at Chance, just an open room away. "All of our fear and pain and anger. He's a sensitive kid. We can't keep…. he's obviously already noticing," he said in an apparent reference to the accident at the dinner table the night before.

Even though I could agree with his analysis of Chance and understood his rationale, I still couldn't accept the proposition. "Finn, no! I want him with us. He needs to feel secure."

My husband braced his hands on my shoulders. "He'll be with Carter. He likes Carter. He's grown up around him. Please, Lara. We need to concentrate on Arinn, and we need to protect him."

"I—"

"I know. Do you think this is easy for me?"

He didn't need to ask. I knew it wasn't. He wiped at the tears I didn't know were making trails down my face. And I touched the rough stubble that I wasn't accustomed to him having on his. I felt a thousand years older. Not knowing what was happening with our daughter was destroying us mentally, emotionally, and physically.

"He'll be okay." I managed to say something that was between a comment and a question.

"I'll stay with him for a little bit. He'll be fine. He'll be back tonight."

"I'll go with you."

"Someone should stay here." He was speaking slowly as if *I* was the three-year-old needing comprehension skills.

"Finn—"

"I done!" Chance yelled out.

"Okay, Little Man," Finn answered him. "Let's wash those hands, and then we're off to Carter's. I bet he'll let you bang on those drums."

"Cool." Chance's eyes lit up.

Finn squeezed my hand. "He's fine. And I'll be back soon."

"Mmmm-hmmm," I mumbled.

Bringing his finger up, Finn touched the scar that resided directly next to the outer rim of my eye. As he wiped, I felt the dampness of the tear and silently urged no more to escape. That night in my teens when the scar was created seemed so bad back then, but nothing could compare to the pain of having your child taken from you. The emotional scars forming in my psyche were a thousand times worse.

CHAPTER NINE

Cayla arrived before Finn returned home. She filled me in on the latest. Officers were still looking for clues at the park, and neither Brianna nor any of the childcare workers had criminal records. She also informed me that she wasn't going to stay long, as she wanted to assist more with the phone and e-mail hotlines. Of course, if we needed anything, we had her direct number.

What I needed was solitude. I had too many thoughts running through my head, and I just needed a quiet space to calm them. I gave her free reign of our downstairs and escaped to our master bedroom after emptying my bladder...again. I got on my laptop and started searching the internet for answers to all the questions that were invading my mind. And when I didn't really like the results I was getting, I abruptly stopped, took a change of clothes into the master bath and decided to start afresh with a shower and new attire.

When I reemerged, I found Finn standing next to the bed and looking stunned. "Lar? Are you?" he asked. "Are you pregnant?"

Finn and I were one, but I couldn't possibly understand how he could have read my mind. "How did you...?"

"Your laptop." He glanced in its general direction on the bed and referenced my internet symptoms search. "You left the page up."

"Oh."

When I didn't offer more, he said, "What? What's going on?"

"I have to find out if I am for sure first."

"What makes you think you are?"

"Well, my period was supposed to start, and I'm never really late, I'm peeing all the time, my stomach, my insecurity, Cayla's perfume...." My allergies were even more on alert when I was pregnant.

"Yeah, but—"

"I'm sorry." I practically cried.

"Lara..." He sighed and took a step toward me. "It's not—"

"I'll have to take a pregnancy test and go to a doctor, but—" I stopped myself, not being able to emotionally go on. I knew I was, and it was further wrecking my mind.

"What can I do for you?" He was walking on proverbial egg shells while reaching out to touch me, but I was just staring like I had never met him before in my life. "What are you thinking?"

All of this was too much. All of it. All at one time.

"Lara?"

Feeling pressured for a response, even though I knew it wasn't his intent, I blurted out what was immediately on my mind. "How can I be pregnant?" I asked, knowing I was methodical about taking my birth control pills. "I mean, I know it can still happen. But I can't have a baby...not now. I... I can't."

"What are you saying?" His hands went to his sides, obviously repelled by the mere thought of me alluding to not having a baby.

"Not now. Not now with Arinn...with how everything is."

"Lara...." He tried.

"I can't. I can't, deal with it, Finn. I need Arinn back. I don't want anyone else. She's my baby. I want her. I just want her. I want our little girl."

"Let's just take it one step at a time. You don't even know for sure."

"No. And I don't think I want to know—not with how I'm feeling," I admitted. I needed to let it be until I could think rationally. And that wouldn't happen until I got my daughter back. "I... how can all of this be happening?"

Before he could answer, Cayla knocked on our open door. "I'm sorry for interrupting." She took a second to note the expressions on both of our faces. "But there is someone at the gate claiming to be your brother." She directed her comment to me. "I need to know if I should tell them to let him in."

My eyes got big as Finn's scrunched. We went to look at the monitor in our bedroom. There, sure enough, was Lane at the gate—not in North Carolina where he lived and worked as a hotel food service manager.

"Uh, yeah. That's ... that's my brother. Let him through," I said as Cayla started exiting. "Thanks."

Finn turned to me. "Did you know he was coming? Why didn't you tell me?"

"No. I had no idea. He didn't say...In fact, I told him *not* to come."

"Okay." He took a huge, deep breath. "Okay." The stress penetrating from Finn was visibly evident—his father, our daughter, my pregnancy revelation, and now an unexpected guest.

"I'm sorry."

"You didn't know, Lara. Let's...c'mon." He grabbed my hand. His need to connect us was so automatic and always a calming, protective source for both of us.

I stopped our stride, though, a couple steps in. "Chance? He's all right?"

"No matter how much he begs, we are not buying that kid drums." Finn's comment was the first light-hearted one I had heard in days, and it actually brought a semi-smile to my face.

We made our way downstairs just as Cayla was opening the door for Lane. I hadn't expected him, but seeing my brother in front of me suddenly made me so glad that he was there. He was a shot of comfort when I needed it the most. I walked straight up to his open arms and let him hold me for a lengthy, solid, quiet hug.

"What are you doing here?" I asked when we finally broke our embrace.

"I had to come," my brother answered. "I needed to be here for you and for Arinn. I needed to help…whatever you need." He reached out and shook Finn's hand who brought him in for a quick pat on the back.

"Finn? Lara?" Cayla thankfully called us by our first names—I was so sick of the Mr. and Mrs. crap. "I'm going. I'll be monitoring the hotlines. Call me if you need anything."

"Yeah," Finn said and showed Cayla to the door.

"What can I do? What do you need?" Lane was asking me.

"I need my baby," I said, followed even louder by, "I need Arinn."

Finn was lightly shaking his head. I knew he felt hopeless. We both did. He was used to being able to console me and make things better. This…this was beyond his control, reach, and capabilities.

"I know, Lar," Lane soothed. "I'm sure everybody is doing everything they can to make that happen. Let me help, too. I'll run errands or talk with people or even just sit here with you if that's what you need."

I saw Finn look at me as if he were measuring my temperament. He took a moment and then said to my brother, "Lane, can you do that? Can you stay here for a bit? Just be with your sister and try to get her to relax? She needs to relax."

Something about that riled me up, but, then again, it

didn't take much. "Relax? I'm not going to take a yoga class when my daughter is missing."

"Lara, I'm not—God!" Finn threw his hands into his hair. "Talk with your brother, okay? I need...I need some time, too."

"Great." It was one word, but it was pure Lara sarcasm.

"Stop. You're exhausted and emotional." My husband was firm but kind.

"Of course I am!"

Finn took a couple deep breaths before turning around and then back again to face me. He had learned a lot of calming, coping techniques through his PTSD therapy. "I'll be back in a little bit," he finally said.

I didn't realize he was actually leaving. I thought he would just retreat to some other part of the house and give me and Lane some time. But leaving? Oh, no. Here we go again.

"Where are you going?" My anger switched to concern.

"I want to go to church. And I would love if you would come with me, but I know you won't, and I understand." He knew I wasn't a big believer in organized religion, and he respected that— just as I respected his need to find solace in it.

"No. I'm not going." I quietly replied and, even more internally, gave thanks that his destination was a church...a much better solution than a "drive" or a bar.

"I know." His voice was softer now, too. "You and Lane... you talk. That will be good for you. I won't be long." He leaned in and kissed me on top of the head before grabbing his keys and heading to the garage.

I buried my head back into my brother's chest. "Sorry you had to see that," I lamented.

"What?" He stepped away. "You're both facing a horrific situation. So, for once, you're not the sickening sweet super-couple you usually are. You don't need to be. Lara, fall apart. Let me help."

I wiped a few tears and managed a laugh. "Super-couple, Lane? What kind of daytime dramas have you been watching?"

He chuckled back. "Piper is all into that stuff."

Wanting to get off the Piper topic, I regained some strength and manners. "Come on in. Give me your coat. Let me show you around the place. You've never been."

"No. I have to say, though, the rock star has some kind of entrance."

"Wait till you see the rest." I managed another smile. Having my brother around was good for me.

***

When we finished the house tour, complete with tears in Arinn's room, I called Carter to check on Chance and then sat down with Lane to update him on the case. My brother waited a while, but he did ask the question I knew was most likely coming. He wanted to know what Brianna had to do with our family, in particularly Finn. Because the media, along with her physical description, had provided details about her amateur singing career.

When I purposefully skimmed the truth, saying that they just had similar career choices, Lane challenged me. "Lara…?"

"It's not what you think. And he told me everything from the very start."

"But there was something?"

"No, yes…no." I stumbled. Something or not, it was between and resolved by Finn and I. "It's…no." I settled on. "I don't know what she wanted or expected, but she can't get it from my family."

"Okay." Lane, if not content with the answer, at least let it be.

To further assist a change in conversation, Lane's phone rang. I started to get up to give my brother some privacy, but he pulled at my arm, willing me to stay. I learned from listening to his end of the conversation that it was Piper he was talking with. He first let her know how I was. And then I was shocked to learn that she was in town with him. They were staying at a nearby hotel. Lane concluded by telling Piper he would be with me for a little while and that he would pass something on.

When I shared my surprise that Piper was in town, Lane, I'm sure trying not to take offense, explained, "She's part of my life. So, she wants to help, too. You know it's that social worker in her. But she doesn't want to interfere."

"Oh."

"She's really a nice person, Lara. You would like her." He knew my feelings, but we had never sat and talked about it in person.

Right then was probably as good of a time as any. "I'm sorry," I offered because, if anything, the past couple of days had made me realize how petty some things could be and how cherished other things like love and family should be. "It's just McEllie...." I spoke of his ex-wife, to whom he had been married to for over ten years.

McEllie had been family. *She* was a part of our lives. And then she wasn't. As Lane had explained months before, they had just faded—no major drama, etc. But now there was Piper.

"I didn't even meet Piper until after McEllie and I had separated. And, Lara, the separation happened before any of you knew about it," Lane explained.

"We saw you together last Christmas." I tried putting the pieces together.

"She had already moved out weeks before that. But I tried to tell you, we're still good friends. It truly is amicable. She wanted to come last Christmas, and I wanted her to, too. I'm glad she did. Neither of us wanted to ruin the holidays with that announcement."

"Why didn't you say anything later? Why did we have to find out with Finn walking in on you and Piper in March?"

"I know. It … what can I say? It's embarrassing. I felt like a failure. It became easier not to say, even though the divorce was really happening. And Piper? We were just starting out. I didn't even meet her until after the holidays."

"I didn't know that," I said quietly.

"I know you didn't. You never gave me a chance." At any other moment, my brother would have said that comment with spite and possibly anger, but having his niece missing affected how he was acting, too. "It doesn't matter now. Let's concentrate on your little girl." When his phone rang again, he looked at the screen and said, "It's mom."

I sighed. I had yet to actually talk to the woman since the news broke, and I knew I should. "Answer. I'll talk with her for a little bit." Family…love…I needed it.

Lane answered his phone and talked with our mother, explaining that he was, indeed, with me. And then, God bless him, he pretty much warned my mom to try to keep it sane—to just listen to me and not project. I almost laughed. Yes, he had grown up in the room next to mine for seventeen years.

My mother started my part of the conversation with, "I'm glad you have your brother. I'm glad that you're having him help."

The way she slightly emphasized the word "him," made me cringe and comment. "I didn't ask him to come down here, Mom."

"I know. Doesn't matter." She brushed off her unwarranted hurt about not being the one sitting next to me. "Are there any leads? Has anyone seen little Arinn?"

"No," I lamented. "No one has seen her or Br—" I started to say Briar but quickly changed it to her proper name—the name the media had promoted. "Brianna."

"You'll get through this, sweetie. You both will. How is Finn? Maybe I should say something to him."

"He's out. He's… he's doing okay." No, he wasn't, I

thought. How could either of us be?

"I can imagine he's just as torn up as you. God, watching him while you were in that coma…" She spoke about when I fell and miscarried years before. "He was an absolute wreck. You two hold onto each other and keep the faith that everything will be all right."

My mother was religious. But, because my father hadn't been, it wasn't enforced on us kids growing up. I looked over at Lane and did the blessing yourself cross symbol. He closed his eyes and shook his head probably knowing, without actually hearing, the exact words our mother was saying across the line.

"I'm having a hard time doing that, Mom. The longer she is gone, the…the….God knows where she could be. I'm scared." When I started to cry, Lane gave me a quick side arm hug.

"I want to be there with you." She was a mom also.

I tried to pull it together. "Can't," I partially lied. "They don't need any extra bodies around." *I* didn't need my hyperactive mother around. "You should see all the different people calling and going in and out of the house as it is." That *wasn't* a lie.

Miraculously, she let it drop but retained her stance on her previous comment. "There will be a good ending," she said.

"God, I hope so." I dried my eyes and looked at Lane. "But, y'know, I wonder if this is, just like Chloe, my penance. After giving up that kid after high school, I always thought I didn't deserve a child, and now…now, I am going to have another baby taken away from me."

"Lara Ann Faul—" She started calling me by my maiden name, surely out of pure aggravation. "Murphy," she corrected. "Lara, that is not true! You gave that boy a loving home. We all know that." We might not have known his name or where he lived, but we did know his family loved him very much because of all they did to help him live, including contacting me about helping to find a successful bone marrow match for him a couple years before. "Your miscarriage was a sad accident," my mother continued. "It had nothing to do with anything you did in the past. And your children—Chance and Arinn—are blessed, blessed let me tell you, to have both you and Finn as their parents. They are far more blessed than you and Lane were."

"Mom…." I appreciated her words of encouragement, but I knew what it was going to turn into.

"I'm sorry about that, Lara. I didn't stand up for you. And your father shou—"

"Mom, I can't. I can't get into this right now." I looked at Lane who did another shaking head/closed eye combo. "I love you, but I have to go."

"What?"

"I have to go, Mom. There's…there's just too much right now."

"Okay. Okay, sweetie. Let me say goodbye to your brother."

"Sure thing." I handed Lane his phone. "Wants you.'"

As I paced the room, I listened to Lane promising our mother that he would watch me and that one of us would get back to her with any new developments. But I was really in the midst of my own internal thoughts. It was weird. My mother had me both a little more upset, recalling a past I never wanted to relive, and, at the same time, a little more at peace realizing what I needed to do.

When he hung up the phone, Lane and I debriefed in our own sibling way of long exhales and eye rolls, and then I encouraged him to go to the hotel and be with Piper. There wasn't anything for him to do at the ranch. Plus, I wanted to find Finn. Love and family. Yes, that was my brother and mother, but for me it would always…always start with my husband. And I needed to make sure he knew that.

***

Even though he was religious, Finn didn't go to church on a regular basis. It was part of the whole privacy-versus-celebrity thing for him. I had known the church he preferred in New York, but Nashville was still semi-foreign to me. So, I found out the name and address of the church from the officer at the gate. The police wanted to always know our locations, both for security measures and in case there was any news.

It was, fortunately, an easy drive. And I was even more grateful to find the quiet church nearly vacant upon my arrival. The first thing I noticed was the multitude of candles aglow, and I couldn't help but wonder how many Finn had lit. He had so much to pray for. Without an active service taking place, there were only a few parishioners in the holy building. So, it was easy to spot him. Finn was all the way at the end of a pew a few rows from the back. Had I not known my husband so well, I might have mistaken him for a homeless individual. His tan cargo pants hung loosely on his legs and his blue hoodie tried its best to cover his whiskery face. And... he was asleep.

Careful not to disturb him or the other attendees rows and rows away, I sat down next to him and adhered to his side. I heard him instantly murmur, slightly stir, and then relax into my touch. Even though asleep, he knew my body next to his. Listening to his soft breathing and feeling his chest move up and down against the side of my face, I felt like I was almost relaxed enough to sleep myself. And then the on-the-hour church chimes rang.

He moved more definitively then, causing me to sit up next to him. "You're here?" He connected the dots of location to me.

"You're here," I simplified, hoping he understood that I would go with him no matter what or where.

He touched my hair. "Is there anything new?" When I shook my head, he tried not to look discouraged, but how could he not be? "Good talk with your brother?" He forged on.

"Yeah. I haven't given him a fair shake," I admitted.

"You tell him about...?" He let me know the subject of his question by looking at my stomach.

"No. Some things should just be us." I spoke not only of the possible pregnancy but more.

He tilted his forehead onto mine for an extended moment. I could feel his love and appreciation even before he said, "I'm glad you came."

"Me, too."

"Have you eaten anything?" he started out asking but, knowing my likely answer, changed his comment to a concerned command. "You need to eat."

"You need to take care of yourself, too," I countered.

"I am. I promise." He stared at me for a while—our faces only mere inches from one another. "I've been talking with Dr. Bartola." He spoke of the New York therapist he would see on occasion. "I called after everyone left last night and then again on my way here. I know I've got to keep myself in check with the meds and counseling. I know I have to for you and Chance and for Arinn."

"Thanks, Cowboy," I said, with relief. I guess I should have known he was taking extra precautionary measures to regulate his PTSD because, for the most part, he had been a solid, sturdy, reliable pillar since everything started. I didn't want to have to worry about him on top of everything else. But, at the same time, I would if I needed to. "I'm glad, but if you want to let go or talk with me, it's all right. Finn? We cut through that, right?" I thought about the night we returned from Louisville, as well as what my mother had said. "We're in this together. Don't think you have to be Superman all the time."

"Oh, baby..." He sighed. "I feel so far removed from Superman right now. I feel so helpless."

I leaned back into his side, appreciating his honesty and

knowing how closely my feelings mirrored his. He placed his hand on mine, which was resting on my stomach. That was when I noticed one of Arinn's fancy little hairbands wrapped around his wrist. His sentimentality brought tears to my eyes.

"One step, one breath at a time. All of us. All of us."

After sitting in silence for a couple more minutes, Finn got up, went to the front of the church, and knelt down at the altar. He stayed there with his head bowed for a while, letting me soak in the peaceful setting and his hopeful words. If I didn't have faith in higher powers like my husband did, I definitely had faith in him.

***

After church, Finn picked up Chance and met me back at the ranch, bringing some Italian takeout for dinner. Immediately afterward, though, Reese came over to strategize with Finn. So, Chance and I withdrew upstairs to color some pictures before his bedtime.

But, even after teeth brushing, pajamas, prayers, and no bedbugs, Chance still wasn't quite ready to go to sleep. He seemed okay with spending his day with Carter. He wasn't clingy or afraid, but I think he just wanted that extra time with me. I laid down beside him and quietly read one of his books until he fell into dreamland. I stayed there for a while in the near darkness of his room, looking at all the items surrounding him—autographed music and sports memorabilia, loving family photos, games and stuffed animals galore. It was everything a child could ask for. The same with his sister. But, yet, none of it, in the end, could protect them.

My eyes refocused on the simplicity of the white ceiling. I tried repeatedly, as if it was a mantra, to send good thoughts to my other child…to let Arinn know wherever she was that we loved her more than anything and that we were doing everything to get to her. I willed her to know that love and not be scared.

I thought and hoped and even prayed for so long, I must have put myself to sleep right there in Chance's room. Because, the next thing I knew, I was feeling Finn sink onto the bed next to me. Plugging in our treasured lava lamp, which always remained in the master bedroom, Finn stretched across to kiss our sleeping son and then wrapped his arm around both of us, creating an even tighter bond. Knowing that no news was just that— no news, I didn't bother to ask Finn for an update. I just wept...both for not being with my daughter another day and for my husband knowing exactly where we both needed to be at that moment.

CHAPTER TEN

God! How could it be Monday already? How could my baby have missed an entire weekend away from her family? How did Friday afternoon even happen? Where was Arinn? Please let her be safe.

I managed to ease myself out of bed without waking Chance. Finn was nowhere to be found, but the lava lamp was still gurgling its contents just as my stomach seemed to be. Entering the hall, I quietly closed Chance's door behind me. Hearing voices coming from the downstairs, I stopped and listened. I immediately recognized Finn's, and sadly, almost as quickly, I recognized Cayla's. I removed and then replaced the childproof gate from the top of the steps and sat two steps down, just to take a moment to myself before it all started again—before Cayla tried to say something encouraging without actually having the facts to back it up, before Finn walked his tightrope of frustrating outbursts and pacifying me, before looking online to the growing media outlets that all thought they knew something more than the other, before keeping up appearances for our son...before I completely fell apart.

"Lar?" Finn was standing a couple steps down from me with his hand outstretched in my direction.

I hadn't even noticed him approach. "Starting early," I said, not moving.

"It's almost nine. You slept. I'm glad."

"Huh." I had no idea.

Seeing that I was reluctant to make a commitment to upstairs or down, Finn nudged his hips next to mine and sat down next to me. I leaned my head into his side. How could I be so tired when I just woke up? And I had actually slept a good number of hours consecutively.

After a couple of breaths, but without lifting my head, I said, "Tell me. I'm ready."

He delved right in. "Nothing credible on the hotlines. Just a lot of nutcases."

"That's what I was afraid of." I sighed and arched my neck so I could look at him. "They all want a piece of you."

"We had to do it, Lar."

"I know."

"There seems to be quite an outpouring on social media, though. People are sharing the police postings and wanting to get out there themselves and search."

"Hmmm…that's good, I guess." But it wasn't—it wouldn't be good until Arinn was back in my arms.

"I just talked with your brother. He's agreed to come over, get some of the flyers, go to some local places, and get more word out."

I scooched apart from my husband. "I want to go, too."

Finn looked at me as if he was a doctor doing an eye exam. "I don't know, baby."

"Finn, I'm not doing anything here. It's driving me crazy. I need to do something. I need to be there for her. I need…God, I need to do something."

Standing at the end of the staircase, Cayla interrupted our conversation, but she appeared to be on my side, so I didn't mind. "It might be good. We really do need to get the personal aspect out there. Ideally, we'd like both of you. But putting Finn out on the streets just might be more of a hindrance. We're working on that. But, Lara, if you want to, especially with your brother, I think that's a good idea."

Before he could agree or refute, I clamped my hand on his thigh, kissed his forehead, and got up. "Let me just get some coffee," I said as Finn grabbed my hand and starting walking with me down the stairs. "Then I'll get cleaned up a little and get Chance ready to go, too."

Now a couple steps into the great room, Finn halted our stride and broke our hand lock. He looked from me to Cayla to me again. "You want to take Chance? I don't know that that is—"

"You don't trust me? I won't lose him, Finn," I interrupted, hearing the instant doubt in his voice.

"That's not what I said," he quickly denied and then looked at me dead on. "Is that what I said?"

"No," I admitted, but he had to think it. God, I did a little.

"That's not what I said." Wanting to make sure his point was clear, he would not let his eyes even blink in front of mine. "And you know I trust you." He paused before saying my name, making me think of all the things that only I and sometimes his family were privy to. "Lara?"

"Okay," I said softly, knowing we had a witness to our intimate conversation.

"I just worry about him hearing and seeing too much," my husband explained.

"I'll make sure that doesn't happen. I think he needs to get out. I can maybe take him to some fast food place, get a kid's meal, jump in the balls. You know, be a kid."

Finn looked at Cayla, who responded generically to both of us with, "That's your decision" and walked away.

"Up to you," Finn relented. "If that's what you want to do…."

I didn't want it to be up to me. I thought it was fine in the beginning, but then he raised doubt. I couldn't handle making one more decision, even if it was about what top to wear.

"Take him, Lara." My silent internal struggle must have been obvious to my husband. "You're right. It'll be good for him." When I plowed into that strong man's chest, he instantly enveloped his arms around me and rested his lips on top of my head. After a moment of pure, escapist comfort, he said, "C'mon, let's get that coffee first."

***

While I was getting dressed and Lane was downstairs entertaining Chance—or was it the other way around—Finn decided to take a break with a shower. I completely understood. The luxury of those few solitary, soundproof minutes really seemed to be a mini-escape from the chaos of the world spiraling out of control around us. I heard the water start and, out of the corner of my eye, saw him begin to discard his clothes. That was when his phone, resting on his nightstand, started to ring.

"Lar? Can you get that?" His voice rose in nervous anticipation—something that now happened to both of us any time any of our electronic devices chimed.

I did a hurried two-step over to his phone and read the caller ID. My reaction wasn't a completely deflated shoulder shrug, but I also knew the caller wasn't someone who could tell us our daughter's location. "It's Dr. Bartola." I looked at Finn whose face kind of mimicked mine.

As he continued to strip out of his boxers, he said, "Talk to him. Tell him I'll call him back in a little while."

Before I could counter with the fact that I had never spoken before to Finn's therapist, he was in the shower. Doing as he asked, though, I picked up the phone. "It's Lara Murphy," I answered, wanting to make sure the person on the other end knew who they were talking with.

"Lara, it's Trey Bartola."

Trey? Hmmm…I think that was the first time I had heard the doctor's first name. Finn had always used the formal moniker when talking about him. Knowing my husband and his relationship with the physician, I gathered it was a show of respect.

"Dr. Bartola, hi." I respected him, too…for so much. "Finn just stepped in the shower. He told me to tell you that he would call you back. I don't want to overstep any confidentiality or HIPAA hoopla."

"You're not and couldn't, Lara. I can call you that, right?"

"Absolutely," I replied.

"Finn has told me—in fact, he has it in writing— that his wife is privy to any conversation we have." While I let my heart melt a beat with that "no omissions" comment, the doc continued. "It's nice to actually talk with you. I'm sorry it is during such a horrendously stressful time."

"You're probably used to that. In fact, I think we might be asking for a two for one rate."

I tried to joke. But there was nothing funny about it. I probably needed therapy as much as my husband did right then.

"You can call and talk with me any time." He was a therapist. He saw right through my sarcastic shield. "And that can be just between the two of us if you want."

"No. No," I denied. "Finn and I have no omissions. Dr. Bartola? It means so much to me for all that you do for Finn. You have helped him through so much. I…I can't thank you enough."

"I think you underestimate your influence."

"No. Finn definitely has been the one holding it together for us. I'm sure that's because y—"

"He's taking on that role for you, right now, Lara. He feeds off of being there for you and the kids."

"But I don't want him to—"

I was hesitating with the truth because I was used to keeping things private. But this was Finn's therapist. He knew.

"What can I do?" I amended anyway.

"Be there for him. Forgive him."

"I have," I responded, assuming the forgiving was in reference to the hook-up with Briar, which I was positive Finn told his doctor about.

"Not just that." As a good therapist, Trey Bartola was also part mind-reader. "Forgive him when he gets angry. Forgive him when he just can't stay in control anymore because he won't be able to all the time."

"I know. I do. I just wish he would let me help him."

"He's trying," he said in a way that let me know Finn and the doctor must have had a conversation or two about the battles we got into about me wanting to help him through his PTSD moments. "Let him know you love him. That is what he needs the most."

"Yeah," I managed to spit out. It was kind of weird and yet so reassuring to talk with someone besides Finn's immediate family who knew him so well. "Thanks. I'll have him call you back."

"Just touching base...trying to do my part to help...for Finn...for both of you. We're praying for your little girl."

"Appreciate it." I teared up— those words got me every time. The enormousness of the danger Arinn was in, that required so many prayers, scared me every time.

***

I was in the great room bustling Chance into his coat when Finn reemerged, appearing only slightly more refreshed. He managed to look at me with the slightest, briefest of smiles before his phone rang. Picking it up and acknowledging Reese as the caller, he started walking into the nearby dining room where Lane and Cayla were strategizing.

Knowing that I was actually, hopefully, going to be an active participant in helping bring my daughter home, I was feeling a little bit energized. That was until I saw the missing child flyers on the mantel. I had seen them before, but somehow knowing they were going to be in my hands and the seriousness of our mission, suddenly crippled me all over again. I heard Chance ask something about what the papers were before I literally just sank to the ground. I didn't want to stand anymore. I just needed a pause...a break...before I had to be the public mom who had lost her child.

"Mommy, what you doing?" Chance called out next to me in a mixture of worry and fun puzzlement. After all, his mother just suddenly sat pretzel style on the floor as if we were going to play.

I had a clear shot of both Finn and Lane's heads swirling around in my direction. Finn, still on his phone, took an instant step toward me. But Lane touched his arm to hold him back and approached me himself.

"Go get your tablet." I managed to direct my son as Lane squatted down next to me.

As Chance ran off, Lane spoke, "I know you're a mess, but you are a fighter, Lara. You and I had to be from birth. And that guy over there may have his faults, but he loves you and your kids, and he is doing everything to make sure everything is all right. And I am, too."

"I know. I just...I know." I looked up at Finn, who nodded once in my direction, wanting my confirmation that I was all right. I nodded twice back and allowed Lane to help me up. "Where's Piper?" I questioned my brother once we were standing.

"At the hotel."

"Would she want to help? We could pick her up. It would be nice to have an extra hand while talking with people and—"

"I'm sure she would love to, Lar."

Finn, now off his phone, made it over to where we were standing just as Chance reentered the great room. "You sure about this?" Finn questioned me.

"Yeah. I'm fine."

He brought me into his embrace. "I'll see you soon." Then he hauled Chance up into his muscular arms. "Same goes for you, Little Man."

And we were off. Coats, tablets, tape, and missing flyers intact, we were ready and determined. The only thing we needed was the right result.

***

Chance held up pretty good. And Piper was a huge help. She kept Chance entertained when store owners and people on the street wanted to speak with me directly. The hospitality and willingness to help was at times overwhelming. Thankfully, most of the time, it was out of the deepest concern over Arinn and not the fact that I was Finn's wife. But there was some of that.

When we broke for a late lunch at a local restaurant, it was quick. We had passed flyers out at a number of places, but there was so much more we wanted to do. Knowing that my three-and-a-half-year-old had pretty much reached his limit, though, and an indoor playground was located right next to the restaurant, we divided and conquered. Lane and Piper continued their pursuit around the surrounding neighborhoods, while I sat and watched my little boy jump, bounce, and laugh in a safe, enclosed, eyes-on environment.

My eyes may have always been on Chance, but my mind was sometimes elsewhere. In between cries of "Mommy, watch this" and "I love this place," I let my mind wander to my other child who, although she would not have been able to do a lot of the activities in the center, should have been there with us. I was thinking of her exuberance for life and the utter joy that she brought to ours, as Chance's "Mommy" yells changed to "Piper" yells.

I looked up to discover Piper halfway across the room

next to my son, and Lane towering next to me. "What are you doing here already?" I asked my brother.

It had been a little while since they dropped us off, but it was definitely not our designated time to meet back up. Or, so I thought. Needing the clarification, I started to fish my phone out of my purse to check the time.

But Lane's voice halted my action. "What have you been doing?"

"Just watching Chance …and trying to keep it together," I admitted. But I was perplexed by his question. "What else would I be doing?"

"People need you." He seemed to take a huge exhale after his statement as if he had been running or worried and was trying to catch his breath.

"Who? Who needs me? You didn't answer me, Lane. What are you doing here already?"

"I was trying to call you. Finn's been leaving messages on your cell. He called me because he couldn't get you and…" His voice was racing. "Haven't you gotten them?"

"No. I…maybe there's not good reception. Maybe it's too enclosed?" I spoke while finally grabbing my phone from my purse. Seeing the dark screen, I swore. "Damn it. The battery is… I forgot—"

"What? Uh, never mind. Finn needs you."

"Why?" I asked. But as I stood to meet my brother, his words since he arrived at the indoor playground started reverberating, and I didn't like them or the way he was frantically delivering them… at all. All of the sudden I understood. "No. No, no, no, no, no! No, don't tell me. I'm not going to listen to you. No, you can't. No." I may as well have had my hands up to my ears. I knew I was acting like a deranged lunatic in an insane asylum. But, I absolutely refused to hear what I knew for sure my brother was going to tell me.

"What? Calm down. Oh, my God, calm down."

My shoulders and his hands on them were both shaking. But was it because he was shaking me into some sort of sense? Or was I shaking so bad that it was causing his hands to bounce?

"Please, Lara." My brother tried to steady me.

"She's not. She's okay. I know she's okay. I would know. You can't tell me she isn't." Mother's instinct, I tried desperately to rationalize. I would know if something happened to Arinn. I knew I would.

"It's not that."

Oh, God. Thank God. I tried to catch my breath.

"What then?" I attempted to steady my jittery eyes on my brother. "Why are you so upset?"

"Neither of us could get a hold of you. We thought…." He started as I glanced back over to Chance with Piper. "Never mind. Call Finn."

"What?" After the scare I just had, it was taking me a moment to refocus.

"Call your husband," Lane reiterated plainly.

"My phone's dead!" I partially yelled, since that fact seemed to be what had started the whole frantic conversation.

Lane pushed out air from his lungs, pressed a few buttons on his phone, and handed it to me. "Here."

I hardly had it up to my ear when I heard Finn's panicked voice coming from the other end. "You got her? You got Lara?"

"I *am* her," I answered, while looking at Lane, who was shaking his head—no doubt in relief.

"Oh, thank God. Shit!" And it was my husband's turn to exhale exuberantly. "Why didn't you answer my calls?"

"The phone died," I explained while still in some kind of shock as to what all the commotion was about in order to find me.

My husband's temper was instant. "Lara, keep it char—" But he managed to reign it in pretty quickly, too. "Okay. I'm sorry. You all right? Is Chance okay?"

"Yeah. We're…yeah."

"Where are you at?" After I gave him the name of the

fun center and asked him why, he finally explained the whole reason why he had been trying to get in touch with me. "Everyone thinks the best idea is to do a live-stream press conference. They're setting it up at the police station. Reese just headed down. They need both of us to appeal to Briar."

"Really?" I asked as Lane walked toward Piper and Chance, providing me some privacy. "She's probably mad at you. And God knows the smug way she glared at me at the CMAs…. she wanted to rub my nose in what happened between the two—" I couldn't, shouldn't, and didn't want to finish that sentence.

"I don't know, Lara," he said with pure exasperation. "This is what everyone is saying to do, though. It's how we get my image and personal plea out there. We have to give it a try. They know what they're doing. Listen, I'm pulling out of the garage right now." As he said it, I could actually hear the garage door descending. "Tell your brother to stay with you guys until I get there, and then they can bring Chance to our place and watch him."

"No. I want Chance—"

"Baby, please." He cut me off, knowing we had already been on the Chance stays versus goes merry-go-round too many times in the past few days. "He'll be with his uncle, and you know the ranch is secure."

The horses and the music were going around too fast, though. I wanted to get off. I didn't want the overwhelming sick feeling any more.

"Lara?" His voice came across the line again.

"Yeah. Okay," I managed and then said, "God knows what she is planning. If she's not asking us for money, what is she going to do? She could have our baby in another state or country by now."

"The police have that all covered," he said in an effort to reassure.

"I know, but people have slipped by before." Then with honesty, I added, "Finn, I'm so scared."

There was a lengthy pause and then an audible breath before he acknowledged, "I am, too."

While I normally admired his usual strength and self-assurance, I also appreciated his candor. Sometimes sugarcoating didn't make anything better. Sometimes I just needed to know that what I was feeling was legit, even if it wasn't what I wanted to face.

"I know," I quietly responded. And then, "Finn? Do you remember it? Do you remember being in that park?"

He knew the park I was referring to. It wasn't the park that flipped our world upside down just three days before—Centennial. In fact, it wasn't in Nashville or even Tennessee. The park I was talking about was in Louisville, and Finn had been just a couple years older than Arinn.

"She won't," he said, without directly answering my question but alluding to the fact that there was definitely some type of remembrance in his brain…hence the PTSD trauma. "Dr. Bartola said she's way too young."

I took a moment to silently thank Dr. Bartola. "God, I hope so," I said. "We've just got to get her back."

"We will." And there was his confidence again…real or not.

"You called him back, then?" I referenced the helpful physician.

"Yeah. He seemed quite taken with you. But who isn't?" Even in extreme moments of distress, my husband could pour on the charm.

I ignored the compliment. "He seems very down-to-earth. It was nice kind of getting to meet him."

"You'll have to for real some time. I just never thought about it. But, you know, Lar, I'm an open book where you're concerned."

I smiled, recalling Dr. Bartola telling me Finn had told him the same thing. And I also remembered the advice the doc had given me. It seemed a most apropos time to follow it.

"I love you," I said.

"Baby, I love you, too."

The scene I made hearing my husband say those words must have been quite a sight. The adults and children who were nearby seemed to venture a little further away. And, from across the room, I saw Lane's concerned eyes meet mine, which were actively flowing along with my labored breath. Finn had never, ever shied away from telling me he loved me—even during times when we were furious with one another. I had said those three words then to help him, but I think I needed to hear them equally as much. I cried, not because they brought sadness but because they brought security and hope.

But, unfortunately, my reaction created the opposite for my husband. "Shit, Lar, don't... don't cry. I'm not there to hold you."

"I'm fine," I lied, while managing to swipe at my tears.

After a beat of silence, he said, "Listen, the GPS says I'm about twenty minutes away. I'll be there sooner." Determination and a sleek car would make that very probable. "Do you need me to stay on the line with you?"

I knew he thought I was strong, and I should be. But my response came out wavering. "Um...yeah if that's all right. Please. Don't hang up."

"I won't," he replied, and I could swear it sounded like a relief to him, too.

There was silence for a while as I calmed myself down and Finn drove. "Finn?" I needed to hear him some way...somehow.

"I'm here."

"I—" I thought about telling him that I was all right, but that would be a lie.

He rescued me from my minor deceitful thoughts. "Wanta know something?" I wiped more tears and waited until he spoke, knowing that it had pretty much been a rhetorical question, anyway. "If I tell you, you can't tell Vanessa." Finn knew my best friend bond with Vanessa, but I'm sure he also knew my bond with him was a million times stronger.

"Aw, crap, I can't deal with a secret or—" I started.

"It's a good secret, Beauty. And Carter wanted me to tell you."

"Yeah?" I was definitely interested, especially knowing it was good and Carter was involved— a secret might be doable.

"He bought a ring."

"Really?" Although they had been dating for a while and it seemed serious, the former playboy had given no indication that an engagement was a possibility when I had flat out asked him in the beginning of September.

"Really. He's a bundle of nerves but good ones."

"Really, Finn?" I asked again, doubting that anything good could possibly be happening.

"Yeah," he confirmed. "He told me yesterday."

"That's so great. I'm so happy for them."

"Well, he hasn't proposed yet. So, shhh."

"Yeah…yeah, of course. That's so great." I wanted to cry again out of pure happiness for my friend and Finn's.

"Do you think you might be the bridesmaid to my groomsman again, Rapunzel?" He was referencing my hair at Sam and Olivia's wedding when they got married right out of college and both Finn and I were, indeed, in the wedding party.

"Huh, yeah. Yeah, maybe." It certainly did seem like a Deja-vu moment, hopefully with a better ending than the nasty divorce Sam and Olivia went through.

"Just so you are always the bride to my groom." My husband's sentiment made me sniffle again, to which he soothed, "Lara, I'm almost there."

We talked for a little bit more until Finn was almost at the indoor playground. Then I knew I had to hang up so I could gather Chance, Lane, and Piper and fill them in on the plan. Saying "see-ya soon" to my sweet little boy was hard. But I was hoping that the reason I was leaving would help me be able to see my little girl soon, too.

CHAPTER ELEVEN

My eyes followed Finn's as a frown creased his face, and he quickly got back into the driver's side of his metallic roadster. There were a couple adults and children getting out of a car parked directly in front of his. And then I understood. He didn't want to be seen. He didn't want to be recognized...especially in Music City and especially with the added publicity. So, I walked a little faster and made my way to the passenger side of his car.

Awaiting my arrival was Arinn's stuffed mouse, sitting solo on the seat. The sensitivity of that man I was blessed to call my friend and husband never ceased to amaze me. I didn't have a chance to tell him, though, as Finn quickly tore out of the parking lot.

Before I could question the abruptness, he found a nearby street that was vacant of any type of building structure or vehicles and pulled over. He unfastened my freshly buckled seatbelt, got out of the car, and came over to help me out. And then I was in his arms— securely, soundly, silently...for a while.

"I've got you," he eventually said. "Everything's going to be okay."

I dropped my hands to his waist and met his eyes.

"We've got each other. Let's go get our baby back."

"That's my girl." He smiled and let his lips sweetly brush mine.

***

Before I knew it, the two of us were in front of a makeshift podium, and there were cameras, and mics, and people all around. Finn took the lead in reading the statement we had prepared, stating how much we wanted our baby back home and that there would be a reward for the safe recovery of our daughter. He answered most of the questions, too, because he was familiar with the press and, quite frankly, it was him they were there to hear from. That was absolutely fine with me. While I was used to having my photo taken on special red-carpet occasions, I most certainly did not like being in the spotlight.

The cameras being so close and the crowd being bigger than I expected didn't help ease my tension or my breathing. I fought it hard. I fought it long. I was all about pushing and persevering, especially because what we were there for was so important. But I couldn't. When I felt like I was spinning or completely drugged up in another world, I knew I had to say something. "I'm a little dizzy. I need to sit down or something." I dropped Finn's hand, which I had been holding the entire time, and kind of teetered a few steps away.

Finn instantly grabbed my side. "Here. Come here."

I tried to look at him, but he was swirling. I knew that wasn't right. I could feel that he was the steady one of the two of us. It was me. I felt like I did during the pregnancy where I miscarried.

I saw the bench that I think Finn was steering me toward when I heard someone say, "She's going to faint."

***

Thankfully, when I woke up, I wasn't in a hospital and I hadn't spent over a week in a coma like I had years before when I miscarried Chloe. I was lying on the ground of the police station. Finn was down there with me holding my hand, and a couple of officers were standing guard. I could hear other people pleading with the press to be respectful and stop the feed. Still groggy and a little dizzy, I tried to sit up slowly. I managed to make it to that bench just inches away. But, as soon as I did, nausea came rushing to my head and stomach.

"I don't feel good," I murmured.

As soon as I said that, someone had a garbage can next to me. And it wasn't a moment too soon. I ended up vomiting what little contents my stomach had inside it into the receptacle.

"Lara, hey...." Finn was brushing my hair back with his hands and then attempting to cradle me.

"Maybe we should get her some water or something to eat."

I looked up at the police officer who said that and replied with repulsion in my voice. "I can't eat."

"Let's at least get some water on your lips," she countered.

"Are you all right? Do you feel like you're going to throw up again?" Finn asked.

"I feel better," I said, mostly because I could see the tremendous amount of concern on his face and only partially because it was the truth. "I just need to breathe." I tried looking at those gathered around us, but it made me lightheaded all over again. A big part of that, I'm sure, was the attention and embarrassment.

"You all right to stand? I'm taking you to the hospital." Finn was now squatting in front of me.

"No. No," I protested. "We've got to finish here."

"Reese," he said swinging his gaze to the podium that his publicist was already walking toward. "Reese will take care of it. We need to make sure you are all right and that this didn't do anything to the pregnancy."

He said it out loud. He said it in front of people. No, not only people, but the press. And I knew they had all heard. I knew because there was a new flurry of movement and pencils writing on papers and Reese looking from Finn to me and then physically trying to get the cameras in her direction. I had no idea what she was going to say because she may as well have been in line with the reporters to ask the same question they were. Was I pregnant?

But Finn ignored all of them. He didn't care. His only concern was me and making sure I was all right. With that objective in mind, he glued me to his side and, with the help of some police interference, walked me gingerly but directly out to his car.

"I'm sorry," I said when we were both in the car and he was pulling out. "I was trying to ignore it, and then it was just too extreme."

"You should have said something sooner. We need to get you checked out."

"I'm fine. I'm fine now. I don't need to go to the hospital. We know what it is. They'll just waste time figuring out that I'm preg—"

"Shut up!" he yelled. "You are going to the hospital. I don't want to hear another word about it."

I shook on his forceful words. I knew he was scared, on top of being stressed, and that was why he reacted that way. But I wasn't expecting it. "I'm okay," I managed to squeak out.

"You're not a doctor!" he belted out again, but I noticed he was at least controlling his driving to a decent speed. "I'd like to switch places with you so you could see what it feels like to watch someone fade away like that— to wonder if they're ever going to wake back up." He looked over at me to make his point but then just as quickly reverted his eyes back to the windshield.

I know the day I miscarried years before was forever

embedded in his mind. I had fainted, fallen, lost our child, and nearly didn't wake up. It was something, though, I still did not remember.

"Don't yell at me." In a disagreement, I would usually give as well as I took, but this time, I whimpered, sounding as defeated and scared as I felt. It was strangely like the eight-year-old version of a hurt and frightened me. Finn's eyes flashed on mine in silent recognition, and we both took a breath or two before I conceded. "I'll talk with a doctor. I was fine with Chance and Arinn."

He didn't say anything for a while. He was getting what he wanted, but I was still hemming and hawing, which I knew he didn't like. He wanted me to take it more seriously. The only thing I could take seriously, though, was getting the daughter back that was already here on this Earth.

"Do you need some air?" he eventually asked, using a much calmer approach than his previous statements.

"Yeah," I agreed mimicking his tone. "Do you mind? I know it's cold."

He pressed a button to open my passenger window slightly. "Okay?"

"Yeah."

"Finn?"

"Yeah?"

My stomach was rumbling so much I think I was actually shifting in the seat. I wasn't going to throw up again, though. I was just a little nervous about what I knew I had to tell him. The angel and the devil were tossing their shoulder ideas around in my head, debating if this was the right time. But I didn't want to wait. That would be almost like keeping a secret…an omission.

"What?" he asked again.

"Before my phone died earlier, when we were at lunch, Miller called. He left a message just saying he was concerned about Arinn."

Knuckles actually do go white when they are applying

an extreme amount of pressure. I was witness to it via Finn's hands on the steering wheel. It wasn't just his hands, though. His face went rock hard on the mention of my high school boyfriend's name.

"Why are you telling me this?" He spoke in a controlled, yet clipped, tone and did not look at me.

"Because we have no omissions. I needed to tell you. And I'm not calling him back. I just didn't want you to find out somehow. I couldn't bear to go through what we did before."

It was the fight that had started it all at the end of August. Finn had seen a text from Miller come into my phone, and he had lost it. The text and calls from my ex were innocent and legit, but Finn hadn't seen it that way, especially with the amount of stress he had been dealing with. The fight snowballed into so much more—events that led to Briar and that, ironically, led to us sitting in that car on our way to the hospital.

"Honestly, Lara, that's the last thing I wanted to hear right now."

"Not the last thing," I said softly. A million other things ran through my mind that would be far worse...Arinn being hurt topped the list.

He read me instantly. "No. No. You're right." He breathed in deeply. "Thank you for telling me, but I trus—" The speaker system in Finn's car alerted us that a phone call was coming in. "Yeah?" he answered after pressing a button on the dash.

"What the hell happened?" It was my brother, who, by his question and tone, had seen the press feed.

"She's all right. I'm taking her to the hospital right now just to make sure."

"Lara?" Lane needed my voice for confirmation.

"I'm fine, Lane. Chance didn't see, did he?"

"No. No, of course not. He was nowhere near the screen," my other protector replied.

"Hey, we're pulling in," Finn interrupted, and I looked

up to see that the hospital was, indeed, in front of us…just a convenient ten minutes away from the police station. "I'll keep you updated." He finished and hit the red disconnect button without another word.

Despite Finn telling Lane I was all right, we entered the hospital with Finn acting like Shirley MacLaine in *Terms of Endearment* when she was trying to get help for her dying daughter. I let him do what he needed to do. The air in the car had momentarily helped me, but the busy atmosphere of the emergency room threatened to make me feel like going sideways again. I sat down on a sofa near the window and waited until everyone else figured out my world for me.

After some water, a private exam room, nibbling on some type of nutrition bar, and a couple of tests run, I was feeling, legitimately, much more refreshed. Finn and I sat in the room together, awaiting the doctor's reentrance and diagnosis. Finn was much calmer. He was definitely not as panicked or angry. Although he still looked worn and weary, as I'm sure we both did over the days since Arinn was taken. He did not apologize for his outburst in the car. But I neither expected nor needed him to. We had been together long enough to know that it wasn't the words that made the difference. It was the love.

A nurse popped his head in. "Mrs. Murphy, the doctor should just be a few minutes. But there is someone here named Lane who is insisting on seeing you."

I guess I shouldn't have been surprised by my brother's arrival, but I was. Lane probably was even more concerned than Finn at that point because he had only seen me pass out, and then the screen cut to black. And with everything else that was going on since we arrived at the hospital, Finn hadn't contacted Lane again.

"Can you let him in, please?"

The nurse nodded his head and was almost instantly replaced in the room by my brother. "Lara…." He came to the side of my bed not occupied by Finn.

"Where's Chance?" was my immediate concern.

"He's with Piper at your place. He's fine," he added.

"He's okay?" I knew my brother had just said that, but I was a mom—a stressed, emotional one at that. "I mean, it's just Piper. Chance doesn't really know her. I don't really kn—"

"Lara, geez!" Lane exclaimed. "Piper is fine. She's a social worker. Don't you trust that I know—"

Finn interrupted Lane firmly but not aggressively. "Don't yell." He was obviously recalling our incident in the car but wouldn't directly acknowledge it by looking at me. "We're all stressed," he continued. "She can't handle any more." He inhaled a longer-than-usual breath. "But we trust you *and* Piper." Finn then took my hand and applied a little bit of pressure. "Trust, Lara. I know it's hard for you. But you need to trust." He kept hold of my hand but looked at Lane. "What's Little Man up to?" Finn's way of talking with us Faulkner siblings helped calm both of us down.

"He's singing karaoke songs with Piper," Lane relayed.

"That's my boy." Finn managed a smile thinking of Chance.

"I was going to bring him, but Piper convinced me he would be scared seeing you here like this."

Finn squeezed my hand and emphasized his first word. "I'm scared seeing you here like this."

I ignored my husband, knowing there wasn't anything I could do to keep him from worrying. "That was probably the right thing to do. I…I just…I'm sorry. The last time I trusted one of my kids to someone I didn't really know—" I stopped myself. I looked at Finn again. "I know, trust…trust."

I squeezed his hand, and he squeezed back. It was a mantra Finn had been stating to me since we first started dating. I had a lot to let go of back then. Trust had pretty much been a four-letter word in my book. But that wasn't the case with the two men in front of me, and it shouldn't have been with Piper, either.

"I'm sorry, Lane," I said. "Tell Piper thanks for watching him."

The air seemed to be a little lighter as my brother said, "Not needed. What's going on? Are you preg—" Lane started only to be cut short by the doctor's entrance.

When the man in the official white coat looked at both Finn and Lane, I said, "They can both stay."

But Finn seemed a little upset. Maybe it was because he thought an official pregnancy reveal should be first and foremost just between the husband and wife. Maybe it was because he thought he was the most important man in my life—which he was. Or maybe he was just anxious. Regardless, Lane picked up on it, too, and graciously bowed out to call Piper and check on Chance, for which I was doubly grateful.

Finn stood up, with my hand still firmly in his, and waited for the doctor's proclamation. But it wasn't what we expected. I was not pregnant.

"I'm not?" I questioned, looking from the doctor to Finn, who only seemed to grip tighter.

Then, a sickening, sad feeling rushed to my brain. I had such mixed feelings just thinking about being pregnant again. I had even said I didn't want another baby other than Arinn. God, did I mean that? Did I unintentionally hurt it? Was this another of my penances?

"Was I, though?" The second question came out slowly and softly. "Was I pregnant? Did I lose it?"

"No. No, Mrs. Murphy," the doctor explained. "You weren't pregnant."

"Oh," I said, trying to let it settle in. "But I have all the symptoms."

"You also have all the symptoms of stress overload, malnutrition, and exhaustion," he continued as Finn let go of my hand, shook his head slightly, and walked in a mini-circle. "Obviously what is going on right now has put a tremendous strain on you emotionally and physically."

"Yeah," I admitted.

"I want you to stay for a little while. We're going to see if we can get you a little more balanced. And then we'll make the decision later if we want to admit your overnight."

"No!" I said vehemently. "I'll eat. I'll drink. Just…my little girl needs me."

"Mrs. Murphy, you are not going to do yourself or your children any good if—"

"God, Lara—" Finn started but was interrupted by Reese entering the room and insisting that she needed to talk with him. "Now?" Finn directed his irritated query to Reese.

When she nodded her head affirmatively, I said in a more calming voice, "Go ahead. I…let me talk with the doctor. I'll listen."

"Please." Finn said his one-word plea and then followed Reese out of the room.

I did listen to the doctor. And I tried to think about everyone's feelings and perspectives. I didn't want to be sick. I didn't want to be so weak that I was more of a hindrance than a help. I didn't want my little boy scared to see me or my husband even more stressed worried about me. I encouraged Finn to take his meds, talk with Dr. Bartola, and let me help him, but I wouldn't do the same for myself. Fainting was my reaction to stress, just like Finn's temper was his. I thought of all of those things and agreed with the doctor about staying and making sure I was regulated.

That was, until the doctor left and I caught a glimpse of all the activity going on just outside my slightly opened door. Undetected, I propped myself against the door frame and listened to the gathering of people, which included my husband, Reese, and a number of police officers.

What I found out was terrifying. If we didn't know it before, it was now confirmed that Briar had Arinn. The police got a call into 9-1-1 claiming to be Briar. She had said she was watching the live feed and was wondering about me and the pregnancy. Brianna knew about losing a child. She was calling from an old abandoned red farmhouse not far from our home. I had seen it before and could clearly picture it in my mind.

She wanted Finn to meet her there. But she only wanted Finn. She was adamant. And she made a point of saying she had a gun. The police were already near the premises but not letting Briar know they were close.

"What about my daughter?" Finn asked.

"She says the baby is fine. She's with her," one of the detectives I recognized from the press conference answered. "Of course, there's no proof."

"I'm going," Finn said simply but with a boat load of determination.

"We can't let you go in there...not with her armed," another police officer spoke. "We don't know what she'll do to you or your daughter."

My gasp must have been more pronounced than I realized because Finn whirled around in my direction. "Baby...." His eyes looked so sad. He put a finger up to me and then turned back to reiterate his intent to the police. "I'm going."

"We can have you talk with Miss Yorwood over the speaker," the detective offered.

"I'm going, too," I interjected.

"No. No way." Finn's attention swung back to me at the same time as Lane entered the scene, taking a spot at my side.

"What?" he questioned. "What's going on?"

Stepping closer to Lane and I, Finn directed his commanding statement to my brother. "You keep your sister here. Understand me? Under no circumstances is she to leave this hospital."

"Finn!" I screamed.

He was now right in front of me and the doorway. "Lara—"

"I'm—" I started.

"No," Finn said clearly and firmly. "You're not."

"I—"

This time my speech was interrupted by Finn physically picking me up and carrying me back into the room and onto the bed. Lane was at our heels. Thankfully, the door shutting drowned out most of the noise from the mini-meeting just outside of it. It did not drown out the chaos in my brain, though.

"I love you," Finn said while bracing his hands on either side of my thighs as I sat. He leaned in and held his lips on mine for a moment. He then tipped back slightly so he was looking directly into my eyes. "I love you so much...and Arinn and Chance. Always remember that. I will make this right."

That sounded way too much like goodbye to me. And not the goodbye as in "I will see you in a little bit." No, this was the forever, eternal goodbye. He knew the danger he was putting himself in. And now, I was even more scared and more determined for him to either take me or not go at all.

"Finn!" I screamed out as he started to back away.

"Keep her here!" Finn directed his demand to my brother and looked one more time at me before exiting.

Again, "Finn!"

I attempted to get off the bed, but Lane was fast and seemingly as determined as my husband. He clamped his hands on my biceps and locked his knees against mine, restraining me to continue sitting on the hospital bed. He came to the show late and didn't even know why Finn had given him that request. But it appeared my brother's protective side was equivalent to my husband's at that moment.

"Lane, God, let me go!" I tried to squirm out of his grasp to no avail.

"No. I have no idea what is going on, but there is no way I am letting you go an inch until you at least calm down and then probably not after that. The doctors—"

Maybe if I explained he would let me go. "They know where she is! They know where Arinn is!"

"What? Who?" he asked but didn't give up on his grip.

"Finn and the cops," I explained. "They are on their way to get her."

"All right. Good." His voice seemed to relax instantly. "That's good news. I'm sure he'll bring her back here."

"No. You don't understand." I stopped struggling so much and tried, instead, to rationalize. "Briar has her, and she's holed up in a place near the ranch…with a gun." I managed to get the details out without bursting into tears. "And she's demanding to see Finn."

"Lara…" Lane moved his hands down so they were on my knees, but he wasn't any further away. "Finn knows what he's doing, and if he doesn't, the cops do. You just need to stay here and try—"

"My baby is kidnapped, and my husband is probably walking into an execution!" I exclaimed.

"Lara!"

"Lane!" I mimicked, while attempting to get up again.

"Sit down." He pressed those hands on my knees again. After he knew I wasn't going anywhere and at least appeared to be calmer, he asked, "What are you going to do? How are you going be any help?"

"Arinn's my little girl. I need to be there. Oh, God. She has a gun. She's going to kill them. She's going to kill both of them."

"Lara, the cops won't let that happen. I'm sure they have negotiating teams and protective gear and won't let Finn be in—"

I didn't want to listen to any more of my brother or his Pollyanna ideas that everything was beautiful and would work out. We didn't grow up like that. We, if anybody, knew better. So, I interrupted him. "I need to be with them. Finn needs—"

But he was ready for his counter attack. "What Finn

needs is to not worry about you. He wants to know that you are safe here."

I knew that. I knew that rationally. And I truly didn't want to add to Finn's worries. But I also knew that it didn't matter. I knew that beautiful girl that I had given birth to just over a year before needed me, and I needed her. I needed to be where she was no matter…no matter.

I took a couple deep breaths and then, speaking so chillingly calm that I almost frightened myself, I said, "I'm going, Lane. I'd really like it if you will take me. I could use your support. But, if not, I'll get a cab. I have to be with them."

It was Lane's turn to exhale…sharply. "God, he's going to blow a gasket."

"That's his problem and mine." I said, knowing that there were no truer words to how my husband was going to react. "But I'm going," I finished, relieved that my brother was implying that he was on board.

"I know," he breathed out more than said. But when I attempted to once again get up, he pressed down on my shoulder indicating he wanted me to stay put. "Please, let's just confirm things with the doctors."

"The doctors will take too long," I partially whined.

"Whoever then. Let's just get someone here on staff," Lane compromised. "Let's tell them you are leaving and find—"

I cut him off, growing more impatient by the second. But I agreed. "Fine. Ten minutes. That's it."

Instead of going to find some kind of medical personnel, though, I saw Lane look at his phone. And I knew exactly what he was thinking. He wanted to let Finn know of my plans.

"Don't, Lane," I said. "Don't call or text him. Like you said, he has enough on his mind. Let them concentrate. I'll be with you."

His mouth curled down and his eyes squinted as if he were debating with himself. But, thankfully, he landed on my side and put his phone back in his pocket. "Damn straight you will be. And nowhere else."

GREA WARNER

CHAPTER TWELVE

I could have sworn Lane was purposefully driving slowly. If there was a traffic light just turning yellow, he made sure to stop instead of coasting through or speeding up to make it. And I couldn't handle it. There had already been too much time wasted talking with hospital personnel and finding a way out of the building without being spotted by the damn lingering press core. At a certain point, when we were close to the ranch and I knew exactly where we were and where I needed to be, I threatened to jump out of the car and run the rest of the way unless his foot found the gas pedal more often. My brother grumbled a few times, but we got there.

Thankfully, the police let us through the first set up of guards that led to the abandoned farmhouse. We were instructed to stop when we got to the second barrier, though. While Lane was parking the car hundreds of feet back from the old, red brick residence, I started scanning the mini-group of cops and others who were gathered in the area. But I did not see Finn, which worried the hell out of me. Before Lane even had the car legitimately in park, I released my belt and opened the door to exit.

"Damn it, Lara!" my brother yelped. "Hold up."

Lane was directly behind me as I approached Reese. "Where is he?" My anxious body felt like there were millions of tiny creatures trying to escape from under my skin.

She had not seen us approach. Her focus had been entirely on the farmhouse in front of us. So, it startled her a bit to see me suddenly standing right there. Looking more troubled than I had ever seen her, she didn't bother to ask what I was doing there or who I was talking about. She just delivered the news I feared. "He's inside."

After closing my eyes to try to unsuccessfully wish it away, I asked in more of a hushed tone, "Are there cops in there, too?" My skin was absolutely crawling.

"No," she said in a similar scary, quiet voice and then turned to face the farmhouse once again. "Just Briar and Arinn." Her speech rose a little when she added, "He's gonna be so upset that you're here."

Mine did, too, out of pure anger and fear. "I know!" I was sick of hearing from everyone else what I should be doing and, in particular, what they thought Finn thought I should be doing. "Tough," I punctuated.

I focused on the house now, too. Directly surrounded by law enforcement in heavily-shielded gear, I knew the situation couldn't be any more serious for both Arinn and Finn. There was no visual inside the building. All the drapes appeared to be closed, and the front door was the solid wood variety, devoid of any type of window. One could only imagine what was happening just on the other side of that entry. And when you knew it involved two of the most precious people in your life and a gun, imagination was not your friend. It was the deepest, darkest kind of horror.

When I saw the police officer who had been at the hospital, I took the few steps and quickly approached. "I thought you said you wouldn't let him go in!" I managed to keep my screech to a minimal roar.

"We weren't getting anywhere with the mic." He tried a

calming voice, but we both knew it was a pretense. "Your husband insisted. We have him vested. He was adamant," he reiterated.

"Stubborn like his wife." Lane rested his hand on my shoulder.

I shook it off and started toward the house. "Maybe I can—"

The officer cut me off both with his words and his sudden stance directly in front of me. "We need you to stay back."

"I can help. Maybe I can say something," I tried, as my brother became a second barrier in front of me.

"Let's let this play out a little first, ma'am. Miss Yorwood wanted to speak with your husband and your husband alone. We don't need her any more agitated."

"And Chance needs a parent." My brother's statement was chilling, making me realize he wasn't as optimistic as he had first tried to make himself appear.

I took in both of their statements and tried to accept the truth in what they were saying. My eyes remained fixated on the house, but my feet refused to stay still. I paced and paced and rubbed my arms while Lane and Reese just watched. I think they were slightly on guard, wondering if I might still attempt to go to the house. But I didn't...not until the gun shot.

Knowing it came from inside the decaying former residence, I gasped, "Oh, my God!"

Lane caught me just as my feet lifted from the ground to go to the sound... to the building... to my family. "No!" He denied me any further progression by forcefully wrapping his arms tightly around me from behind.

"Oh, my God! What happened? What's happening?" I struggled in my brother's arms. "Lane!" I screamed out in pure terror.

He spun me around but kept those hands secure on my biceps. "Lara, look at me. Look at me."

I tried. But there was too much commotion happening

directly behind me to be even remotely successful. I turned around to discover that the deep bellowing and pounding sounds were that of the police showing no mercy as they gained immediate access into the house. The officer/my guard put his hand up in the universal stop symbol in front of me. He had been witness to my behavior long enough to know my natural instinct. But it was a moot point. Lane was not letting me budge.

The silence that followed seemed, if possible, worse than the just previous chaotic noise. Minutes felt like hours as we got nothing. There were no more sounds of voices or banging or, thank God, gun shots. And there was no visible movement as the officers had closed the door immediately upon entering the house of horrors.

"Lane!" I wailed, feeling like I was either going to totally collapse or literally split from reality and lose my mind. It felt like I had strings attached to my body that were trying to pull me like a balloon up and away—it was all too much.

"I know," I heard my brother say, and I tried to hold onto his strength.

Finally, a police officer emerged from the front door and then...then out came Finn holding Arinn. He blew out an extensive gust of air and took a few steps before spotting me. There was a look of initial shock and then a slight smile.

The imaginary strings released along with my brother's grip, and I ran like an Olympian track star to my husband and baby. "Are you okay?" I asked, meeting them a little more than half way to the house. "Finn, is Arinn...? Finn?" My words and head were bouncing from both relief and adrenaline. "Arinn." I reached my hands out to our daughter as Finn placed her in my arms. "Oh, baby, you beautiful, sweet, little thing," I said while repeatedly stroking the back of her head.

"Ma-ma-ma-ma-ma," she cooed out innocently while rubbing her little hand on my cheek.

"Yeah." Wiping a tear, I smiled at the sweetest name I could ever be called.

"Secure!" I heard some police officers calling from inside the house.

My main focus, though, was on the two people directly in front of me. I looked Arinn more thoroughly over. She was wearing a baggy cream-colored onesie and fuzzy green pants that were also ill-fitted. Her hair was in the same band I had put in the day of the play, but she seemed clean and taken care of.

"Is she okay, Finn? Is Arinn all right?"

"Yeah. I mean, she's seems to be. Look at that smile." He bent a little to wrinkle his nose and smile directly in our daughter's vision.

"And you?" I questioned as he straightened back up.

"I'm fi—" Finn edited himself as Lane approached. Shifting his eyes from his two girls to my brother, Finn strangled a growl. "I told you to keep her put."

"I'd like to have seen you try," my brother countered as he reached out for little Arinn's hand. "You try to get in between a woman— warrior Lara, nonetheless—and her child...and you."

Surely knowing there was no arguing with that, Finn decided to let it be and enveloped Arinn and I into his chest as best he could, considering he was still wearing the protective vest. "Everything's fine," he spoke softly.

After a second or two, I pulled away and, looking toward the house, cited something that made me know it truly hadn't been okay. "The gun," I said. "We heard a gun go off." It literally made me shiver recalling that terrifying moment just minutes before. "Is she...?" I suddenly realized there were three people in that house when the gun sounded and two of them were, thank God, bullet-free in front of me.

Finn shook his head. "Everyone's good," he started. "It was me. I was stupid. I asked her to put the gun down, and, at first, she wouldn't. She wasn't really threatening me with it, but I just…I didn't like it being there when I was trying to talk with her. But then, when she went to put it on the floor, I kicked at it to make sure it was away from us and it… it somehow went off. I should have just let her set it there."

"My God." I swallowed hard. "Where was Arinn?"

"She wasn't even in the room."

"But Finn, you—" I started.

"We're okay." My husband wasn't going to let me verbalize my ominous thought.

"Did she tell you why? Did she say why she did it…why she took her?" Now that I knew everything was, indeed, okay, my rapidly moving brain wanted answers.

"It wasn't planned." He stroked Arinn's hair and did a little smile at her. He was obviously as mesmerized and relieved at seeing our child as I was. "She just saw you and… and, well, lost it, I guess. She wasn't really making much sense. I think she had a mental break. We know the label wasn't working out, and she blamed me for that. That much I got. She blamed me."

"For God's sake!" I started and then managed to bring my bellow down a notch. "You helped her out." And then, even quieter while side glancing at Lane, I said, "And you didn't need to do that."

I saw the guilt swipe my husband's face. It was something he would always live with. "She wanted what I had, I guess."

"She can't have our baby!" My voice rose once again.

It was then that I saw the police leading Briar, or whatever her real name was, out of the house. She looked so different than when I had seen her at the CMAs. Her uncombed hair, now dyed an off-blonde, looked greasy, yet dry and split. Her mismatched clothes were loose and covered up her body, unlike the tight, revealing outfit she had worn at the awards ceremony. Thankfully, I couldn't see if she still had her nails long and red because they were secured with handcuffs behind her back. Those eyes, though—those blue eyes—darkened when they met mine.

If I had not had the baby in my arms, I would have done more than just a lunge. "Don't you ever, ever think about getting anywhere near my—"

"Hey, hey." Finn pulled me into his side and shushed me before saying, "She's completely unstable. Don't engage."

Even if I wanted to, I couldn't have, as the police rushed her into the back of a squad car, and Finn nudged me by walking in the opposite direction. Calming down by knowing we were blessed with the most positive, safest outcome, I realized there was only one thing that would make everything completely all right. "I want Chance." I looked in my husband's eyes.

"You need to be at the hospital." Now that his dance with danger was behind him, he was back to focusing on me.

"I'm fine." If I didn't sigh out loud, it was a damn strong internal one.

"God, Lara, why can't you just listen for once?" Finn's anger was instant as he stopped us mid-stride.

Not wanting to poke the protective beast any further and knowing his minor outburst was out of love and concern, I took a breath and rubbed my free hand on his forearm before speaking. "I am listening. I'm listening to you telling me how much danger you were just in. I'm listening to my baby girl who I haven't seen in days, or knew if I ever would again, calling out for me. I'm listening. I'm listening to my body telling me I'm fine and my heart telling me I could not bear to be separated from any of you right now."

To his credit, my husband let a third party become the jury in our domestic dispute. Knowing that Lane was just as invested in protecting me as he was, he turned to my brother for input. "Help?"

"First of all, man, I am with you one hundred percent on the not listening part." Lane shook his head.

"Lane...." I rolled my eyes.

"But I made sure we talked with the medical staff before leaving," he continued. "They said they weren't going to admit her. She was free to go but she needed to get fluids, and eat, and relax."

When Finn shook his head like he was still disagreeing, I tried a little sweet sass. "What? You don't want me to be okay?"

"Don't, Lara. I'm worried about you." He burrowed his eyebrows at me but smiled at Arinn.

"I know, baby. But listen to what Lane said. I'm okay. I just need to be home."

A burst of air left his mouth before he relented by saying, "You're going to have your feet up. You'll be in bed—"

"Geez, Cowboy, I think I might be too tired for a little action tonight," I teased.

"Shit!" Finn exclaimed, initially upset but then started to laugh because Lane had, too.

We all needed the release from an extremely stressful few days. Even Arinn started to giggle in my arms. And that was the most beautiful sound of all.

***

It was a while until we got back to the ranch and an even longer time until we were alone. There was so much to be done—procedures, formalities, statements. But, most of all, we needed to make sure that Arinn was all right. Because of the looming press stationed right outside the first barrier to the decrepit farmhouse and knowing that they would follow us when we left, it was arranged to have a medical professional come to the ranch to examine our little girl. It would be the safest, most secure, and close-by environment. In addition, the police would finish up with anything they needed from us there.

I could not have been happier than when I was

reunited with Chance. Knowing that both of my babies were with me and that the four of us were in the house made my heart overflow. Unfortunately, it wasn't just my heart overflowing, though. Tears came, too, when the physician arrived and started chronicling the different things she would be examining Arinn for. I could not handle it. I was not that strong. I wouldn't even pretend to be. I wanted to be there for her. But I couldn't. So, Finn stayed with our baby while I, after pawning Chance off to his uncle downstairs, hibernated in our master bedroom alone.

***

"She's fine." Finn found me curled up in the fetal position on our bed.

"Yeah?" I only slightly looked up.

"A wee little diaper rash, but that's it. The doc gave her a clean bill of health. She's fine. She's beautiful. She's perfect."

I got off the bed since he hadn't sat down with me. He had said all the right words. And I could see the honesty and sincerity of the truth in his eyes. But, yet, he was still and silent.

"Finn?" I queried and attempted to wrap my arms around him.

But every muscle in his body seemed to be wound to its tightest limit. It wasn't that he was emotionally rejecting my embrace. It was that the physical strain in his body was too fierce.

"Ah, fuck!" he yelled and took a few steps toward the closed balcony doors. He strung his arms up in a "Y" formation to hold onto the frame. "That..." He dipped his head down and then turned around to face me. "That was hard."

"But she's all right." I cried just seeing him so upset.

"She is. Oh, God. Thank God." He wiped at his own

tears. "I just need to gather myself for a minute before we deal with whatever else we need to downstairs."

I breathed for a second or two. "I want to see her."

"She's in her crib."

"K," I managed and started toward the door.

"Lar?" He called out my name, and I turned back around. "Try that hug again. I could really use it."

Reaching him in purposeful, fast strides, I sank into his torso. His seemingly heavier than usual arms draped over me. And even though he was still tense, the connection was solid. And our combined support made us even stronger.

***

After all the reports were filed, people thanked, and precious children put to bed, we were left with just family and honorary family. Under Finn's close scrutiny, I made sure to have something to drink and eat amongst the company of my brother, Piper, and Reese. We did our best to unwind, but I knew it would take a lot more than an evening for any of us to forget what horrors we had been witness to.

Lane and Piper left after promising to call my mom. But Reese stayed a little longer. She had already been dealing all afternoon and evening with the fallout of the press conference, my non-pregnancy, and, now, Arinn's return and Briar/Brianna's arrest. Finn wanted it to all just go away—to brush it off with no comment. But we all knew that wasn't bound to happen. There would most likely be a trial and additional press and questions. My nerves riled right back up just thinking about having to relive the ordeal of my child being gone, the guilt over my part in it, and the potential of Finn's connection with Briar coming out. The best we could hope for was her copping a plea, remaining silent, and getting the help she needed.

Reese wanted to get the upper hand, though. Her

suggestion was for us to sit down with one exclusive reporter, make a simple statement, and answer only preapproved questions. She blamed the later on not wanting to influence or taint the police case, but we all knew it was to protect Finn, too. After making sure I was all right with doing an interview and hearing the name of the reporter Reese had in mind—someone Finn had a great standing with throughout his career—Finn reluctantly agreed. And with comforting hugs to both of us, Reese left to make those arrangements for the next day.

Finally, it was just me, Finn, and our safe, slumbering offspring. I checked on Arinn one more time while Finn called his parents. It was late, but it was a phone call that surely anyone would be happy to awaken to.

When I came back into our bedroom, Finn was lying in bed staring straight up at the ceiling. "So?" I asked generically, knowing he understood.

"He's okay," Finn answered, regarding his dad. "In fact, a little energized. He pretty much tore into me about trying to keep anything a secret from him."

"Well, you figured that, didn't you?" I turned off the light and took off the slightly sweaty clothes I had been wearing all day.

"Yeah. But it turns out, he knew all along."

"Your mom?" Too tired to do much more, I let my top and pants remain on the floor, and I slid into bed in just my bra and panties.

"Yeah."

"Sometimes, moms know best," I teased, being a mom myself. "Speaking of, maybe I should just—"

Finn placed his hand firmly on my arm as I started to get out of bed and go to Arinn for nothing more than to simply watch her breathe. "She's fine," he reassured. "Plus, you promised me you would sleep."

"I know," I admitted.

"You feeling all right?"

"Finn, I'm fine. No dizziness. No queasiness. I'm good.

If I pee too much, it's because of all the water you're insisting I drink." I trailed my index finger from his nose to his lips before lying completely down.

After an extended moment of simply staring at one another, he asked, "What?" Because, even in the darkness, he could tell that my mind was swirling with something to say.

I sat up and lightly pushed on his shoulder as tears threatened to emerge from behind my eyes. "Don't you ever think about saying goodbye to me like that again."

He didn't even bother pretending he didn't know what I was talking about. He knew what he had said and how he had said it when he had left the hospital earlier. Sitting up to meet me, he started, "Baby, listen—"

"No," I interrupted. "I know you would do anything for our kids. I know that. I know you would risk anything for them...for us. But don't you ever even have it as the slightest of smallest thoughts that you will not return to us. We need you, okay? We need you." It had taken me until then, until everything else in that crazy day had been settled, to retrace back to that moment. It was also our first chance to truly be alone. And I wanted him to know exactly how I felt.

"I—" he started again.

But I wasn't done. "And I'm sorry that when you told me you loved me that I didn't tell you just how much I love you, too. I was just so scared. But I should have told you no matter what."

"It's okay. I knew." He paused. "My turn now?" When I nodded my head affirmatively, confirming no more Lara interruptions, he relayed his emotions. "I know you wanted to come, and you had every right. But, shit, Lar, you know the same goes for me. I couldn't handle you being in danger...the possibility of losing you. And I'm sorry for putting us in this mess in the—"

I did interrupt, though, because I truly didn't need his apology. I put my finger up to his lips to silence his thought. "So, just to clarify, I love you."

"Forever," he claimed, which doubled the meaning of the three traditional words. Bringing me into his strong and comforting embrace, he added, "And 'goodbye' is officially out of my vocabulary."

CHAPTER THIRTEEN

Ignoring most of the calls flooding our individual phones, Finn and I tried to take that next morning to revel in the beauty of just the four of us. We sat on the floor with the kids and watched as Chance showed Arinn how to drive his cars around the carpet. Of course, she didn't get it, but she tried to follow her big brother around.

Out of the blue, Chance gave her a smothering hug. "I miss you, Arinn. I glad you not on road anymore."

Finn, tiny green muscle car in hand, looked at me. "Did you tell him that?"

"No!" I laughed, thinking our son must now associate anyone being gone to his dad touring on the road. "All right, Chance, she missed you, too. But you're gonna smush her. Just play. Wait," I stopped myself quickly. "On second hand, give her a hug again. I want to take your picture together."

Chance, a natural performer like his father, boasted a big beam with his arms wrapped around his sister. Finn laughed, and I snapped the picture on my phone. But just as I was ready to stretch from my seated position and place it back on the coffee table, it rang. And I knew that ring.

"It's my mom," I partially grumbled. "I should

probably talk with her."

"Give her my love." Finn grinned with a touch of sarcasm, knowing I loved my mom but also knowing the drama that she could create when there was even a hangnail, never mind a kidnapping recovery.

"You want to answer then?" I teased my husband.

"Too busy playing cars," was his non-legit response.

"Hi, Mom," I spoke into the phone while watching Chance "vroom" his car around Finn's car.

"Is she there?" My mom's voice shrieked over the line. "Is Arinn there?"

"Yeah, yeah. She's here," I answered. "She's beautiful, Mom." I got a little teary-eyed and Finn rubbed my back.

"Why didn't you call me yesterday?" she yelled.

"Lane did, right?" I asked, knowing that if my brother said he would, he did.

"Yeah. Your brother—not you. I wanted to hear from you!" she practically shrieked.

"Mom, there was so much going on way into the night. There still is today. Did you get my text?" I *had* done that.

"Yeah. I just wanted to hear your voice," she answered.

"We're good," I replied. We were.

"It's that hillbilly, hick town you're living in now. Nothing but in—" she started.

"Stop!" I got up to walk because I couldn't stay seated any more. I knew she was being her typical, coming down from nerves Elise Faulkner self, but I couldn't deal with that yet—not when I was finally trying to soak in a few moments of peace. "You didn't want me living near Manhattan because it was too big of a city and now you don't like Nashville?" I looked at Finn, who was paying closer attention to me. "Where do you suppose we should be? Certainly not back in Pennsylvania. We all know I was never safe there." She had brought it up in our last phone conversation, so it was fair game for me to do it now, especially when she was undermining my happiness.

As if he sat on a tack, Finn sprung up and bounded to

my side. He knew, as well as my mom, about my troubled youth—an abusive alcoholic father, underage drinking, a hazy sexual encounter with my boyfriend's brother, a teenage pregnancy, and giving the baby up for adoption. What my mother considered home was definitely not the safest or fondest of places for me. I had escaped years before and knew I had finally found the place where I belonged— right in the arms of the man next to me.

Finn took the phone and spoke to my mother. "Elise, hey…." When I tried to take a step away, Finn used his free hand to rest my head on his chest. I listened to the vibrations of his voice as he sweet-talked my mom as always. "Yeah, we feel unbelievably fortunate. Everything is good, okay?" There was a pause, and then he said, "I know. She knows. I will never let anything happen to any of them. You believe that, don't you?" He listened some more. "Tell me about it. I have to live with her." On that comment, knowing he was throwing me under the proverbial bus, I smacked his chest. "Owww!" he exclaimed in protest and then said to my mother, "I'm sure you want to talk with Chance." Pause. "Yeah, here he is and, by the way, we'll need some more of those cookies when you come next." When he got hit again just for showing me up with his nice son-in-law routine, Finn handed the phone to Chance. "Here, talk to Grandma for a minute."

"Grandma," Chance handled the phone like a pro. "I playing cars with Arinn." Chance continued to babble to my mother.

But it was my husband's voice that I was listening to. Finn flanked his palms on my cheeks and tilted my head so I was looking directly at him. With confidence, he said, "You are not that girl any more. You are brave and strong and fierce. And when you can't be, I am here. You got it?" When I nodded my head, because that was all I could manage in his sentiment, he added, "And quit hitting me. If anything, you owe me." He pressed his finger to his lips in a smile, and I obliged with a sweet kiss. "That's more like it." He grinned and added a soft kiss of his own.

***

Lane and Piper stopped by before heading to the airport and then back to North Carolina. It was nice to actually sit down and legitimately chat with them. Sure, our phones were buzzing, but we weren't in that desperate of a hurry to react to them. Nothing but family mattered.

After telling us about her job and family, Piper, who was sitting next to Lane and across from Finn and I, asked, "So how did the two of you meet?"

My husband and I had relayed the story of us meeting in college a million times. We pretty much knew each other's exact dialogue when we would recite the story together. But something, most likely because I was so lighthearted over having my daughter back, caused me to stray from script. "I was a backup dancer for his band."

Finn literally spit out his drink. I mean, there was an actual spray of caramel-colored liquid shooting across the coffee table. He immediately placed his glass down and started belly-laughing like I hadn't seen him do in months.

"Oh, yeah," I continued, making up a completely fictitious tale while trying desperately hard not to laugh myself. "It was one of those things, though, where the student outshone the star. He couldn't compete with these moves." I waved my hands over my body.

"Yeah, that's right, baby," Finn managed. "Go ahead, show us your dance moves."

I did laugh then as Piper, a little thrown, said, "I'm guessing that's not the truth."

"Can you believe my girl hates to dance?" Finn tugged me momentarily into his side, kissing the top of my head.

"It's true. I hate it," I admitted.

"So...?" Piper prompted back to her original question.

"Our story is kinda boring. It's the traditional," I

expected to hear Finn say how we were friends first, blah, blah, blah, but, instead, when "mail order bride deal" came out of his mouth, it was my turn to burst into laughter. "I needed someone to, you know, cook, clean, and she was the only one left. They actually paid me to take her off their hands."

"Finn Murphy!" I bellowed.

His response was to kiss me and say, "Yes, dance star?"

Arinn's fussiness throughout our conversation had grown increasingly worse. I recognized it as her tired whimpers and understood why. She had not slept well the night before. She had been sleeping through the night for months but had woken up the night before, causing both Finn and I to rock her until she eventually fell back asleep. It made me wonder what kind of crazy schedule she had been on during those horrific days away.

Since we wanted cheerful, happy children during the interview, which was set to happen at the ranch later that afternoon, I decided to see if I could get her to go down for a mini-nap. "I'm sorry." I picked Arinn up from where she and Chance were playing with blocks. "I'm gonna put her down for a little bit." And then I directed my next comment to my daughter, "Come on, sweetie, let's go see Mousey."

Finn stood up to meet us. When he rested his lips on top of Arinn's head, her little eyes began to flutter trying to fight off slumber. "Sleep tight, little bug."

"I help!" Chance called out. He really did seem to have missed his sister and was being so protective of her. "Piper, too!" he yelled, and before I could even shrug my shoulders at her wondering if she minded, Chance had Piper's hand and was pulling her up the stairs.

While Chance was getting a fresh diaper out of the drawer for Arinn, I turned to Piper. "We met in college." And added, "Honestly."

"Are you sure?" She smiled.

"Yeah." I laughed and had the new diaper on as

expertly quick as only a mother of two can. I started swaying my little one in my arms, knowing it wouldn't take long for her to fall asleep. "It wasn't love at first sight. We were just friends," I continued. "It actually took us seven years to become a couple."

"Huh."

I placed Arinn in her crib and started rubbing her little nose. "There were other people and worlds to conquer in between."

"I know about that," she said.

"You and Lane?" I looked up, knowing my daughter was just about asleep.

"Yeah." She smiled like a woman in love.

Before I could reply, my phone rang, and Chance belted out that he wanted Piper to read him a story. "Oh, honey…" I said to Chance. "Piper's our guest, and she and Uncle Lane have to leave."

"It's fine." Piper reassured. "We'll read a quick one."

"I have one in my room!" Chance exclaimed.

I looked at my phone. It was Vanessa calling. I really did want to talk with my best friend.

Piper, seeing my glance, said, "Take your phone call. We'll be fine."

"Thanks," I acknowledged her kindness. As we walked out of Arinn's room, I couldn't help but wonder, after witnessing Piper's connection with my normally shy son and her lovey-dovey eyes when talking about my brother, if Lane might one day become a father himself, after all.

I put it out of my mind, though, and answered the phone. Starting down the stairs, I listened to an emotional and excited Vanessa after I confirmed that Arinn was, indeed, safe, healthy, and home. Taking a mental note that Finn and Lane were not in the great room where we had left them, I continued to fill Vanessa in on some of the details of the day before. I ventured a little further in the house until I heard the faint sound of my husband's voice. It seemed like it was coming from the family room, which

Finn used as part exercise area and part game room.

"You want to get into this, Lane, let's talk here. I don't want Chance hearing."

My brother's voice equaled Finn's even and controlled tone, but I could tell there was also a bit of strain. "I think we need to. Arinn has been the priority. And she should have been. But you need to know…you need to understand, I know what this was all about. You can deny it all you want, and Lara will, too. But whether it was something you did…" He paused, and I knew my brother well enough to know, without actually seeing him, that he had taken the moment to eyeball Finn. "Or it was just a consequence of your career, this was on you."

"It was," Finn replied straight-away, and I knew I had to intervene.

"Vanessa?" I said into the phone. "I'm going to have to call you back. I'm so sorry. Everything's fine. I just have to deal with something." I felt bad, but I abruptly cut her off for the second time in days and scurried the last few steps toward the family room.

As I entered, it was Lane who said, "It's not in me to sit by and watch Lara get hurt."

"Me ei—"

"Lane, don't!" I demanded, causing Finn to stop mid-sentence and both men's eyes to swirl in my direction. "This isn't any of your business. Finn is my husband, and I love him so much. More than…well, he knows how much," I twerked one side of my mouth at Finn. "That's what's important. Just as I know how much he loves, protects, and is there for us."

I needed the crap—all of it—to be done. I was tired of it. Why couldn't we just be happy? Did I actually have to build those Lara walls just to bubble the four of us inside?

"Lara, let me finish," Lane said.

"No. If you are going to lay into him about what happened and think you know that he hurt me, then no. No. You are the one hurting me right now."

"Beauty, it's all right." Finn reached out for my hand. "He has a—"

"I love you," I said to my husband but, admittedly, it was partially for my brother's benefit.

"I love you, too," Finn echoed calmly but then turned to my sibling. "I do."

"I know that." Lane did a little breath. "I've known that for a long time now, and that's what I was going to say. I grew up trying to protect you. But I know I don't have to. I know rock star here—"

"Lane…." I cautioned, as somehow using a mocking name for Finn didn't seem like a good call if he was truly trying to keep things copacetic.

"Loves you insanely," Lane concluded while ignoring my tone. As I looked at Finn who slightly smiled my direction, Lane continued. "And I'm glad. I just needed to say my piece."

"Oh… all right," I said.

"Still okay with us coming for the vows?" Lane asked as Piper and Chance entered the room.

"Still okay with giving me away?" I bounced back, even though the whole thing was a sealed deal/moot point.

Lane nodded upwards at Finn and said, "Yeah."

It made me smile. "Thanks for being here, Lane. I mean it. It meant a lot."

"I haven't always been," he lamented.

"You shouldn't have had to be," I refuted.

Thank God for my brother. Only about a year older than me, he had been my saving grace for as long as I could remember. He guarded and defended and literally took hits for me when we were young. The year after he left straight out of high school was the rough one he was referring to. But he had every right to move as far away from there as he could, and, eventually, I had, too.

"And I certainly haven't been, either." I looked at Piper as if there was any confusion about what my attitude had been concerning their relationship. "Thank you for coming," I spoke genuinely to hopefully a new friend. "Thanks for your help and for being there for Lane. I'm sorry I haven't been more welcoming."

Finn had said earlier that I was brave, strong, and fierce. But he had forgotten to add stubborn. And that I most certainly was. Everyone in the room could attest to it. I didn't want to be stubborn at that moment, though. I wanted to strip myself of the unkind feelings I had bared toward Piper and admit it out in the open.

I felt Finn grab my hand, understanding what it took for me to say those words, as Piper helped ease the awkwardness verbally. "I wasn't expecting a hostess," she joked.

But I didn't want to be left of the hook that easily. "You know what I mean."

"It's nice to finally meet you, Lara."

I felt my shoulders ease. "You, too."

"You have a beautiful family." She smiled.

"I'm very lucky." I squeezed Finn's hand and encouraged Chance to give Lane a hug.

"See you soon, tough guy," Lane said on their release, and Chance flexed his muscles, causing his mini-audience to laugh.

"I take care of my baby sister." Damn...his little sweetness could bring me to tears every time.

"Just like your Uncle Lane." I smiled, smoothed Chance's hair, and gave my brother a hug. "Have a safe trip back," I said, and then whispered for only Lane to hear. "Piper's a keeper."

Lane replied with, "I think so," and reached his hand out to my husband.

"They're my life." Finn shook my brother's hand and then tossed Chance into his arms.

"I know. I know that," Lane said. "Just never forget it."

I wasn't sure if Lane was referring to his self-proclaimed faded relationship with his ex-wife or what he thought might have happened between Finn and Briar. It most likely was a mixture of the two. But it was nice knowing both of the comments from Lane and Finn were said out of love and protectiveness of me.

After watching Lane and Piper get into their rental car and head down the long driveway on route to the airport, Finn shut the front door. Still in his arms, he touched Chance's nose. "Chance, bud, we need you to go clean your room, and then it's going to be time to get ready for more guests."

"Who?" His little face looked puzzled by the onslaught of people in and out of our usually reclusive residence.

"Reese, and that lady Cayla, and a reporter named Hal, and maybe a couple of people who might want to take your picture. But you won't have to talk with them. You can play upstairs." He put our son back down on the floor.

Neither Finn nor I wanted Chance to be a part of the interview. The subject matter was not one for a three-and-a-half-year-old. Not that I liked it as a thirty-six-year-old, either. Plus, Finn had always kept his private life just that. And the interview, for as much as he could help it, would follow suit.

"Go clean that room first. We don't have any mail order brides around here," Finn reminded him as I burst out a bit of laughter.

"Music," he semi-whined. He was talking about when I would set a song for him—he would usually pick one of Finn's—and he would have to get a chore done before the song ended.

"Can't," I replied. "Arinn's sleeping."

Seeing his sad little face, Finn made an offer. "I'll come up and personally sing to you if you get started."

"Yay! Daddy, it be the cleanest ever!" And with that, his little legs scurried quickly toward and up the stairs.

Standing behind me, Finn wrapped his arms around my waist and dropped his chin onto my left shoulder. After a moment or two of soaking up the rare silence, he spoke softly in my ear. "We haven't had a chance to talk about it."

"What?" I tried to keep the serenity but anticipated his topic matter had something to do with Briar or Arinn's kidnapping.

"The non-pregnancy," he said, and the presence of his hands on my stomach seemed even more pronounced.

Oh. I turned around to face him. "Guess there's nothing to talk about." I used a more clinical approach. Besides, after the doctor's reveal, it had been pushed out of my mind due to the immediate, fast-paced recovery of Arinn.

He exhaled before speaking. "I sorta feel like I lost something, even though it was never there in the first place."

"Hmmm." I needed a moment to take in Finn's words and then try to legitimately process what my own feelings were. I eventually took his hands in mine and looked into his patient eyes. "You want to know something?"

"Absolutely, Beauty."

"I don't think I want another baby. If it were to happen—if I got pregnant—then, yeah, sure I would love that child unconditionally. But I like our family just as it is." When it came out, I knew it was the truth. I just wondered if Finn and I were on the same wave length. "Is that all right? Are you good with that?"

"One hundred percent...all of it." He kissed me before backing up. "I think I owe my son a song."

I ran my hand across the stubble that had overtaken my husband's normally bare face. "You also need a shave."

"You need to fix your hair." He purposefully rummaged his hand through my hair.

"Finn!" I hit his torso but laughed just the same.

"I love you, Rox."

"You too, Cowboy." To my chagrin, he tousled my locks once again, causing me to push him out of the room. "Get out of here!" I couldn't help but smile as I listened to his natural, yet unfamiliar as of late, laughter as he exited.

Knowing I had a few minutes, I reclaimed my phone and started cycling through a few messages and texts from friends and family. When I came across an unfamiliar number, I almost skipped it. But then I realized my unlisted number was very hard to come by...for obvious reasons.

The message was from the preschool we had enrolled Chance and Arinn in. We had given them my phone number because Finn's was, of course, even more obscure. Our babies were supposed to start at the center that morning. We had not had any plans originally for the day, so Finn and I had set up an appointment so we could be there with them, meet their teachers, and stay a little while before letting the kids adjust to the environment on their own for an hour or so. The school had called because it was regulation to contact someone when they didn't show up for their time slot. But they also said they completely understood why. God, who didn't in the Nashville area? And, for that matter, in the country? The preschool representative said they would be more than happy to set up another day and time to meet with us and our family. I stared at it awhile and pressed delete. I wasn't sure that I would ever be able to trust my kids with a stranger again.

CHAPTER FOURTEEN

About twenty-four hours after we had participated in the police station press conference, we were sitting in our great room ready for the exclusive interview, which was surely going to trend in multiple other outlets. Hal, his producer, and his camera man were extremely considerate and respectful of the boundaries that Reese had set up prior to the interview. Cayla spoke when there were questions regarding Brianna's arrest and future but gave limited information, as it was still a case very much fresh and in progress. Finn and I talked about our fear during those four days and the relief and gratitude at the conclusion. Purposefully using her real name to divert any further music connection, Finn spoke a little about the rescue itself but said he wanted to respect Brianna's rights and not jeopardize the case. And, of course, we asked that the public respect our privacy as we continued to decompress from the traumatic few days. Finn and I were filmed, but the kids were only present for a couple still shots of the four of us reunited. In one, Chance clung to me while Arinn was joyfully bubbly in her father's arms. And in another, Chance leaned over and gave Arinn a kiss.

Even though it went as well as could be expected, it

was still very emotional. Everything was still so raw. My emotions—anger, relief, and still a lot of fear—were right at the surface. And I wasn't used to sharing my innermost thoughts with anyone besides my husband. But, regardless, they came out during the questions Hal asked. According to Reese, who stayed a little after everyone else left, it was just enough to show the human side of our plight, as well as the special connection between Finn and I.

After dinner and a long, soaking bath, I found a couple-plus glasses of wine. I didn't usually indulge in more than one, but I needed their smooth, soothing powers to help me put away some of the remnants of anxiety I had felt during the interview. Chance went to bed earlier than usual due to not taking a nap and the extra excitement of all the guests. Arinn held out a little longer, which we hoped meant she would sleep continuously until morning. While I brought her to her nursery to get her changed and rock her to sleep, Finn returned some phone calls.

With just the nightlight as his guide, he found me sitting in the rocking chair with Arinn blanketing my chest sound asleep. Finn lifted our daughter from me and placed her sweetness in the crib. After humming a few bars of what sounded like a nursery rhyme, he turned back to me. "You next."

"Mmmm-hmmm." I agreed, and shut the door behind us as we made our way to our own room.

"Lar?" Finn questioned when I sat on the bed. "Lara?" he asked again, and this time it was definitely with more concern.

It was only when he crouched before me and wiped my wet face that I realized I was crying. "Uh…" I started. "I'm fine. Just a little too much to drink." But the tears didn't stop.

"Yeah, probably. But, that's not all of it. What's wrong?" Sitting next to me, he touched under my eyes with his thumb pads. "Tell me." He spoke in the same manner that the quiet, nighttime room demanded.

"You won't get mad?" I hated it, but just like Finn, I had my own scars. I had my own demons and fears stemming from childhood. I tried to avoid anyone being mad at me. I wasn't as bad as my mother, whose solution was to pacify, but I still tried to get around it.

"Baby...no."

I took a deep breath and told him what had been cycling through my mind in the nursery prior to his arrival. "I was thinking about how close we came to losing this. How close we came to losing us—you and me...our family." I grasped his hand to prove that we hadn't, though.

"Oh." I'm pretty sure a little bit of sad air deflated from his lungs.

"Everything kinda just hit me. We finally have our baby back, and I was able to breathe again and think," I tried to explain while adjusting my sitting position slightly. "And it's made me think of everything...everything...all that happened... even back to late August and September—"

"Lar—"

"Finn," I interrupted. "I'm crying because it made me think of all the doubt and pain and, God, what a horrible time that was. God, how I missed you. I missed us so much. It was bad. It was so bad...every part of it," I said, as if he didn't already know. "I think now being on the flip side of that—on the good side...the great side—of *all* the trauma made me realize how scarily close we really were." I couldn't help it, a fresh tear emerged in my eye. "How close we came to losing us—Arinn and you and me."

"Lara..." His voice was emotional now, too, as he stroked my hand. "What your brother said was the truth. I *did* hurt you."

"I—"

"And it will be something I live with forever."

"But what I'm saying is—what I was saying to Lane—I don't doubt us for a second." I tried to clarify. "Not for a second. That's just it. Us. You. I want you to know that. I want you to know that I have complete faith in you and in us. And I wouldn't have gotten through everything with Arinn if it wasn't for you. I don't know how you manag—"

"Baby, I couldn't get through *life* if it wasn't for you. That's how I managed. Knowing you needed me to…knowing the kids needed me to." His pronounced statement made me remember what Dr. Bartola had told me about Finn, and it rang so true. "We are not going to lose us. Not ever." He said with honesty and determination.

He hardly got my hand up to his lips when I just lost it and started to uncontrollably bawl. I was crying for his sincere words and crying for the pain we had suffered. But I was also crying out of relief that we had made it through. He pulled me into his taut torso and held me as if I was part china doll and part the softest of comforting pillows.

"Geez, Lar. It's okay. It's all okay." He held on as I tried to slow my sobs. "God, I hate when you cry."

"Maybe I *am* pregnant." I teased, dotting my eyes after being able to finally pull slightly away. "I'm a hormonal mess."

"If you are, you're going to give birth to a bouncing baby bottle of wine," he jested, trying to get me to smile.

And I did grin, even adding a little chuckle. "I shouldn't drink." I swiped at the remnants of tears.

"You can drink. Just stick with Fat Boys kind of drunk." He referenced the bar in our college town. "Drink when you're happy. Not because you're upset or are thinking too much."

"Yeah," I said softly and leaned in to kiss him just as sweetly.

As his arms encircled my body, I felt like I was melting into him. His touch was a little bit of heaven. "Come on, Beauty," Finn cooed. "You should really get some sleep."

"I am so tired." Between nerves, wine, and little sleep

over those previous days, it was no wonder. My eyes slowly blinked as he pulled down the comforter and laid me under it.

Turning off the light, he crawled in beside me. "Y'know, my shoulder sure feels lonely."

"My head needs its favorite pillow." And I rested it on his shoulder.

"There is one thing for sure your brother was right about."

"What?"

"I *am* insanely in love." He curled his arm around me, kissed my forehead, and tugged my body into his even tighter.

"Me, too."

★★★

I wish he hadn't encouraged me to go. I understood why and actually agreed after a little debating. After all, it really would have been a great way to relax and release. My husband had the home treadmill and meditation earlier in the morning. I had my hair in a ponytail, limited make-up on, and a Pilates class in town where, hopefully, no one would recognize me as Mrs. Finn Murphy.

But, as I was semi-racing my car back home, I regretted going. Of course, neither of us could have ever predicted what happened. But it did, and I had to leave what was supposed to be a relaxing class before it had even begun.

I touched that same shoulder my head had rested on the night before. "Finn?" I said his name carefully because I knew, somehow, he hadn't heard me enter the house nonetheless the dining room— most likely because his mind was processing the same information mine was.

He twirled around to face me, shock filling his misty eyes. "I…I didn't expect you. I thought…."

"I bailed when I heard. I came straight back."

"Cayla?" he questioned while running his hands over

his face and then placing the lid back on the bourbon bottle without pouring.

"Yeah."

"I told her not to call. I said I would tell you." He turned from the liquor cabinet and started to walk away.

Recognizing the irritation in his voice, whether it was because Finn and Cayla never quite hit it off or because he didn't want someone interrupting my peaceful outlet, I clarified. "She didn't. I was early." I still didn't know the town well enough and was always mortified at the prospect of being late. "I had a few minutes, so I thought I would call her from the parking lot to thank her for her help." I followed him into the family room.

"Oh."

I was still trying to determine his exact demeanor. "We should talk about it."

His gray eyes momentarily minimized on mine. "Yeah." He paused. "I'm glad you're here. I'd really like to hold you." He then secured his arms around me. "How are you?" he asked. "You okay?" That was just like my husband—asking about my well-being had to be his number one question in life.

"Finn…" I gently pushed away so I could see him and get an honest answer. "How are *you*?"

"I don't know, Lara. I…" He took a few steps away and seemed to be searching the room as he was searching for words. "I haven't been able to process any of it. Everything around her just feels like a dark hole. Everything…from the beginning. The regret I feel for what I put you through…" He paused and let the guilt transfer from his eyes to mine. "And then what she did to Arinn. I was…I am…I…furious." Without him even saying those words, just mentioning our daughter's kidnapping caused tension in his stature. "I wanted her erased altogether, but yet I feel guilty."

"For her killing herself?" My voice was laced with disbelief, both over the fact that Finn would feel that way and that Brianna was dead.

When I had called Cayla, she had pretty much just gotten off the phone with Finn, detailing the news that was surely going to spread like wildfire in the local and, most likely, national scenes. It hadn't yet, only because it was too new. Besides Brianna's family, we were the first to be contacted as, sadly, we were an invested party. I didn't get the exact details, but I probably wouldn't have been able to concentrate on them anyway as I was still reeling from the initial declaration. However, I did find out that, while in jail, she had manipulated a piece of her bed or mattress or something that was poking out and then slit her wrist with it. By the time they realized it, she would never wake up again.

"Finn?" I asked again, trying to refocus both him and I.

"Guilty about everything, yeah."

"She was mentally unstable. You only tried to help her—with her career and even when she had that gun. God!" My body cringed with the flashback of hearing that gun go off in the farmhouse.

"But it was all because of me... because of that stupid night." His voice rose, too.

I knew he wasn't wrong, in a way, but there was also a much bigger story...long before that revolting night at the club. "No." I took a big, hopefully calming, breath. "There was a history... a history you didn't know about. She suffered and never got the help she needed. I saw the scars on her wrists in the photos. This wasn't the first time."

"You feel sorry for her?" he asked with a coating of disbelief.

That wasn't what I had said, but it did make me think. "I know what it's like to lose a child. But I had you. I had you and our family to support me. So, I guess maybe I do a little. I don't know, maybe it's hindsight, too. Because this morning, like you said, before finding out, I probably wouldn't have said that. The fact that she thought she could just take anything or anyone—"

"I know."

"But all of that was on her. Everything was her decision—from taking Arinn to slitting her wrist. It was her decision…psychotic break or not. We're all safe. That's what matters." After a moment of silent air hanging between us, I said, "Finn? I want to know what you're thinking."

"You, too, Lara." He took one of my hands in his and began to stroke it. "I know you have to be feeling more than—"

"I'm okay," I denied.

He didn't believe me. It was apparent by the frowning frustration in his face and the way he now clasped my hand instead of caressing it. His question took me by surprise. "Will you make love with me?"

"Yeah?"

"You want to know what I'm feeling. I want to know what you're…. I think we need each—"

He was so right. There really wasn't anything else for either of us to say. We were both really in the same proverbial boat—an overwhelming state-of-shock boat that was trying not to sink in the up and down waves of life. And he wasn't angry and screaming out to the world. He was reaching out to me as if we were life rafts for each other.

I kissed him then… in the tongue diving, giving every bit of passion and possession kind of way. When he instantly reciprocated, I started on his light gray, ribbed sweatshirt. There were a few white buttons on the top that I began to undo. But after the first one, the next couple got stuck and were stubbornly refusing to unfasten. Frustrated, I grasped both sides of the open part and tugged in opposite directions and down. The buttons not only opened, but the sweatshirt tore a little.

Finn started laughing and simply removed his shirt over his head revealing those damn distracting abs. "You actually *are* tearing my clothes off."

"What?" And then I remembered our sexting right before our world collapsed, a.k.a. Arinn being taken. "Oh." I laughed a little, too. "Kids?" I asked quickly.

"Still napping." he gave the answer I suspected because he had just put them to sleep while I was getting dressed for the Pilates class.

Wearing probably the most unsexy outfit possible, I pulled off my own black sleeveless yoga top exposing my pink sports bra. With that movement, my ponytail was left half done. Finn finished the process, fanning out my strawberry blonde locks, and then he went to his knees. He untied and took off my gray tennis shoes and socks, tossing them simultaneously to the side. His hands met the waistband of my gray with white trimmed leggings, and he began pulling them down. Once they were mid-thigh, he started slow, sensual kisses inside both of my legs and continued that way until the pants were to the ground. By the time he got to my ankles, I wasn't standing still. I was squirming and backing up. Without saying a word, he got me to lift my feet so the pants could be completely removed.

Finn smiled and proceeded in reenacting his delicious deed. This time, though, he started at my ankles and kissed my wobbly legs in the same erotic, methodic way until he reached my panties. Taking those in his hands, he lowered them and moaned in a way that drove me absolutely insane. I could hardly wait for him to get my underwear off my feet. The instant he stood back up, my hands were on the belt encircling his khakis. Luckily, I managed the buckle better than the buttons of his sweatshirt.

He tried to unfasten my bra but it was a sports bra, and he didn't know quite... "How?" He sounded frustrated, like I had been with his shirt.

"Say, please," I teased, gathering my hands at the bottom of the bra.

"Please. Now." In the moment that I released the bra, his mouth found my breasts.

As we made our way onto the sofa and Finn discarded his bottoms, I understood how much I needed us...how much we needed us together. I had never felt threatened by Briar when it came to Finn's relationship with me. Deeply disappointed and horrendously hurt? Absolutely. But I knew she had meant nothing but a drunken, off meds, deepest depressed moment for him, and it would never happen again. We had reconciled our feelings on the matter until Arinn was taken, and then they couldn't help but be dug back up. The girl we knew as Briar was most certainly gone now and, admittedly, I felt both a little sad and glad about that fact.

But, yet, I needed my claim. I needed him. I needed him to just be thinking about me and about our love. Surely because of my actions and our deep connection, I knew Finn recognized that. Grabbing my hand, he guided me onto him, allowing me to take charge. I could feel the pistons firing in my heart and in between the two of us as we collectively let our emotions and bodies go.

"Lara...." he called out my name as his eyes rolled in ecstasy.

But then I couldn't see him. My eyes were suddenly betraying me. They were filling up with tears. But they weren't the sad variety. It was just the opposite. They were flooding with love and relief.

"I love you," he murmured. "I will always be here for you." His eyes wouldn't leave mine as we continued to rock in exquisite union. "You'll always be safe and happy."

Those words didn't help the tears, but they warmed and secured my heart. Happily spent, I closed my eyes and collapsed in the afterglow on Finn's chest. And, after a moment or two, he lifted my head and kissed me on the lips.

"Thank you," he said, while strumming his hand through my hair.

I'm pretty sure I had the "cat ate the canary" smile. "Did you just ask me to make love with you and then thanked me for it?"

Finn's laugh was light and relaxed. He touched my lips and smiled. "Yep. I guess I did." And then he turned serious. "Thank you for loving me as much as I do you."

Those had been my words that very first time we had made love all those years before. Although, I had substituted "caring" for "loving" back then, as I had been too insecure to flat out admit the whole truth. God, did I love that he remembered all those special moments between us so many years later.

"Loved you then, love you now, love you every day after." I circled my index finger around his chest.

"Can't think of any other words I would rather hear."

"Daddy, Arinn and me wake up!" Our little boy's voice seemed to be coming from—

"Da-da! Da-da!" Yep, upstairs in his sister's room.

"Well, those words are pretty special, too." Finn smiled and then hollered in the direction of the kids, "All right, bud. Stay with your sister. I'll be up in a minute."

"He's really looking after her and glad she's home."

"Yeah. Me, too."

I kissed him sweetly before literally sitting up and tagging him. "I'll race you to get to them."

Finn's amused eyebrows raised as he said, "I just have to put on my shorts."

Realizing he totally had me beat in the properly dressed department, I whined, "Help me!"

Finn, sitting up next to me, started stringing on his boxer briefs as I reached for my bra. I had it over my shoulders when I felt Finn's fingers trailing up the back of my spine to finally meet where my hands were attempting to close the clasp. His wet lips met my back at that precise point, but he did finish putting the bra properly back on. Stretching, he grabbed my panties off the floor and looked at my ankles very mischievously.

"Go!" I laughed. "I don't think you are helping." I snatched the underwear away from him.

"Probably not. That was too damn hot."

As I put on my panties, he stood up and tossed on his now ripped gray sweatshirt. He sat back down and turned a little bit serious, "Lara, I can only imagine the calls on my phone right now. It's not over. It just spun in a different direction. I'm gonna have to deal with it."

"I know." I realized the new questions that would arise from Briar's suicide and how all the focus would now solely be on us but most of all Finn. "I'll be right there next to you."

"You shouldn't have t—"

"I think I've proven that I've got your back," I smiled. "And… your front."

He let out a light chuckle at the sexual reference and then sucked in a powerful, thankful kiss. "Most importantly, you have my heart."

***

As predicted, news of the suicide, right on top of the already very active press coverage of the kidnapping and arrest, brought everything to a new level. There were rumors galore about the reason why Briar had taken Arinn and why she felt such despair as to kill herself. Of course, with the music industry as a common denominator, there was the automatic connection to Finn. And with each media source wanting the scoop and to outdo each other, hearsay and suspicions became "fact." But no one, absolutely no one, had any type of proof. Because, in reality, it wasn't true. They were not having an affair. He had not tossed her aside. I didn't even want to know the rest of what people thought.

We had a couple of advantages on our side. For one, not a lot of people were talking. The theater did not make a statement to any media source. I'm sure they were fearful of possible litigation. But Finn and I did not want to press charges. It was something we realized was a legitimate error and everything, thank God, worked out in the end. And, the label wasn't talking, either. A couple of Brianna's neighbors were on the local news, but they appeared disheveled and semi-illiterate and had nothing to say about Finn.

Brianna's emotional mother, supported by her sister, was the only one who gave a slightly negative impression of Finn but mostly of the music industry. She spoke about how Brianna had been abandoned by men all of her life. First her father, then the baby daddy, and now, although she wasn't positive, Finn and the "people who rule what is deemed music nowadays." She spoke of her daughter's incredible talent and what a loss the world was suffering through. It was quite an exaggeration, but she was a mother and, in that respect, I understood.

The other advantage we had was Finn's nearly spotless reputation with the industry and his fans. He did have his issues in the past. There was his drug abuse in the very beginning of his career and the altercation with Macon— Miller's now-deceased brother and the biological father of the child I gave up. But Finn and his life with me was one of the positive cornerstones in country music. So, any misdemeanor on his part was hard to imagine, except for the trolls on the internet.

Finn felt the pressure, though. On the advice of Reese and his lawyers, he made a short statement, basically acknowledging Briar's passing, and then let our interview at the house speak the rest. Sadly, everyone in "Camp Finn" was hoping for some other tragedy to happen to someone else to divert the negative coverage away from him.

Even though he did his best to shield it from the kids and me, I could tell how much it beat him down. He was dealing with these murmurs of accusations, a high-octane career, and his father's health, which we knew, more from Nola than his folks, was declining. Every time we would hear something ugly or he would get off of a stressful phone call, he would come and give me a hug—strong and long—as if I was going to flee. After all, his greatest PTSD trigger was being left.

"Baby...." I said after being the recipient of many of these.

"I know." He sighed. "I need to, though."

He relaxed and somehow held me tighter at the same time. We had a lot going on in our lives. But the best and most important thing was love.

CHAPTER FIFTEEN

"In here," I loudly whispered after hearing Finn down the hall, opening and closing the kids' bedroom doors.

My husband appeared at our master bedroom doorway next. Illuminated by the sitting room light and our flowing, red lava lamp on the nightstand, I could see the curiosity screech across his face as he looked down at me in our bed. Glued to my side was our three-and-a-half-year-old, thankfully sound asleep.

"What's going on?" Finn returned the nighttime whisper while looking from Chance to me.

"Rudolph," was my single word response.

"The reindeer?" His inflection was downright hysterical.

"Do you know any others?" I softly chuckled while disarming myself gently from our son and standing to join my husband at the edge of the bed. I took his hand to walk us into the sitting room. I didn't want to disrupt Chance's sleep with our chatter, especially about something that had already disturbed him.

Kissing me sweetly but quickly, Finn said, "Hi, baby."

"Hi." I smiled...it would never get old.

"Tell me about the red nosed caribou." He touched my

own nose.

"We were watching it on TV, but he didn't like it... at all. He was shaking during the abominable snowman parts, and then he kept wanting Rudolph to find his way home. He was so worried about him being lost in the cold."

"Oh, man." Finn sighed and momentarily looked up to the ceiling. He didn't have to say it. We both knew Chance's reaction was because his sister had been missing...lost.

"I never even looked at the movie that way," I continued.

As a child, I remembered loving the fact that the reindeer left those bullies and ventured out on his own. But that was the difference between having a bully of a father at home versus a loving family like our son had. Chance saw his sister needing to be back where she was loved... not with an ugly creature made of snow.

"I made him finish watching it," I continued. "I don't know if that was good or bad. I wanted him to see that there was a happy ending."

"God, Lar, have we screwed this kid up already? I thought that wouldn't happen until he was in his teens." He said it in jest, but I knew he also meant it seriously.

"Overachievers," I bounced back, trying to keep it light.

"Uh-huh."

"Anyway, he wouldn't go to sleep. I know we don't usually, but I let him come into our room."

"That's fine. Do you want me to carry him back?"

"No. He's still doing a lot of tossing and turning."

"All right," he concluded.

"How did things go with you?" I put my hand up to his chest, adorned with a steel gray button down that exposed just enough to accent a red T underneath.

"It was good," he said with what I determined true peace in his voice—something that had been lacking for so long. "It felt good to sing. It felt good to do something good." Finn had agreed to participate in a local country music fundraising concert prior to Arinn being kidnapped. And while he strongly debated about still attending just a few days after Briar's death, he had. "No issues. Everyone was there for one reason... the right reason."

"That's great." I breathed in a sigh of contentment. I was happy for him. I was happy that he could go somewhere and feel like he wasn't going to be questioned about what happened. "I have to say, Cowboy, there's no group stronger than the country music family. They've proved that to us time and time again."

"They have." Finn's smile was more in his eyes than his mouth, as if he was reflecting himself. When he saw me stifle a yawn, he quickly added, "All right, bed time." And he looped his arms around me from behind and walked us back into the bedroom and our sensitive, sweet, sleeping child.

***

The fact that things went well for Finn that night gave me hope. It gave me hope that things were slowly starting to turn around—that the media and public were moving on and that we could, too. Our baby was safe in our home and there had been resolution—although dramatic and sad— with the woman who took her. It needed to be put it in the past for everyone's sake.

We hoped that the focus would now be on celebration and family and new beginnings as the Christmas and New Year season always symbolized. With Finn's newest album set for release just before the holidays, it was the perfect time to also concentrate on his music. We were relying on his huge fan base to not only buy the tunes but promote his professional side more than his personal. Of course, Finn had his own promoting to do, also. He was set to make the rounds of a couple talk shows in New York City, where he would be singing and talking about lyrics and collaborations, not alleged affairs and kidnapper's suicides.

He wanted me and the kids to go with him for those few days, while he not only promoted but checked in with Dr. Bartola and closed on our house in suburban New York. It was tempting. We could stay in our Manhattan penthouse and see all the magic that the vibrant city exudes, especially during the holidays. There was the Rockefeller tree, the skating rink, the store window displays along Fifth Avenue, and so much more. But, in the end, I decided to stay in Nashville.

For one thing, Vanessa was actually, ironically, coming into town the day after Finn was leaving. She was going to spend the holiday with Carter and his family and most likely become engaged, but that was still a secret between Carter, Finn, and I. I missed my best friend and really wanted to see her.

But another reason I decided not to make the trip to New York with Finn was a biggie. I wanted to see if I could do it…if I could handle him being away. It would be the first time since he got home from the summer tour and our mini-separation immediately following, that he would be away from us for more than a few hours or so in a day. And, of course, it would be the first time I would be completely alone for days with the kids since Arinn was taken. Rationally, I knew one had absolutely nothing to do with the other. But there was that underlying twinge of uncertainty. I knew Finn had it, too. But it wasn't about any kind of distrust in my mothering capabilities. It was that he always wanted to be nearby in case any of us needed anything. So, in that sense, it would do him good, too.

"I think we're bordering on too much togetherness, anyway." I teased as he was waiting for the car service to pick him up for the airport.

"Do you? Do you really?" Finn replied, not detecting my humor.

"You're not sick of me?" I tried again.

"Are you being serious?" His face looked a little puzzled and a little hurt.

"Finn, I'm kidding. But I need to feel secure when you're away. It's going to happen sometimes, and we're not always going to be able to pack up and go with you. It's a few days." I tried a sexy smile. "Besides, absence and the heart and all that."

"So, you *will* miss me," he said with more confidence.

"Hmmm …." I pretended to think.

"There better be a good answer at the end of that hesitation," he jokingly warned. Before I could come up with a sarcastic comeback, though, he verbalized something I knew he had just figured out. "I've never left you at this house. It was always the other way around." He spoke of the times before we were married…it was me who visited him in Nashville and then had to leave to go back to New York.

"I know."

"You realized that already?"

"I did," I said. "You know what that means, don't you?"

Pure puzzlement streaked across his face. "No. What?"

"It means this is our home."

"I like that." He gave me a serene closed-mouth smile followed by a quick kiss.

"It also means I need to find a spot where I wait for you." My spot had been on the cushioned bench in the foyer of our New York home. I could tell he wasn't completely listening, though.

That was confirmed when he said, "I forgot something upstairs."

"What?"

"Uh …just a contact I need for New York. It's in the bedroom. I'll be right back. Maybe you can see if you can coax Grumpy McFly over there," —he motioned to our pouting son on the other side of the room— "to come say goodbye to me. My ride will be here soon."

I thought it was odd that Finn needed to get a contact. All his numbers, addresses, etc. were surely programmed in his phone. But I didn't have much time to ponder since I, indeed, had to try to convince Chance to see Finn off. We had already talked to our son about Finn being away for a few days, and he was not handling it well. He was old enough to understand what it meant but too young to comprehend the short time it involved.

"So, look, Chance," I said, now in the kitchen with the despondent preschooler. I was pointing to the calendar, which was a great visual representation for him. "We can't count today since Daddy's still here. So, count with me." I pointed to the square days, and we counted in unison to three. "And then, when you wake up, Daddy will be home." I marked that day with a smiley heart. "You can count that many all by yourself all on one hand. It's only a little bit of time."

His little face, eyebrows furrowed similar to his dad's, peered up at mine. "Like when Arinn gone?"

Yeah. God. Yeah. It actually would be very similar to the amount of time that Arinn had been missing. But to her parents it had seemed ten times longer.

"It's not long at all." Finn's voice behind us made Chance jump, since neither of us had seen or heard him enter the kitchen.

Our son's words and then actions made me so sad. It was dear that he held his sister so close to his heart and mind, but I was afraid we hadn't shielded him as much as we should have when it came to her disappearance. And then for him to be scared by a sudden sound behind him? He shouldn't have been having those fears. He was too little. He was being raised so loved. But, as much as he was like Finn both with his looks and performer-self, he was like me...reserved around people and afraid of being hurt.

"Sorry, bud." Finn apologized when Chance sucked onto my side and both of us turned to face Finn. "Chance, I need that hug, Little Man. It will make me so happy."

"Don't want you go away," he pouted.

"I know," Finn consoled. "But I will talk with you every day, okay?"

"Weally?" With one-word Chance sounded somehow surprised, optimistic, and doubtful.

"I always do. You know that," Finn reassured.

"You no call last time."

"Of course I did," Finn answered our son in a puzzled but affirmative way.

Right before Chance refuted with his "no" again, I got it. The last time Finn was away, without the kids or I, was not the time he was touring. It was actually days after— when Finn and I had separated. It had happened suddenly, and Finn fell hard, not contacting us at all. On tour, yes, he spoke with the kids and I daily. But the last time he went away, Chance was right— he actually went completely away...and it was longer than three days.

I made my eyes grow wide at Finn who instantly then understood. "Bud, I promise. okay?"

He bent down to Chance's level. And when he didn't get a reply even after saying our son's name, he looked up at me, and I wondered who was hurting more in that moment—Chance or his dad.

Not wanting to miss out on the action, Arinn came toddling in to join us. She was just the happiest little girl. She had the silliest toothy grin on her face, and the laugh she projected was as if she was amused by her own crazy waddle. I hoped she never lost that infectious love of life.

Scooping her up into my arms and running my finger on her back, I said, "Arinn, want to say bye to Daddy?"

She actually reached her arms out to Finn and said, "Bye-bye, Da-da."

If you call that a complete, comprehensive sentence, that was her first one. And, of course, as her proud parent, I accepted it as so. My eyes grew wide again—this time with pride. Finn probably didn't like that his child's first sentence was saying goodbye to him, but he also understood that it was a milestone. I crouched down closer to the floor with Arinn so she could go to Finn. He gave her a warm hug and kiss while looking at me. I knew his emotions were all over the place.

"Ans." Arinn said, which we now recognized as the name she said for her brother.

Just feet away, Chance looked at her and, after a slight hesitation, joined the duo in a hug. I think he gave in to his resistance because a) his sister wanted him, b) if Arinn could do it, a big boy could… but most importantly c) he adored his dad like no other. After a second, I reclaimed Arinn in my arms and let father and son have their own hug moment.

"I love you, Little Man," Finn said, standing up with Chance still in his arms. When Chance held out his arms extra wide—their special love meter—Finn, just like his own dad, said, "Double that."

**

A little after he left, I found out why Finn had to go back upstairs "to get the contact." Using one of my dark lipsticks, my husband had written a message directly on the master bath mirror. *I miss you* ♥ *Finn*

I grabbed my phone and took a picture of his handiwork. Although the shade may have been slightly different, the location and message were exactly the same as when I had written it to him seven years before—the first time I was in Nashville and the first time I had to leave to return to New York. I forwarded the picture to my husband with an accompanying text. *My sweet sentimental man* ♥, *just so U know, that made me cry.*

Finn's return text came immediately. *I still have the original saved in my photos.*

U do not!

Really, Lara. U doubt that?

Of course, I didn't. I knew when it came to all things

me, he kept them treasured in his heart. He had proven that time and time again by remembering and celebrating our love.

Now I want to B on that plane w/U. I texted and then quickly sent another one. *& U know how I feel about planes!*

But U love me more than U hate them. He recited another thing I had told him years before regarding my detest of flying. And then he sent a follow-up text of his own. *I can send a car & wait 4 the next plane, baby. Just say the word.*

Thankfully, my sigh couldn't be detected via text. *I know U would. Can't. It's hard, but I think this is a good thing esp. 4 Little Man.*

Chance needed to see that Finn would live up to his word by calling and returning very soon. It might be a little rough but, in the end, it would give him more security. And me, too.

After a second, Finn texted back. *How's he doing?*

He's fine. I typed and then added, *Really* for extra reassurance. And then, recalling one of the first things our son had said after Finn's car drove off, I typed, *Thanks BTW 4 telling him I promise 2 play that dance game w/him every nite. I WILL get U 4 that!*

Ha! Ha! U R sooo welcome, dance star. I expect video.

In your dreams.

Always ;) He didn't need to put the wink emoji, I already felt it from him. *I'll let U know when I land. Love U, Rox.*

Love U 2. Have a safe trip. xoxo

***

I watched as Finn plied on the charm and handled two live broadcasts beautifully that next morning. They were pretty much back-to-back interviews, but he somehow managed to change outfits and look just as handsome in both. The kids and I were having a lazy start to our day, which worked out perfectly for me to be able to watch.

When my phone rang, I knew it was him calling. Of course, I would have known simply by the designer "Roxanne" ring I had assigned him. But I also knew it was just enough time after the last interview for him to shake hands, do the mandatory signings, debrief with Reese and others on his team, and navigate away from everyone else to finally be alone. I knew then that he would immediately call me. I knew that from past experiences.

"Hey," I answered casually. "You in the car?"

"Hi, Beauty. No. Just got to the penthouse." He changed his voice to acknowledge the friendly front doorman at the building that housed our Manhattan apartment. "Hi, Graham."

"Tell him I said hi, too."

I heard Finn do just that and then laugh before saying to me, "He says he wants to see the prettier of the two of us in person soon!"

"He's sweet."

"Baby, I'm getting on the elevator. Just in case I lose you."

"Okay."

"How are the kids?"

"They're good. I'll go get—"

"No. Hey, do you mind? Can I just talk with you for a sec.?"

"Yeah. Yeah." It made me a little apprehensive, hoping he didn't have some bombshell to disclose. We had been subject to enough drama for a while. "You all right?"

"Yeah. I just…I need a minute. Just need to talk with you." There was the slightest of pauses before he said, "You see the interviews?"

I should have figured. Finn was a performer, and he did a spectacular job. But I also knew he was much more comfortable singing than speaking, especially when it involved anything personal. I knew those piercing eyes on television earlier had shown anxiety or anger during the questions about Arinn's kidnapping. He had done fine, though. I could only imagine how I would have handled the pressure of being in the national, live spotlight with those questions being thrown at me. My eyes wouldn't have pierced. They would have teared and closed.

"Yeah, I watched. You did great."

"I hate that they asked—"

I knew what they had asked, and I didn't want to hear it again. So, I interrupted. "Finn, that's their job. I'm sure you and your team expected it. You handled it well... both times. You answered briefly and sympathetically and kept referring to your music. I'm ready to buy your new album." I tried to put a little humor on at the end as I looked at Chance who, hearing me call Finn by his first name, was ready to pounce on the phone.

I heard Finn opening the door to the penthouse as he played along. "I think you may have a personal in with the artist and get comped an album."

"And maybe even a private serenade."

"Hmmm." He still sounded reserved and distracted.

"Finn, the interviews truly did seem good." When he didn't respond, I asked, "You all right? You're not really upset, are you?"

"No. No. I'm good. Nothing a little joint Pilates workout in the family room when I return won't cure."

"Ha! Ha!" I knew from him saying that, that he must be okay. "That was a little more than a Pilates workout, Cowboy."

"It better be." I could hear the devilish smile in his voice. Then he went directly into his protective mode. "Listen, if any press contacts you at all—at all—you let me know right away, okay? They shouldn't be bothering you."

"Finn?"

"Yeah?"

"I love you."

He knew me and my tactics so well. "Lara...." He wanted me to take his request seriously.

I did. But I also wanted him relaxed. I used my

mommy voice. "Say it back."

His sigh was audible, but his words were true. "I love you, too."

"Let me get the kids. Chance might have another potty accident. He's dancing around so much because he's so anxious to talk with you."

"God forbid." Finn lightly chuckled. "Let me talk with him."

"Finn..." I tried to reassure across the miles. "We're all good. And as long as that's the case, nothing else matters."

CHAPTER SIXTEEN

When Vanessa and I met up the next day, we did such a normal thing, I almost cried. Kids in tow, we went shopping at the Opry Mills Mall. Only a handful of days before Christmas, the shopping center was abuzz. But that only added to the fun. It was great to see Vanessa. It was great to be out. It was great to feel free again.

I had a lot of shopping to do. Between the move, CMAs, planning our vows, Thanksgiving, and the kidnapping, there had been about zero thought put into the holidays. I knew Finn had taken care of his staff, crew, bandmates, etc. Well, in essence, he had someone do that for him. We had also decided to host Carter and Vanessa's engagement party, provided he actually popped the question soon. But we still had family and the kids to consider. When I would find something for Nola or Kelsea or the kids, etc., I would text Finn to get his opinion. Being in meetings and closing on our suburban New York home, I'm sure he wasn't exactly thrilled with my interruptions, but he would always briefly text back in agreement. Then he texted wondering what I was finding for him.

I replied honestly, but it was also quite conveniently

sexy. *Looking @ lingerie right now. Just pick a color. ;)*

Is edible a color? was his quick comeback.

I stared at a rich brown negligee. *Chocolate it is, then.*

I love U, Roxanne.

U 2. Sorry 2 keep bothering U.

Never. He protested via text.

In all truth, Finn and I didn't buy much for each other. At least not extravagant items. We had everything we needed. And if we wanted something, we usually bought it together. Although, I held onto my tradition, starting from the first Christmas we were dating, of buying him one sentimental gift and one practical gift. I already knew my sentimental one, which was one of the main reasons we went to the mall. I was going to get Chance and Arinn's picture taken with mall Santa and have it laminated to put in his collection of photos inside his favorite guitar case. We had yet to get a photo with Santa with either of the children. Arinn had just been born the year before, and the one time in the past that I got Chance to the mall, he was scared of the white-bearded, jolly man in red. This year, thankfully, he was excited. Adding to the sentimental gift, I put Carter and Hawk in charge of getting and setting up a holiday tree at the ranch while Vanessa and I were out. Carter was more than happy to not go shopping and instead do a manly thing with Hawk. We usually didn't set one up since we always spent the holidays at Finn's parents. And we were going to again. But I thought we needed some additional cheer. It would be a beautiful surprise for both the kids and their dad.

I was still having a hard time thinking of the practical gift, though. So, I asked Vanessa, "What are you getting Carter?"

"I don't know!" She tossed her long wavy brunette locks around in frustration. "We are in a completely different place than before."

"Mmmm-hmmm." I murmured, thinking how damn hard it was not revealing the ring secret. I tried to see if she had any inkling or I could figure out when it was going to happen. "So, are you two doing anything special before going to his family's?"

"Tomorrow we're going to some restaurant that looks over the skyline of Nashville. I forget its name. Sounds kinda foo-foo."

I knew the way she said it that it wasn't Carter's normal jeans and T-shirt type of venue. Before she could delve further, though, I lamented, "I wish Finn and I could do that."

"What do you mean? You go out. I know sometimes the fans—"

"No. It's just…I don't…the kids. I don't know who to and how to trust someone with the kids. It was easy in New York with our relatives and friends. But now I don't know anyone, and with what happened…." I looked at my happy little girl as we stood in the LEGO store. I wondered why I couldn't be as strong as her. I still had yet to return the preschool's phone call.

"Oh," Vanessa understood. When I attempted a smile back at her, she went into her full best friend mode. "Well, you two need a date night, too. Saturday, when Finn is home, Carter and I will watch the kids."

"You have plans!"

"Tomorrow, but I don't think for the weekend. Let me call Carter. I'll make him."

She instantly had her phone in her hand ready to dial. And all I could think was: Carter is going to kill me if I ruin the night he was going to propose. Although, I did think the romantic Friday dinner reservation was probably the main event.

"You never see him," I tried again.

"I will be seeing him. We'll watch the kids together. It's a done deal."

"If things change…." I started.

But she was already on the phone. "Hey, hottie, how's the tree business?"

While Vanessa was on the line with her unbeknownst soon-to-be fiancé, I started to coax Chance into giving up the LEGO and exiting the store. I promised that if he did, Santa might deliver a few of the famous connecting plastic blocks on Christmas. We were just about to make our getaway when something I had feared would happen during our outing came to fruition. I was one part amazed that it hadn't happened sooner and a bigger part pissed that it should even happen at all…especially since we were just about done with the shopping experience and ready to exit for the day.

Wearing all white, except for an orange scarf and dark boots, I had first noticed the shoulder-length bleached-blonde because she seemed more interested in her phone than her naturally blonde daughter, who was near Chance. I knew I was guilty of texting Finn during our excursion, but I had Vanessa to watch the kids. This woman seemed alone and not at all engaged with the child who kept calling "Mommy" out to her. It was when she pointed her phone in the direction of me with Arinn in my arms, that I started to suspect we had been unmasked.

Normally, unless I was with Finn and he wasn't under the disguise of a ball cap and shades, I was not recognized as Mrs. Finn Murphy. And, in some circles, just being related to someone famous made you a celebrity yourself. But despite me being most casually dressed in jeans and a paisley peasant top and only wearing a pale lipstick and some eye-liner, I knew this woman recognized me. Whether it was from red carpet outings, where I was much more dolled-up, or from the press conference or exclusive interview, she knew who I was. Besides a couple look-ups from store personnel when I handed over my credit card, we had been unscathed for the day.

I wanted to say something about respecting our privacy and especially about not taking a photo of my daughter. But the woman, sensing that *she* had been had, approached me first.

"I see you're keeping a close eye on your daughter now." Her southern accent came out like a hiss.

"What?"

My head practically whipped around with the implied accusation. I should have said that she had no room to talk, but I was too stunned. To take my picture or to approach me or Finn with a "I know who you are" kind of thing was bad enough, but—

"It's not your fault, though. I blame your husband. I think there must have been a little hanky-panky with the starlet, huh?" She was no-doubt a tabloid fan. "Nobody goes off the deep end like that, otherwise. Oh, well. Stand by your man and all that."

My eyes grew wide as I first looked around the store to see if anyone else had heard her. But, thankfully, everyone was much more engrossed in their preholiday worlds. I then looked to her obnoxiously big white purse to see if there was a bottle sticking out of it. The woman had to be drunk to say something like that about someone and something she knew nothing about.

"First of all—" I started and just as quickly stopped.

First of all, I shouldn't engage. I knew that. It was Celebrity Confrontation 101.

First of all, Finn wouldn't want me anywhere near this. It wasn't because he would be afraid of what I would say or how it could potentially end up in the press but because he wouldn't want me upset. And he definitely wouldn't want the kids nearby.

I was a good mother. I was a decent human being. I took the high road and Chance's hand at the same time. I was going to just leave and not say anything.

But my best friend did. "You are the one that's off the deep end, bi—" Vanessa, inside a store full of children, managed to censor that word at the last second. But despite being petite, she was bold and fierce, and she continued. "You have no idea what you are talking about. How dare you attack someone that you don't know at all and someone who isn't even here to defend himself, especially…especially when none of it can be further from the truth." She looked to the woman's daughter, impeccably dressed with a red bow in her hair, and concluded with, "What kind of mother are you? What example are you setting?"

"Put your claws in," the other woman countered. "I was just—"

"Vanessa…" I said to my defender. "Let's go." We didn't need any more attention.

"Ness!" I heard Carter's voice coming through Vanessa's phone. They had obviously not hung up before Vanessa went on her rampage. And he could hear exactly what was going down.

Hearing Carter's voice made Vanessa do one last glare at the beast of a woman and then turn away. As I fastened Arinn into her stroller, which also housed our shopping bags, Vanessa took Chance's hand. He seemed to understand that Mommy and Aunt Nessa were upset and that he should simply obey. We walked out of the store and simultaneously started toward a main mall exit.

"Vanessa!" We both heard Carter again through the phone lines.

Vanessa's light brown eyes did an "eech" look at me and then she picked up her phone once more. "Sorry, sweetness," she said to Carter. "I had to take care of—" She stopped her vocals, but we continued our stride. "Carter…" She started again once the drummer obviously had his say. "I wasn't going to let that woman say that stuff." She paused to listen once more. "I know. I know." Another pause. "Yeah, we're all good. Lara and I can take on anyone." She did a smile slash smirk in my direction. When I motioned for her to hand me the phone, she obliged. "Lara wants to talk to you. I'll see you in a bit. We're heading back now." I think there was a small blush on my best friend's face as she said, "You, too" into the phone before handing it over to me.

Vanessa gained reins of the stroller as I spoke with Finn's drummer and friend. "Carter, don't tell Finn, okay? Tell Hawk not to say anything, either."

"Lara, he's gonna wanta know," he countered.

"He has enough on his plate," I tried to reason. "What good would it do? It was one ignorant...." I searched for a kid-appropriate word, being so close to my two impressionable youngins.

"Ass," Carter said for me.

"Thank you," I replied. "It's part of this world, right? He doesn't need to know."

"I don't know, Lara-Li." He used his personalized nickname for me. "You'll double-owe me, considering the kid gig I now have on Saturday." His words may as well have had a shaking head emoji floating above them. He had obviously gotten through the babysitting question with Vanessa before we all were so rudely interrupted.

"Oooh. Oh, yeah. Sorry about that. I tried. That's not ruining anything, is it?" I carefully and tactfully asked, knowing that Vanessa was within arm's length and in earshot.

"No," he confirmed. "Tomorrow would have been a whole other story, though."

I smiled. "That's what I thought."

"I'll keep your secret if you keep mine," he offered.

"Definitely a deal," I replied. "Thanks, Carter."

"Sure. You *should* tell him, though."

"Yeah. I will. Once he gets home."

No omissions and all that. I just didn't want him to hear and, more importantly, get upset, when he was so far away. I hung up the phone and handed it back to its owner.

Once again carefully monitoring the words coming out of my mouth, I spoke to the only adult in my mini-posse. "Why haven't you asked?"

"About what?" Vanessa replied genuinely curious.

"You know," I looked down at Chance who was

happily swinging his arm in sync with Vanessa's and, thankfully, only paying attention to his baby sister pointing at random things from the stroller. "With what happened with…with Brianna."

She brought her brows together with the most innocent look and then spoke purely. "Because I don't have any questions."

I reached out for her hand. "You're the best, Vanessa."

"Lara, it's Finn. Anyone that even remotely knows him knows his devotion to you. It's just the media trying to keep latching onto a story that should have ended with that poor, sad, love-struck's death."

"Yep. That is the truth."

And it really was. I didn't need to worry about what some random stranger in person, online, or wherever thought. As long as my family and friends knew the truth and the real us, Finn and I had nothing to fear.

***

The old rocking chair, which had been displaced from the great room due to the humongous, decorated evergreen now invading its space, rocked obnoxiously when I bounded from its new spot in the foyer. It was Friday night, and Finn had just walked through the front door. He was finally home from his trip to New York.

Actually lifting off the ground momentarily, I bounded into his arms. "Welcome home."

"Hi, baby." He set his bag down and kissed me.

"I missed you," I cooed and burrowed myself a little deeper into his chest.

We stayed like that for a few serene, secure moments, just taking each other in before Finn eventually pulled away to remove his leather jacket. After he hung it on one of the foyer's coat hooks, he commented about my location. "I like your new spot."

"Yeah," I said. "It's kinda comfy. I was just sitting here

rocking and thinking of you."

"I'll have that in mind next time now." He smiled.

"So," I grabbed my phone, found the recent text, and showed it to Finn.

Next to the words *Will B wearing some new bling babysitting 2morrow!!!* was a photo of Vanessa's hand adorning a beautiful halo-cut diamond.

Finn didn't say a word but responded by flipping his phone over and showing me his text from Carter. *Get ready, Best Man!*

Then my husband said, "Babysitting? For who?"

"Us. I told her not to, but she's still insisting."

"Where are we going?" Finn asked, both a little puzzled and amused.

"The Ben Winthrop movie?" Only sitting there rocking had I remembered that Finn and I had been planning on seeing it right before Arinn was taken.

"Oh, brother." Finn's abs shook in humor. "It's a good thing I love you."

"It's a great thing." I repeated the words he had told me in early November. "You all right with that?"

"Me loving you?"

My stomach bounced in laughter. "Going out," I clarified.

"Yeah." He touched the side of my face softly, kindly, lovingly. "In fact, I think we need this—just you and me."

I smiled and grabbed his hand. "Come on, there's some things you need to see."

I led Finn into the great room where a little boy lay sound asleep on the sofa. His arm dangling off the cushion mimicked the droll coming from his open mouth. He looked so peaceful.

"He wanted to wait up for you," I started to explain. "I let him think he could. But my deal was, he had to quit challenging me to the dance game."

Finn started to laugh but cut himself off when he spotted the Christmas tree in the back corner of the room.

"Oh, my God, Lara. What is that? When did you—? Wow. Did you do that?"

"Not really. Sorta," I answered, pleased by his response. "Carter and Hawk did."

"Hawk? Carter?" I think that surprised him even more than the tree itself, which was quite a shock.

"Yeah. Merry Christmas, baby." I smiled as he walked closer to the tree decorated with a string of multi-colored lights, garland, and a star on top. "I know we're gonna be at your folks. But I thought we could do something here, too, for the kids. And it's kinda a fresh start."

"*Our* Christmas." His eyes glistened, and I knew he was remembering our first Christmas dating when he had surprised me with a similar set-up and words.

"Yeah." I formed into his side, both of us staring at the tree. "There's not a lot. I thought we could add things every year." I paused, looked up, but didn't let go. "So, the tree is part of your sentimental gift. The other one is under the tree."

There was only one gift under the tree, so, it wasn't hard for Finn to find it. "Can I open it now?" he asked in his usual can't-wait-to-tear-open-gifts way.

"You are so bad." I chuckled and then said, "Yeah. The practical one will have to wait until Christmas, though." Especially because I still had no idea of what to get.

Leaving the wrapping paper amiss on the floor, he held the photo up for close examination. "You got him to do it?" Finn turned to me.

"Yeah. That was on the first take, too."

"Daddy?" We heard the subject of the photo mumbling from his makeshift bed on the sofa.

Finn placed the photo back in the box and started walking toward Chance. "Yeah, Little Man. Everything's okay." He scooped our son up in his arms. "I'm home. Let's get you to bed."

"Daddy...home." He sounded so content, but, then again, so was I.

We tucked Chance into bed together, which didn't take long, seeing as he was already asleep, and then went in and kissed a sleeping Arinn. We walked into our master bedroom hand in hand and, as if on instinct, both stopped at the same time and faced one another. Without a word, we began soft, sweet, endless kisses. I felt like I was being rocked to sleep myself by the easy rhythm and love. We stopped just as simultaneously, and I rested my head on Finn's T-shirt-covered torso.

After a couple beats, I heard him ask, "You all right just going to sleep?"

"Oh, thank God," I said a little louder than the softer tones we had been using.

"Well, that didn't bruise my ego at all," Finn jested, pulling me slightly away.

"Sorry," I apologized with a laugh and then explained with honesty, "I'm just beat. I forgot what it's really like having these two nonstop."

"Sorry, baby. Maybe we should make a five-day rule."

"What? Of not sleeping together?" I asked, thinking that was a strange request.

"God, no!" It was his turn to laugh. "And, by the way, I am not doing that whole no sex the week before the vows thing again!" He referenced the week we originally got married —me and my stupid, idealistic pact.

"Okay," I agreed and got back to the question. "What five-day rule then?"

"Being apart. You and the kids need to come with me if it's five days or more."

"Sounds like a deal—a vow." I smiled.

CHAPTER SEVENTEEN

Our night out the next day was everything a typical outing looked like for us... unfortunately. We did go to see the new Ben Winthrop film. It had the right mix of romance and comedy so that both Finn and I enjoyed it. The theater was packed, probably due to the holiday season and people being off work or home from college. But the advantage was, I had purchased the tickets and assigned seats ahead of time, and we arrived after the lights were dimmed for previews. And, therefore, we went unscathed by Finn Murphy fans.

We weren't quite as lucky at the restaurant, though. Even with a corner booth reservation, Finn was noticed during our meal. Luckily, only a couple brazen fans approached us, though. And nobody brought up Arinn or Briar. Finn, as he usually was, but especially with our family being so scrutinized with the recent media attention, was considerate and kind but quick when speaking with them.

"Can I take a picture with you?" one red-head asked. At least she asked permission.

When Finn agreed to the request, she took out her phone and handed it to me. I guess I was supposed to be the photographer. I felt Finn's hand under the table touch above my knee where my pink dress met my leg. It was *his* way of asking. I stood and obliged. Really, one picture didn't take up any time, and it was good for public relations.

But when the woman looked at the photo and decided she needed to remove her foofy beige coat, because it made her look too big, and have me take a second shot, I was rethinking my original assessment. I personally thought she should take off the gaudy red lipstick, too. But I kept that to myself.

The second woman, a more petite, subdued blonde, came to our table just as we were finishing our meals. "I just wanted to tell you, I love your song *Dark and Dusty*."

"Thanks." Finn gave the obligatory nod and smile and turned back to me.

But the woman didn't leave. She stood to the side and a little behind Finn for another awkward minute or two. She was definitely one of the nervous-fan-types. Finally, she spoke again. "No. I really mean it. The words resonate with me."

Finn turned once again to her. "Thanks. I appreciate it. But if you don't mind, I'd really like to finish dinner with my wife."

"Oh. Oh, yeah. Sure. Merry Christmas." And she practically tripped over herself trying to leave.

Finn's hand laced on top of mine giving a squeeze. Before either of us could speak, the waiter came to clear our plates, and we decided to order some desserts to bring back to the house to share with Carter and Vanessa. While we waited and sipped the last of our wine, another person approached our table.

"Incoming" was all I needed to say to Finn who groaned in anticipation of another interruption.

But this time it was bro code. The man, maybe in his early to mid-forties, shook hands with Finn, and we were introduced. He was a lyric writer that Finn sometimes collaborated with. I knew the name. I just had never met him in person. They talked jargon for a while as I smiled and accepted the check and packed desserts.

And then, finally, we were out the door and in our Jeep to head home. Even though it was my car, Finn always took the manly role and drove. It was the way he was raised. Plus, there were so many times when he was driven around, that he appreciated being behind the wheel. It was odd that we were in the red Wrangler. I only drove it when I was alone, which was a rarity. But when Carter and Vanessa had pulled in, they had parked in front of the garage right in between our two other vehicles' spots. So, instead of having them move their car, we had taken the Jeep. I liked it, though, for a change. It somehow made me feel freer and younger.

"I love you," Finn said, once we had cleared the urban area.

"You don't have to apologize," I offered, knowing exactly what those three words at that particular time meant.

And he knew I knew. "It gets old sometimes. It's not just fans around here. It's industry, too. I just wanted to enjoy a night out with you."

"You mean you didn't?" I teased, making sure to look his direction.

He rested his right hand on my leg. "Always." He smiled.

As we drove a little further, I realized I was getting to know the area better. I knew I could make it back to the house without using a GPS or any other directions device. It didn't hurt that we hadn't ventured too far from our abode, though. But, still, Nashville was starting to legitimately feel like home.

"You know what I always wanted to do in a Jeep?" Finn's voice broke into my thoughts. If I couldn't tell by the seductive way he asked the question, I could tell by the slight smirk on his face.

"Me, too." I admitted and, for some reason, was a little bashful doing so.

"Yeah?" He questioned and then sounded pleased. "Hmmm."

As the traffic light turned from red to green, something suddenly flitted into my mind. "Wait. You didn't with Audrey?"

I could feel Finn's instant tension on the mention of his ex-fiancé. Although at different schools, they had been dating when Finn had his original Jeep back in college. This version was the one he bought me years later when I innocently told him how much I liked his car in school.

"Beauty, do you think I would have ever bought you this if I had any memories of Audrey with it…no matter how much you said you liked it? Audrey hated my car." He went on to further explain. "She refused to ride in it. If we went anywhere back then, it was in her car. Mine was too loud, junky, whatever." There was a tone of slight mockery in his voice, which I greatly appreciated at the moment. "I loved my Jeep. I hated getting rid of it," he said and, for the first time, I realized he might have done so because of her. "When you said how much you liked it, it just made me love you more."

"I have wanted to be with you in this car pretty much since you first gave me the keys." I let my hand rest on top of his—both of us now creating circles on my thigh.

"Really? Why didn't you ever say anything?"

It truly did take me a moment to figure that out. It was something very internal. I just always thought it wasn't a good idea. And, then, bam! I realized what it was.

"I guess because of your thing with back seats."

The hand motion stopped cold. He hated recalling his wicked past. But it was something he had been honest about with me from the beginning of our relationship. After Audrey had left him, and his star was beginning to rise, the undiagnosed PTSD and depression took over. It led to many liaisons with females who just wanted any part of him they could get. They had the privilege of giving an upcoming rock star a blow job. He never wanted that to be me.

"My thing with back seats," —he said slowly— "is about who and what happened in them…who I was back then. But I have never, ever made love with someone in the back seat of a car. And I would like to, but only to cherish and treasure my sexy, stunning, spectacular wife in our Jeep. The one with our memories…especially if my girl wants to."

"Then, Finn, you better find a place to park pretty damn soon." I brought some levity back to where it belonged.

"Yeah?" His query was accompanied by light laughter.

"Between getting ready to fulfill one of my fantasies, seeing Ben Winthrop on the big screen,—"

"Stop it." Finn's hand squeezed playfully on the mention of Ben's name.

I laughed and concluded with, "And loving you so damn much, I am so ready."

"Okay, okay. Just need some place less conspicuous. All we need is more press."

I know it wasn't my imagination that Finn was driving faster. Unfortunately, the most secluded place on our way home was the property on the ranch itself. But we knew if we accessed the front gate that leads to the driveway and property, Carter and Vanessa would know we were home. So, using what a Jeep was made for—rugged terrain—Finn pulled off on a kind of grassy deer path next to the property. He drove back a little way, turned off the ignition, kissed me very quickly, and exited the car. I joined him as he opened the back door and worked on folding down the rear seats. Still, there was very little room, and the carpeted back drew cause for concern.

I swear Finn may have been physically twitching when I said, "Can you take the top down?"

"What?"

221

"We'll be warm enough. Trust me."

Despite it being around forty degrees, he did take off the Jeep's roof just like I did my dress. I climbed into the back and asked Finn to shut the rear door. Once he did, he stripped himself of all of his clothing and joined me. It was then that he understood. I propped myself up against the spare tire area and held onto the cross bar above.

"Oh, my fucking God." He groaned. "Yeah?"

"Parking brake on?"

"Yeah." He laughed.

And then, God, did we have some fantastically hot sex. It wasn't the longest, and it wasn't the sweetest. But it was pretty damn good.

***

Now reclothed, we entered the house via the garage. Our arms were flitting around each other's lower backs as we stepped into the great room to spot Carter and Vanessa on the sofa. I actually giggled, thinking I could still feel Finn inside me.

"Jesus! You two should get a room." Carter shook his mop of straggly dark hair in mock exaggeration of our display of affection.

"Just did, man." Finn kissed the top of my head, and I lightly smacked him on his button-down covered chest.

"You go, girl!" Vanessa exclaimed, sitting up a little straighter after having been propped on her newly crowned fiancé's shoulder.

"I don't want to know," Carter partially grumbled.

"You're not gonna," my husband answered.

"How were my babies?" I asked, proud that I had only called once after the movie to see how Chance and Arinn were doing.

Finn began playing with my long hair, which had been rustled out of the clip somewhere during the Jeep performance. "*Her* babies...like I had nothing to do with it."

"They're his if they were awful," I added jokingly.

"Uh-huh," Finn murmured.

"They are so damn cute," Vanessa stated. "No problems. Chance was asking about you guys at bedtime, but he did okay. You must have quite the bedtime routine. The prayer list was endless!"

"Ha! Yeah," I agreed. "Should have maybe warned you about that."

"Dude was asking why I didn't bring the drums."

"No drums, Carter!" Finn exclaimed, and I laughed, especially because it would be due penance since Finn, to the chagrin of her parents, had gotten Kelsea drums when she was even younger than Chance. "If *he* gets drums, *you* don't," Finn continued with a false threat.

"Then your career tanks," his best friend/bandmate went with the shtick. "You know they're all only there to see me." When I started to laugh, Carter said, "Thanks a lot, Lara-Li. I thought we were friends."

"*I'm* there to see you, babe." Vanessa sounded like someone in love.

"Hey, listen..." Finn threw in the proverbial towel. "We brought some dessert, and there's champagne."

"We wanted to thank you guys for tonight and celebrate your engagement." I tagged on.

When Vanessa and Carter agreed, Finn got the cork popped and I set out dessert plates and forks. We made a couple toasts and took a few sips. And then we sat casually on the sofas and delved into the scrumptious almond torte and raspberry cheesecake.

"So, besides the obviously satisfying ending of your date night," Vanessa smirked in reference to the way Finn and I had entered our home. "How was the movie and dinner?"

I rubbed my foot on the spot right where Finn's foot met his pant leg and wondered if every couple felt that much in love. Refocusing on the question, I looked across to Vanessa and Carter and answered. "The movie was really good. You would love it, Vanessa."

"Did Ben get all steamy and naked?" Her eyes seemed to dance in anticipation of my answer, while the men in the room groaned.

"No." I laughed and patted Finn's leg.

"At least shirtless?" She still had hope.

I looked to Finn. "Did he? I don't remember." Honestly.

"That's my girl." Finn put his hand on mine and smiled. And then, I am quite sure, changed the subject on purpose. "Dinner was all right."

"Hmmm, I thought that place was supposed to be great. The dessert sure is." Carter, having not been able to decide on which to choose, had devoured both desserts and some of Vanessa's, who was already on the kick of losing weight for a wedding that was probably still a year out.

"Oh, yeah. The food was good. Don't you think, Lar?"

"My salmon salad was delicious, and the service was top notch, too."

"It's just I think we've been used to small town USA in suburban New York," Finn explained, while entwining his hand with mine. "Can't just have a simple night out around here without having two or three tourists or even locals approach you."

"It wasn't as bad as the mall thing, was it?" Vanessa's look recalled the horrible interaction we had with "bad momma."

In contrast, Finn's look and release of my hand portrayed his surprise. He scooted a smidge away from me so he could see more definitively in the eyes. "What? What about the mall? What happened at the mall?"

"Lara, I thought you said you were going to tell him." As Carter spoke, my teeth clenched inside my closed mouth and my eyes grew big at Vanessa.

With Finn now sporting a similar glare at me, I said, "I

was. I just didn't get a chance to yet."

"What happened at the mall, Lara?" Finn's jaw tightened along with his voice.

I took a breath as if trying to will my husband to also. "There was some lady—" I started.

Vanessa made an amendment. "She was no lady. She was a bitch. She went off on Lara about taking care of Arinn and then accused you," —she looked at Finn— "of sleeping with that hussy."

My eyes closed. All of it was true. I just would have presented it in a way where Finn's blood pressure didn't escalate dramatically in seconds...which I'm pretty sure it did.

"Lara," He stood up. "Crap, why didn't you tell me?"

I joined him. "I was. I was going to." I swung my eyes quickly at Vanessa and then back again to my husband. "Baby, believe me, everything is fine. I just tried to ignore her."

"And Vanessa should have, too." Carter, who rarely called his finance by her formal name, seemed to be as serious, if not as pissed, as Finn.

"She had nothing on us." Vanessa was rolling up her sleeves as if she was ready to rumble, which caused Carter to groan.

"What happened?" Finn reiterated.

"Vanessa scared her away." I thought it was going to come out more like a light-hearted joke, but it didn't. I couldn't pull it off because I knew Finn was too upset. "She told her off, and we left. That's it. We just got Chance and Arinn and got out of there."

"Did the kids hear?" he asked, in a mixture of what I determined as horrified and ashamed.

"It's all good, Finn." I tried to reassure with the truth.

"Damn it!" he yelled nonetheless.

There were a lot of slight eye movements between the four of us then. I closed mine in reaction to Finn's outburst. Carter's eyes, as dark as his hair, blinked before he shook his head at Vanessa for stirring things up in the first place. Vanessa rolled hers at Carter in a dismissive way. And Finn looked at me. But I had no idea how to interpret his regard.

It was Arinn needing pacified that actually did the same for the adults in the great room. We heard her whimpering cries from the monitor on the nearby mantel. They weren't bad, and normally we would have let them go, knowing she would most likely put herself back to sleep. But we were both more sensitive since the kidnapping.

I looked at Finn and took a step toward the staircase, but he stopped me and said, "I'll go." He paused. "I want to."

I did a partial, encouraging smile, understanding the many different reasons for his request to escape to our help our daughter. I spoke out loud the most important one. "You're a good dad."

His voice softened. "Learned from the best." Finn's dad was never far from his thoughts. He had even mentioned him in one of the New York interviews. It was almost like he kept saying his name out loud to prepare himself for the inevitable.

"Sorry," Vanessa stated after Finn was up the stairs and Carter was pouring himself another glass of champagne. "I didn't think it was that big of a deal."

"Between his dad and his career, not to mention what happened with…."

I couldn't talk about Arinn's abduction anymore. Not only did it bring us down, but it needed its place. And most people, besides a few ignorant women in malls, were accepting that.

"He's dealing with so much," I continued. "It's not fair."

"Nope. It's not. Neither of you should have to put up with any of that crap."

"But we do, and we will."

"And you'll love each other even more."

I gave my best friend a hug. I needed to hear that. Although I trusted our sturdy, forever love, I was wondering how much of Finn's aggravation was that he found out about the mall encounter from Vanessa and not me. Hearing, via the monitor, Finn coaxing our sweet little thing back to slumber land, I was hoping the other reason I believed Finn made the parenting request was holding up—he was trying to refocus and calm himself. I knew it wouldn't be long until I would find out if that was the case, or if I would have to face the proverbial music.

***

When Finn reentered the room, Carter made some excuse about the logs needing readjusting and drew Vanessa toward the floor-to-ceiling, stone fireplace. The couple was still within earshot, but I didn't mind. It was just nice that he was thoughtful enough to give us the illusion of a little privacy.

I walked over to my husband who was standing at the edge of the room. "I'm sorry," I offered. "I was going to tell you."

"Baby…" he said in a tone a lot calmer than the one he had left with. "I'm not upset with you." He held out his hand to me, which I readily took. "I'm mad at the situation. I'm mad that you were put in that position. I'm mad that someone had the audacity to do that, not only to you, but in front of our children."

"I know. It wasn't right," I agreed. "But it was just one nameless ass." I looked at Carter, recalling the word he had used for the woman initially. "Everyone else has been really kind. And if not, I can han—"

"Look, I know you can handle it. You've handled a lot of tougher shit than that." He knowingly peered at me, without needing or wanting to say any more in front of our guests. "But I just wish you didn't have to. I'm mad because I never want to see you hurt. And no matter what you say, that had to sting." He looked in my eyes as if daring me to disagree.

But I didn't. I couldn't. Of course, it hurt to hear horrible things, no matter their legitimacy, about someone you loved to the core. I squeezed his hand in agreement and appreciation. He double squeezed mine back, and we walked toward the sofa where Vanessa and Carter simultaneously met us.

"Vanessa?" he directed his comment to my best friend. "I'm sorry you had to be a part of that, too. Thanks for helping Lara."

"But walk away next time," Carter added.

"All right! All right!" Vanessa exclaimed and then pulled her long, wavy, brunette hair from her face and chipped a kiss on her fiancé's lips.

I smiled slightly at Vanessa's response. While none of us really wanted there to be a next time, there undoubtedly would be. That was, indeed, the beast of burden of the business. Hopefully, though, there wouldn't be a replay of the mall but something more like our dinner interruptions.

"You know, I think I want to check on the kids, too." I began to knot my hand in the ends of Finn's hair that harbored the back of his neck.

"You need some help?" Finn suggested and gathered his arms around my waist in a familiar close way. "I didn't see Chance."

"I think I might." And then with a lightheartedness added, "Vavoom."

By Finn's light laugh, I knew he instantly caught my reference. The word I had chosen was the one I had used the first time I had been on that great room sofa. It was the time that I first came down to Nashville, and I was nervous and buzzing and Finn had kissed me. It was one of those magical times neither of us would ever forget.

After Finn replicated that kiss, took my hand, and started us toward the staircase, I heard Vanessa ask Carter, "Do you think they're gonna come back down?"

"Not a chance," Carter chuckled his response.

Finn and I swirled back around. "Not a chance," Finn echoed, emphasizing the word "not." "Do me a favor? Can you make sure the fireplace is secure?"

"Sure thing," Carter responded.

"And enjoy the guest room," I said with a partial giggle but also legitimately since they were staying the night.

"Oh, geez...." Finn laughed and we started up the stairs.

After, indeed, checking on our offspring sleeping peacefully behind the doors highlighted with little yellow painted handprints, we entered our own bedroom. I let my hands drift down to Finn's hips and, snuggling our bodies so there was no space between us, I began to kiss him. "Thanks for tonight, Cowboy," I eventually said. "The movie, dinner..." I paused on purpose. "The Jeep." I smiled mischievously. "I'm sorry it didn't end so well."

"What's not right about this?" Lifting my hands so they looped around his neck, he started swaying us to the unheard music.

"You're right." I smiled. "Even if we are dancing."

CHAPTER EIGHTEEN

It was kind of a changing of the guards situation at my in-laws the next couple of days. Mr. Murphy's family had been in town over the weekend and were leaving a little after we arrived on the twenty-third of December. We rarely saw Finn's aunt and her husband, or his uncle and his family, being as they lived in California and Florida, respectively. And since the passing of Finn's grandfather over a year before, they were the only other Murphy family members left outside of us and Nola and her family. So, it was nice to be able to briefly catch up, especially knowing the next time we gathered would most likely be for a funeral.

Arinn, of course, was the positive center of attention. And being the happy girl she was, she didn't mind. Her grandparents, Nola, Will, and Kelsea doted on her every move and sound. It was the first time they had seen her since the abduction, and reliving it through their eyes made me appreciate her presence in our lives even more.

Finn's father definitely looked worse than when we had seen him just shy of two months before. He tried to downplay it by still giving great big bear hugs and shaking off any reference to illness. But he didn't have the stamina to keep going as he once had, and his eyes looked so incredibly weathered, sunken, and beat.

When Thalia, Finn's mom, tried to encourage him to slow down and rest, he jokingly said, "I'll rest when I'm dead."

The group grew quiet. My mother-in-law, who had been up to that point in good humor, burst into tears and left the room. I rubbed Finn's back, almost as concerned about him as his parents.

"Pop...." Finn lamented.

"I know." The elder, now deflated from his burst of energy, went after his wife.

Fortunately, after that, everything and everyone settled down a little bit. We all watched the original cartoon version of *The Grinch*, which I was very leery of since the whole Rudolph/Chance fail. But, thankfully, our son was obsessed with pretty little Cindy Lou Who.

Finn jokingly thought that might be worse than nightmares of an abominable snowman. "We're gonna have to look out for this one early on with the girls." When I laughed, he ruffled our son's hair and said to him, "There's plenty of time, Little Man. I just hope that when that time comes, you are as blessed to have someone as genuine, loving, and beautiful as Mommy." And he leaned over to kiss me.

We celebrated Christmas Eve traditional Murphy style. After being dolled up in dresses and shirts and ties for mass, we came back to my in-laws to put on our Mrs. Murphy-handmade pajamas. Arinn got her first official set, since the year before she was less than two months old. And my mother-in-law made a new set for Chance because he had grown out of his pair from the year before.

I was also able to keep another tradition going by the skin of my teeth. The morning after date night, I had an epiphany on what to get Finn for his practical Christmas gift. I was able to go out quickly that Sunday and buy and wrap it before taking off to Louisville.

I didn't think the whole thing through, though, because the first person to say something, after Finn unwrapped it on Christmas, was Kelsea. "Are you getting a dog?"

And on her coat tails was dog-lover Chance. "We getting a puppy?"

Finn, finally getting to see his own gift, opened his gaze at me and slowly shook his head. He lifted our son onto his lap to look at the box. There was, indeed, a golden retriever clearly on the cover. Yep, I had gotten it at the pet store. But I knew Finn would know exactly why I had bought it. And it had nothing to do with animals.

"No, bud, you know we can't get a dog because of Mommy's allergies." That was very true.

As Chance's little lip curled out in toddler sorrow, his cousin asked, "What's it for then, Aunt Lara?"

"For the back of the car," I said.

"Waterproof, quilted for comfort, perfect for leashes and toys." Finn was purposefully reading the description of the SUV cargo cover in a way that the adults understood but the kids were clueless. "Very practical, baby. We'll have to use it right away."

"Oh, brother." Will rolled his eyes.

"Will, that really is a good gift. With all of Kelsea's gear, we could—"

"Nola, how old and naive are you?" Will looked incredulously at his wife, who I guess I should have put in the kids category. "Your father is even over there laughing."

"I'll get you some watermelon." Mr. Murphy burst out in jest, knowing our inside joke about watermelon rinds being a natural aphrodisiac.

"Oh. Oh. Oh." Nola spit out slower each time. "When *is* the honeymoon going to end?" But she began to laugh with the rest of us.

"Ha!" Finn exclaimed and dramatically dipped me for a kiss. "We're ready to start our second."

***

That Saturday, the core Murphy clan drove the approximate three hours to reconvene on the place where Finn and I had first met and where exactly five years before had recited our wedding vows. We knew there could not be a better venue to renew our commitment and everlasting love than our alma mater in West Virginia. Just like our wedding, we had wanted to keep it intimate and personal. So, my mother, Lane, and Piper were the only other guests, which made my heart warm with the encapsulation of the entire family that I held dear.

The dusting of snow on the ground mimicked the white of my formal cocktail dress. I had chosen it because, although its length was a little shorter and top a little less revealing, it looked similar to my original wedding dress. Wearing a simple band in my hair, I had decided to leave my hair down in contrast to the updo I had worn at our wedding. I wanted things to be similar because our love was steadfast, but I also wanted to acknowledge that we had grown and changed.

Finn hadn't seen my dress, but he knew of my intentions. So, he decided to wear the same black suit he had worn at our wedding with a new white shirt. And, of course, Mr. Workout still fit in the suit. But instead of a white tie, he chose a striking blue one. Well, actually, the color choice was our son's. Finn had let Chance decide because they were both going to wear the same color. And, sticking true to his favorite hue, our son's color selection was blue.

Our other special love was in my arms as I walked up the short aisle. Arinn, decked out in a simple, satiny, cream colored dress, squirmed a little when she spotted her dad and brother standing next to one another in the front of the chapel. I carefully let her down, holding her hand as she wobbled next to me the final couple of steps.

"Ans!" she called out to her brother with pure delight

and then to the other man in her life, "Da Da!"

"So, so beautiful." Finn's eyes were first on me as he practically echoed the words he had said our first time around. He scooped up Arinn, giving her a nose kiss, and said, "You, too, little bug."

"Mommy, I like being in weddings!" Chance exclaimed, looking like a tiny mirror image of his dad.

"You do such a good job," I acknowledged.

"I no even have to carry a pillow this time." He referenced his job as ring bearer at Reese's wedding.

"Nope, you're Daddy's best man."

"I Daddy's *little* man." He thought he had corrected me.

"That, too, bud." Finn ruffled our son's hair as the intimate gathering of family chuckled.

"Can I sit down now?" Our preschooler recalled what we had told him earlier in the day.

"Yeah," Finn answered and gently brought Arinn back down to the floor. "Help your sister."

Chance took Arinn's hand and they walked to where Nola was waiting for them. She had left an empty seat for Chance in between her and Kelsea, who looked like a young model in her red dress. Arinn, however, didn't seem to like being restrained in Nola's lap. She looked like she wanted to take off back up the aisle to her parents. Will, sitting next to Nola, tried to give Arinn a funny face, but it didn't work.

When I was ready to start to go to her, Finn held my hand in a "give it a second" stance. I was still so protective of our little girl. I had been guilty of checking on our daughter multiple times at night when she first came back home. It was just like after Chance was first born. I had been one of those first-time moms that felt a need to go and make sure he was breathing in his crib. With Arinn, I had been much more relaxed until ...until.

Rationally, I knew she was all right—both at night in her room and in that chapel. But I also knew the fears would take a long time to subside …if ever. Finn recognized it in me, but, if he was honest, he struggled with the same fears and urges, too.

It was her brother who managed to settle Arinn from squirming out of Nola's arms. Chance reached over and smoothed her hair just like he had seen his father and I do so many times. If we did anything right, it was creating two magnificent kids who we not only loved but loved each other.

I glanced over at my own brother then. Lane, seated between our mom and Piper, did an acknowledging nod in my direction. In all reality, if it hadn't been for him, I would have never survived my childhood to have grown up to meet the wonderful man I was standing in front of.

Finn winked at Chance, lifted his cheeks in a smile to me, and held both of my hands as the ceremony officially began. Although the minister was now retired, Finn had managed to get the same man who had officiated our wedding to conduct the vow renewal. The gray-haired pastor started by acknowledging our wedding day and then pointed out the blessing of our family. But then, he got right to business. He knew we wanted something sentimental but short, not only because of the two children under the age of four, but because of Finn's father and his lack of energy at elongated events. And on top of Christmas and traveling, we knew the ceremony was already a strain for Mr. Murphy.

"Now…" said the minister. "I remember you two, and I understand that, once again, you have some of your own words in mind."

"I do," Finn agreed and then grinned. "Well, those words, too."

I laughed. It was nice being so relaxed. We had gone through so much. It almost seemed unnatural to not have my shoulders up to my ears and my neck not sore from stress.

"Can I go first?" I heard myself say. I wasn't sure why I

made the request, but I knew Finn wouldn't deny me.

"Yeah, baby. Sure."

"I remember standing here with you five years ago and hearing those vows— for better, for worse, in sickness and in health—and we had already been through so much of that. So, promising that didn't concern me in the least. We were one. We were together no matter what. And since then, we have been blessed with such incredible miracles—our babies being the best of all." I squeezed his hands and briefly looked over at Chance, who looked entranced by his parents, and then at Arinn, who Piper now had in the back of the room, joyfully waving to us. "But even through the challenges we have faced, there has never, ever," —I emphasized the last word for good measure— "been one time when our love has faltered. Not one ounce. I know with the utmost certainty in my heart, that my love for you is forever, and I feel it tenfold back from you. Not just in your words but your actions. You are my forever. I vowed back then, and I vow now to love you with all of my heart in good times and in bad, for better or worse, in sickness and in health, for richer or poorer, as long as we both shall live."

Finn raised our joined hands up to his lips and, after bringing them in unity back down again, said, "Well, talk about upstaging." On my shy but honest shrug, my husband continued. "God, Lar, think back to when we first met. No, it wasn't love at first sight. But you know what? It was better than that. You were my friend. And you are now, more than ever, my best friend…with benefits. Sorry." His apology was to the minister, who smiled knowingly. "Roxanne, my girl, Beauty, dancing star…" Finn announced his liturgy of nicknames for me. "As long as I have you…that you love me, I will never be lost. You make me whole. I love you so much. You are *my* forever."

His words, and the personalization of them, never ceased to amaze me. I knew they always came from his heart. I felt a need to hug him then…to feel that bond of two unbroken bodies and souls, to feel the comfort that we gave one another. He accepted and held onto my embrace for an extended moment before butterflying kisses on my lips.

"Sorry, I seem to not be able to wait my turn at this wedding thing." Finn spoke of kissing me way before the official "you may kiss your bride" directive five years before.

As we reclaimed each other's hands, the minister said, "If you didn't want to kiss her, young man, then I would be concerned."

"True." Finn's light laughter was echoed by members of our audience.

"I thought this Irish blessing was appropriate for you two," the minister continued. "May your life be filled with laughter…May your heart be filled with song…May your eyes be filled with beauty." I squeezed Finn's hands on the song line, and he immediately mouthed "they are" to me after the word "beauty," as we continued to hear the words that seemed to have been written just for us. "May joy be your companion through each and every day…May your soul always know to whom you belong."

***

Our "honeymoon" was spent at a resort near Pittsburgh. It was a purely practical decision. Although the romantic, private suite couldn't have been more perfect, especially since, aside from a few select phone calls, Finn was business and media-free. While our siblings flew back to their respective cities and Finn's parents drove back to Louisville, my mother was going to watch the kids for a couple days in my hometown just outside of Pittsburgh. That way, we were still near the kids in case, God forbid, anything should happen. And when we came back to pick them up, we would spend an extra day with my mom.

Since we hadn't spent any time with her during the Christmas holiday, she wanted to celebrate with us then.

That day was New Year's Day. While my mom busied herself cooking a traditional first-of the-calendar-year feast, Finn and I took the kids out in the yard to build a pretty significant snowman. Snow had fallen fairly consistently throughout those couple of days, leaving close to a foot of powdery, cold, white stuff on the ground. Thankfully, the roads were all clear, though. Chance, of course, was way more into the snowman creation than his younger sister, who would have gotten lost in the dense mass if even attempting a snow angel.

Besides a knitted blue polar bear hat, Arinn was completely decked out in multiple hues of pink winter attire. Bundled in my arms, we were watching Finn hoist Chance onto his shoulders so he could put the blue camouflage baseball cap—which had previously been on Finn's head— on top of the snowman. It accompanied the black scarf already around its neck, as well as the famous carrot nose.

It was then that I heard my name being called from behind my back. I knew the voice. It was one I had known for years. It was one that, unfortunately, brought back painful memories both from my distant and recent past. After Finn and I both turned to face Miller, I silently sought out my husband's eyes with my own, trying to convey my love and encouraging him to be patient.

With Chance still cradled on his shoulders, Finn extended his gloved hand toward my high school boyfriend. "Miller," he said plainly. And, if I'm not mistaken, it was the only time he had ever addressed him personally by name.

The shake exchange was quick due in part to our precocious son. "Miller," Chance giggled an echo of his dad's words. He dipped down, extending his preschool hand toward Miller as Finn held onto our son's legs tighter. Of course, Chance had no idea who Miller was, but it was a nice little ice-breaker from the awkward scene. As Miller clasped Chance's hand, our son proclaimed, "I just like Daddy."

Sporting a heavier beard than when we had seen him four or so years before, Miller looked a little older but in more of a content—not aged—kind of way. He took a natural step back and said, "I see some of your mom in there, too."

The instant tightening of my husband's defined jaw informed me that he did not appreciate that fact that Miller implied he still knew me. He didn't. And even though I was sure Miller's comment was innocent, I knew a peace brokering had to be made quickly.

"At least he has Finn's musical side and not mine," I joshed.

"Another Murphy on the radio?" Miller played along.

"Let's hope not."

I swung my gaze at Finn after he spoke those words. We had never talked about that— our kids going into the music business. It seemed very premature, and, of course, I only wanted Chance and Arinn to be happy like both their father and I had been in our jobs. But I found it interesting how adamantly and quickly my husband had replied in a negative fashion.

"It can be a hard road." Finn seemed to back up his statement with an explanation.

"But we do it well," I said as encouragement and reinforcement. Although I also knew there was a tremendous amount of truth in what Finn had said.

Finn's closed smile at me was loving but tight due to the invader still in our presence. He brought Chance down to the ground and gave him a task to complete so the adults could talk more openly. "Why don't you go find some sticks, Little Man. Frosty here needs some arms. And maybe some rocks if you can."

"On it!" Chance exclaimed and gave us a good laugh as he tried to balance his short, rubber booted feet and puffy, hooded black and orange Cincinnati Bengals snowsuit in the snow— a risky outfit in Steelers country.

"What are you doing here?" My question was direct as I adjusted Arinn a little more solidly on my hip.

"I heard you were in town," Miller replied, and I prayed that meant my mom mentioned it to one of her small-town friends who had a big mouth, rather than him hearing it through some kind of nosy media outlet. "I just thought I would stop by and say a quick hello. This your little girl?" He smiled and leaned just a smidge closer to Arinn. "She's beautiful."

"Thanks," I answered.

"I'm glad everything ended up okay after…after that scare last month." Listening to Miller struggle on the topic of her kidnapping, made me tug Arinn even closer. "Wow. Last time I saw you, you hadn't even had…." Miller started looking in the direction of the stick and rock gatherer.

"Chance." Finn completed the sentence, although I am pretty sure Miller was quite aware of our son's name. "Stay right there. Get those." Finn directed his comment to our little boy when he looked up after hearing his name.

"You're very lucky," Miller commented.

"We are." Finn's voice was full of strength and confidence. After a beat of silence, he went on to suggest, "Do you two want some time to talk?" Even though his tone sounded the same, I'm not sure he felt the same strength internally.

"No," I answered immediately. I would have put my hand out toward his, but holding a well-padded Arinn took precedence. "No," I said again. "You—"

"I can't stay." Miller gave the same answer but in a different fashion. "Hana is at home, and she still has all that queasiness stuff going on." I guess I didn't have my poker face on because Miller started to explain about his wife. "Oh, I guess I haven't talked to you in a while. We're pregnant."

I looked at Finn. That little tidbit of news should have

surely solidified to my husband that Miller was not interested in me. He hadn't been since high school. Finn's left eye did the smallest of twitches that I am sure only I, as his wife, would have picked up on. He wouldn't say or acknowledge anything, but he didn't have to. I knew Miller's declaration made him feel a twinge better.

"Congratulations," I offered to Miller on the impending birth of his first child.

"Thanks." A full smile spread along his face—one that I never, ever recalled on him. "Yeah, thanks. I love Hana's son like my own, but, I admit, this is special. It's a girl, by the way." He looked at Arinn again, and I could tell in just the way that his eyes lit up, that he was more than content. He was truly happy, and he was already a great father. "I'll see you around, then." Miller began his statement looking at me but finishing on Finn.

He would have to know that neither of us, in particularly my husband, wanted that proclamation to come true. He should have known that because I hadn't returned any texts in almost half of a year. But I did need to ask one more question before my ex walked away. It was the reason Miller and I had even started being in contact again years after high school. He was the bone marrow donor for the baby I had given away as a teenager. And even though the boy had no idea that his biological uncle was the one whose donation saved his life, the boy's family updated Miller every so often on his life… out of gratitude.

"Anything more about …about…." I verbally stumbled.

I never knew what to call that boy. Neither Miller nor I even knew his name. And while I may have been the birth mother, I could never claim him as my son. That was someone who was in his life more than an hour after birth. That was someone who knew his favorites, helped when he needed something, went to the practices, wiped his tears, loved him unconditionally. My son was Chance. That was someone else's son.

"Not for a while." Miller bailed me out of the awkwardness. "That's a good thing, though. I'm pretty sure that means everything is all right. Everyone," he emphasized the word and looked from me to Finn and back again. "Everyone seems to be good, huh?"

On my serene smile, Miller nodded his head positively and walked away. I put Arinn down on the sled so that her bottom could stay dry while she reached for the snow around her. I wanted to concentrate on Finn and all that we were and had.

"Thanks," was my one-word acknowledgement for the unexpected encounter with my ex and the way he handled it.

"I don't like him," he replied, as if I didn't already know.

"Thanks for not letting it show." I purposefully pasted on a smile. "… too much."

Finn cupped my gray sweats-covered butt and pulled me into him snugly. Even between our layers of sweatshirts and coats, I swear I could feel our hearts beating against one another's. Pulling my cream-colored knitted hat off to reveal my long, strawberry blonde locks, he first kissed me and then spun me around so he could wrap his arms around me from behind. It gave both of us the proximity of each other while allowing us to watch our two little loves happily playing in the winter wonderland.

"I love you." Finn dipped his words directly into my ear.

I think my body melted a little just like the snow that was ever so slowly doing the same in the sun's rays. I loved hearing him say that. I loved that he always said it and always, always meant it.

"Lara…." He murmured my name, wanting some type of response.

"Always you. Always. Forever."

***

Due to an early start, we were able to make it back to Nashville before sunset. Despite a relaxing, loving, carefree week plus away, I was glad to be getting back to the ranch…back to the place I was more and more every day calling home. I was anxious to establish some type of normalcy after such a chaotic month. The route that Finn took on the very last leg of our trip, though, did not assist in an easy transition back.

"Finn…" My voice quivered. "What are you doing? Why are we going this way?"

My instincts made me look to the backseat. Chance was totally engrossed in a movie and Arinn was thankfully asleep. But, logically, I knew even if she wasn't, it wouldn't matter. She really shouldn't have any cognitive recognition. I did, though. And Finn did. Why the hell would he torture us, especially because, without ever saying it, we had, until that moment, avoided it purposefully.

Finn rested his right hand on my left leg. "Trust, Lara," he spoke mantra style.

It wasn't that I didn't trust him. It was that my stomach didn't trust that it wouldn't unload itself or that my heart wouldn't pound straight out of my chest. I adverted my eyes to look solely at my husband and not out any of the car's seemingly suddenly massive windows. He grasped my hand and put it on his thigh. In just a couple minutes, though, he put both hands back on the steering wheel and turned the car before putting it in park. It had been horrifying enough with the thought of driving past, but stopping? And I knew, without looking, that was exactly where we were.

"Go!" I seethed through my teeth. Hate is a strong word, but at that moment, I did not like my husband very much.

His reaction was polar opposite to mine. He first brought his soft hand up to my cheek and then pecked three gentle kisses on my lips. I didn't move. He looked at me for a second and then after one final kiss, he wrapped his arm around me, drew our cheeks together, and slowly turned me in the direction of my passenger window.

Despite resistance, I was forced to look. "It's…it's gone," I stammered. "Where? What?" All of the five Ws circled my brain.

It was true. The weathered red farmhouse was no longer. There wasn't even a brick left of the house of horrors. There was just a field of overgrown grass and a decrepit cement drive leading to a dusty, low mound of dirt. I glanced back again at our beautiful daughter. She was safe. She was happy. She had survived being in there with that crazy woman. And, because of her age, she wouldn't recall it. But the physical representation had been ever so close to our home. And now it wasn't. It was as if it disappeared. As if it was just a bad memory. But how?

Finn separated from me so that we could look each other in the eyes. "I bought it and had it demolished. They tore it down."

I felt my bottom lip actually drop from the top one. "You did?" I finally managed.

He nodded his head positively. After a moment of silence, which I greatly appreciated, he said, "We can do with the property whatever you want." When I didn't speak, still trying to absorb this new reality, Finn continued. "We can just plant wildflowers, or make it a park, or sell it so someone can build their own home…" He touched my cheek again. "Or, if you're sick of me having the guys over, I can build a big barn and that's where we'll jam."

I managed a smile at that one. There was plenty of property surrounding our house if Finn ever wanted to do that. We didn't need one down the road.

"A park?" I managed, knowing his detest of communal playground areas.

"Okay, maybe not. But, baby, whatever you want. I'd

contract a bakery and coffee shop to make you happy, but it's not a commercial lot."

"Thanks." I smiled at Finn's thoughtfulness—the double-edged sword of the ranch's location was our privacy versus no coffee or any shop, for that matter, nearby. "But I don't need to get fat." I touched his hand. And before he could counter his denial, I added, "And I am happy." Then, with a cleansing finality, I said, "It's really gone."

"It is," he confirmed. "Good, right?"

"Oh, God, Finn, yeah. More than." I let out a breath I didn't know I had been holding in. "We can decide what to do with it later, right?"

"For sure. No rush. I just wanted you to know...to see."

"Thanks. Yeah."

"Where we at?" Chance's voice broke into our conversation.

"Almost home, bud. Almost home." Finn put one hand on the gear shift and the other on the steering wheel, and we started back to where we belonged.

CHAPTER NINETEEN

Champagne and the occasional juice box were the liquid celebrations for Carter and Vanessa's engagement party, which we hosted at the ranch just a couple weeks later. Ham, assorted breads and spreads, cheese and fruit platters, casseroles, and Vanessa's favorite chocolate almond cheesecake were set out buffet style. Finn flew Vanessa and her immediate family in for the weekend, and it was the first time that both the future bride's and groom's family were to meet. It was an interesting social experiment that turned out pretty well. But, then again, I wasn't the one in the center of it. I was the hostess who, even better, had everything catered.

Most of the guests left a little after nine, including Vanessa, who took her parents to the hotel. But the band and Hawk relocated to the family room to pick at some guitar strings and open an additional bottle of beer or two. Carter, who had done a good job with the stress of future in-laws, needed to chill and kill some time before meeting Vanessa back at his place.

By that time, Chance was way too confident in front of his daddy's best friends and was acting more like a human tornado than a civilized little boy. And Arinn was getting fussy because it was most definitely past her bedtime. So, I took the kids up to Arinn's nursery to change them into their pajamas and read a *Berenstain Bears* book. With Arinn in my lap sucking on her little finger—I suspected a new tooth was on its way—and Chance snuggled very sleepily against my side, I was nearly at the end of the Brother Bear, Sister Bear tale when I heard the pounding sound of running feet coming up the stairs.

Placing the book down and standing up with Arinn, I immediately got up to discover Hawk, the obvious foot pounder, in the doorway. "What?" I asked, instantly alerted.

Before he could answer, I heard Finn. The direction of his voice told me he was still in the family room. The volume in which he was speaking said he was in definite distress. "I need Lara! Get Lara."

"What? What's going on?" My panic grew not only hearing Finn's words but because of the look on the normally calm man with closely cropped, dark copper hair and similar-hued beard.

"I don't know. We were just shooting the shit, and he got a phone call. He went berserk. It's just Carter down there with him now. Everyone else left. He wants you." The last part of Hawk's dialogue stated the obvious.

"Okay." I jittered a minute, knowing Arinn was still in my arms and Chance was looking up at me doe-eyed, obviously sensing the uncertainty, yet again, in the house. I was a little uneasy dragging my little ones into the unknown.

"Here." Problem solving, Hawk stretched his bodyguard-like arms out to Arinn. "Give me the baby. You go. I've got them."

"Mommy?" Chance cried in his near sleep state.

"Chance stay with Hawk. Let me see what Daddy needs. Everything is all right." I tried to reassure my sensitive child, who would normally adhere to Hawk like peanut butter on bread. "Chance, all right?" I didn't give him an opportunity to reply but instead reiterated my question in a statement form. "It's okay," I said. Although, by the sound of my husband's voice, I knew it was probably far from it. Having much more faith in Hawk's ability to entertain my children than my ability to resolve what I was going to walk into with Finn, I left the room and scurried down the stairs.

Finding Carter exiting the family room, I said, "Do you know anything?"

"No."

"Okay. I got him. You can go. Sorry, Carter. Sorry if this ruined your day," I rattled off.

"If I'm going to see Nessa, nothing will ruin my day."

I couldn't help but briefly smile at his romantic side. He was far from the playboy I originally met years before. I was so happy that he figured out what he wanted and matured in time for both my best friend's sake and his.

"Let me know if you need anything, Lara-Li," he said, putting on his coat.

"Thanks, Carter."

"Baby?" I heard Finn, now a little more subdued, calling me from just inside the family room.

As Carter left, I walked into the room to find Finn pacing with his hands embedded in his hair behind his head—a startling contrast to the relaxed, jovial man I had left just moments before. "Finn? God, what's wrong?" My stomach was jolting all around in anticipation of the news he was about to bestow on me. I was scared of the possibilities but was pretty assured it would not have to do with Briar, as there had been no more media follow up since the new year, thank goodness. But, then again, when I found out, I wished it had been about her.

His glassy eyes met mine and, with his one word, I knew mine were going to be as equally wet. "Pop."

"Oh." My ability to converse was almost as erratic as his. "Oh...God." I took the final steps to be directly in front of him and reached for his hands. I knew I had to be the strong one, even though I felt like falling apart. "Sit down. Sit down with me, please." When he didn't react, I tried again. "Finn? I need you to talk to me. I need you to tell me what happened…whatever happened." I didn't want the worst confirmed, but I still needed to know. "Who was on the phone?"

"Mom. He's … he's bad. She wants us there. He wants to stay at home to…."

I closed my eyes. My father-in-law was in the final stage of life, and he wanted death to come in the comforts of a place he was familiar with and surrounded by those he loved. When the inevitable waterfalls started to roll down my cheeks, I dropped my husband's hands in an attempt to wipe them away. Finn, never good at seeing me cry, put aside his own pain and used the pads of his thumbs to help. Empowered by his love, I wrapped my arms around his lean torso, feeling a sure tightness that seemed to relax just a bit on my embrace.

"I love you," I said without the slightest notion of letting go. "We're going to be there. We'll be there. You'll be with him. I'll be with you. I love you," I reiterated the words that could never be repeated enough.

Hawk was a huge help, packing some stuff for the kids as they slept, while I stayed with Finn as we, zombie-like, packed our own bag for a trip neither of us could ever be prepared to take. But it was also one that we were blessed to be given the opportunity to do. So many times there is not that chance to say "goodbye." I hadn't had that with my father. And even though ours had been a tumultuous relationship, closure would have helped. Finn and the Murphy clan certainly had not had that with Wyatt. The sudden, shocking loss of that seven-year-old had ramifications on their psyches forever. We had known Mr. Murphy was terminal, and it shouldn't have felt like a cold bucket of ice was thrown on our warm bodies, but it did. I was just glad that we could all be there together with him, with each other, to ease us all through the transition and loss.

Finn relented letting me drive to Louisville that night. I knew he was too emotional, and I wasn't sure how much drinking had been going on prior to the phone call. Although I am sure there's nothing more sobering than a call like that. Hawk even offered to drive us all there, which was sweet but unnecessary. The burly man, with hazel eyes, was a sturdy, strong rock and a true member of our family—one who I hoped would find happiness of his own someday, too.

Of course, we arrived in the middle of the night. There wasn't much more for us to do but tuck our already slumbering offspring into bed, check on a similar sleeping grandfather, and hug and support Mrs. Murphy. Knowing it was important to be well rested and strong for Mr. Murphy in the morning, I tried to encourage Finn to sleep, too. He made a valid attempt, but I know he didn't sleep well because I didn't sleep well, either.

Nola, Will, and Kelsea's flight arrived the next day before noon. Their only other option had been to drive all night, and a twelve-hour drive wouldn't be good for anyone. Plus, they wouldn't have arrived that much earlier, anyway.

In addition to hanging on for all of us to arrive, Zak Murphy made it through one more Cincinnati Bengals game that afternoon. Although propped up with pillows and dozing on and off, Finn's father watched the game to the nail-biting, playoff Sunday end. He even managed to enjoy a few bites of the skyline chili that made Cincinnati famous.

Knowing that Finn had to concentrate on his family, I dealt with as much of his business stuff as I could. Or, I at least talked to Reese, Hawk, and his assistant, Shelly, to see if they could put anything pressing on a wait-and-see list. Luckily, that time of the year was traditionally the leanest in Finn's schedule. In addition, the hospice doctor that stopped by was kind but very honest. He said Finn wouldn't need to do a lot of rescheduling. Mr. Murphy truly did not have much time.

Kelsea helped keep Chance and Arinn entertained. She knew the truth about her grandfather, and she talked openly about it. But neither of our kids understood. Chance did notice that Pop-Pop wasn't as active playing with him as he usually was, but our son had been more fixated on how he had gotten to the Louisville abode. Chance thought it was magic, since he had fallen asleep in our house and woke up in Pop-Pop and Nana's house.

In Finn's childhood room that night, I was curled on my side, eyes closed, trying to lose myself in some classical instrumental tunes floating through my earbuds. Seconds after I felt the bed sag behind me, my husband's undeniably strong hands lifted my gray ribbed tank up to my arm pits and he started massaging my back. As I pulled out the buds and stretched out on my stomach, Finn's muscular frame carefully found its position on the back of my legs to continue kneading, rubbing, and manipulating my back with his hands. I laid there silently, letting him do his thing because I knew he needed to work out the tension…both mine and his.

"Mmmm, you do have magic hands, Finn Murphy," I cooed, truly appreciating the release of my overstressed muscles. "Even if your football season is over," I tacked on in a teasing way.

"It was a gallant fight to the bitter end." Finn spoke of Cincy's loss in the last twenty-five seconds, but I couldn't help but wonder if he was referencing his father's battle, too.

"I'll let you have a complimentary chocolate feast some other time." I tried again to keep things as light as they could be.

"Yeah," he said, but I could hear the melancholy in his voice. "Another time." He planted his lips on my bare back for an extended moment until I eventually turned around, forcing him to prop up on his arm beside me.

"How you doing?" I asked, caressing his jawline.

"I'm all right. Pop fell asleep. I was just talking with Mom. I wish I could spare her this pain…and the kids. They are so innocent… sleeping there so peacefully," he said, confirming that he had checked on them in the room next to ours just like I knew he would. "Kelsea, too, you know. She's not as old and tough as she wants to be."

"Neither are any of us—the tough part that is."

"I know, baby. I wish I could shield all of us from the heartbreak in this world."

"Finn? You know your heart wouldn't break if you didn't feel love. And that is what makes it worth it."

He did a closed-eyes, closed-mouth, elongated exhale. Upon opening them both he said, "God knows I love you."

After I kissed him my "ditto," he stretched out and let me spoon into his front like we had done so many times in our lives. I felt his lips first on the back of my head and then on my shoulder before resting his head alongside mine. It was the rhythmic moving of Finn's chest indicating that he was sleeping that put me to ease and helped me do the same.

***

The following day, Monday, Zak Murphy didn't even make it out of bed. If his pale complexion gave a visual of how weak he was, his breathing was the auditory proof. He sounded as if he was snoring, but he wasn't. He was awake and struggling.

Finn and I sat in the chairs already stationed at his bedside where rotating family members had been coming in to sit and talk with him all morning. We asked him if he needed anything. But it was merely a way for us to feel useful because we both knew there wasn't anything Zak could possibly need besides a clean, healthy body.

"What about water or ice?" I asked on his denial. "I'll

even go chip at some of those icicles hanging from the porch for you." I mentioned the rare snowy blast that had hit Louisville right before we arrived. "But just for you. This one," —I teasingly punched Finn in the arm— "drives me crazy when he chews on ice. It's like fingernails on the chalkboard." I looked at a head-shaking Finn.

"Lara, Gal…" Mr. Murphy partially laughed/partially coughed. "You were the best addition to this family since I married my wife. You knocked that Will character right off his pedestal." I was glad to hear he was going to keep his humor intact right to the end.

"How about the best female addition?" I offered, knowing the love the Murphys had for both Will and I.

"True enough, true enough," he agreed. "Both of my kids really are blessed."

"That's for sure." Finn reached for my hand, the one adorning the baobab bracelet Mr. Murphy had given me, and I could feel not only the love but the need for me to be touching him. He was putting on a brave front for his father, but the pain he was holding in wasn't so internal when our bodies were bound.

"Finn and Nola have beautiful role models for love and family." I gave my husband a reassuring squeeze and soft smile.

"Pop—"

Finn was cut off by his elder. "You keep treating this little lady right, understand?"

"I plan on it." Finn's response was immediate and, for sure, one hundred percent honest, but I knew by the rubbing of my hand that it was also a little guilt ridden. He was surely recalling the conversation I had overheard him have with his father in November—about not deserving me.

"He more than lets me know how much he loves me," I spoke to my father-in-law, but it was equally meant for my husband. "If not," —I turned on the sass meter again— "I'll make sure he knows about it." I grinned this time.

"Oh, I'm sure you will." Mr. Murphy got and appreciated my humor, too.

But, really, none of the situation was truly funny. And I knew I had to take the opportunity, while I still had it, to speak from my heart and tell this wonderful, pillar of a man how I felt about him. That's why we were there. That was the blessing of having that time.

"I love you," I started and reached across the bed to give him a hug. I made sure not to squeeze too tight or too long because his frail body could not take that. But I did make sure that he could feel the honesty in my touch. "You can't possibly understand what you mean to me," I continued while sitting back and now holding his hand. "You are my father. Thank you for all of your love and compassion. Thank you for raising this amazing man." I grasped my other hand with Finn's. "And thank you for accepting me as one of your own. I am so lucky."

"You are an astounding, strong woman, Lara Murphy." Although darkened and bloodshot, his eyes were clearly fixed on me and the bracelet that symbolized strength. "You know, I was just telling Thalia that I think God got me through my first bought with this nasty disease— granted me the remission...reprieve, whatever you want to call it— just so I could see my son truly happy." He looked from Finn to me again. "Otherwise, I would have never met you or seen my beautiful grandbabies born. I just wish I had more time to get to know them."

Ah, hell...so much for being strong. So much for supporting Finn. I just let loose and sobbed.

"Hey, hey, none of that." Mr. Murphy did his talking/coughing act again as he tried to readjust in his bed. "Don't let me down. Y'all promised me a good old-fashioned Irish wake."

Finn pulled me into his chest and kissed my forehead. "You'll get it, Pop," he reassured. "And we can give you more time with those grandkids," Finn was managing to talk while I gathered my emotions back in check. "It sounds like they are tearing apart the parlor right now. I can get them in here."

"Can't be as bad as you and Nola were," Mr. Murphy joshed, and I couldn't help but think that a preschool Nola and a toddler Finn would have been similar to our precious two.

"It was always her fault." Finn grinned, teasing his sister when she wasn't even there to defend herself.

"Oh, boy," I tsked my husband before saying, "I should go check on Chance and Arinn."

"You don't have to," Finn started. "They have plenty of people watching them."

It wasn't my fear of the kids being hurt or scared, though. I knew they were safe and loved with their grandmother, aunt, uncle, and cousin. I just knew I needed to be unselfish and give Finn and his father some one-on-one time. "Spend time with your dad." I squeezed Finn's hand and stood up before bending down to kiss Zak on the cheek.

"Love ya, Gal." My father-in-law managed a wink— a memory I was determined to keep close and dear.

***

While Will was in the adjacent foyer talking on the phone with someone at his Wall Street job, I sat on the sofa with the Murphy siblings as they reminisced about their childhood. I had both of my legs intertwined with Finn's so that I could sit snug against him. I was doing it to bring him comfort, but, admittedly, it was for me, too. I liked being warmed by his touch more than the false heat of the old Victorian home's radiator. And I liked feeling the steady, solid beat of his heart, knowing that there was so much love inside.

As Finn and Nola teased about after school snacks and ugly fashion sense growing up, I told Arinn once again to back up from the television screen. She kept toddling her way in front of it as her brother and cousin sat on the floor trying to watch an animated cartoon. Kelsea scooted Arinn back and tried to sit her on her lap.

"Thanks, Kels," I said, just as my mother-in-law entered the room, looking worn from the days, weeks, etc. of dealing with her sickly husband.

"Hey, Mom," Nola spoke. "Do you want some sweet tea? We were just talking about the time when we took that bus trip, and we left the car in that shady parking lot, and then the bus broke down and Pop was the one helping the driver. We were what... not even in middle school, right? Do you remember tha—"

"Mom?" Finn, cutting his sister's recollection off, was suddenly on his feet, taking me with him.

It was then that I looked at my mother-in-law more closely. Her normally curled hair looked limp and her shoulders deflated. And, yes, she was tired. But she had a mix of resolve and strain on her face as she looked at her two adult children. It was something that her son had picked up on almost immediately. It was a subtle change in demeanor, but I knew then that she was being a mom. She didn't want to hurt her children, but she needed to speak the truth.

"He loved you all so much."

We all noticed the choice of past tense in Thalia Murphy's words. There could be no denying what Finn had sensed upon her entrance. I heard Will abruptly hang up his phone as he walked to his wife's side.

"He...?" Nola couldn't get any more out. She started to cry as Will brought her to him.

"Mom?" Finn repeated in a way that it sounded like he was hanging on to the slightest of denial.

Just like our legs had been moments before, I took my arm and twisted it around Finn's so that we were bound tightly and securely together. I arched my neck so that I could find his eyes. Seeming a little more gray than usual, he nodded ever so slightly at me. I nodded back, willing all of our combined strength to get us through.

Nola was the one who went to her mother. "I didn't think..." Finn's sister struggled to find words in her sudden grief. "I mean, I thought.... Really?"

Understanding exactly what was transpiring without being told directly, Kelsea appeared to be the grown up she was trying to emulate. She got off the floor and went to Will's side as Nola held onto a strong-as-could-be-expected Mrs. Murphy.

"He went peacefully." The new widow restarted her tale now that we all had a moment to digest. "It was what he wanted. Not to struggle...not to have a fuss..."

"...with you by his side," I concluded, imagining that was, indeed, what my father-in-law, so in love with his wife, would have wanted.

"Yes," she admitted, although I doubted she would have said it out loud. She was much too modest of a matriarch.

Hearing those words, Finn snuggled me in tighter, and I was relieved that he didn't feel as strained as I anticipated. Maybe there was still some shock. Maybe he was being strong for all of us. Maybe he realized, as I did, that his dad was no longer in pain.

"I wish—" Nola started.

"Nol...." Finn said his sister's name with a sad sigh but nothing more.

"He didn't want any of you to have to see that." My mother-in-law looked from Finn to Nola. "He didn't want you to beg him to stay because he would have tried. And we know that wouldn't have done any good. He was at peace. He knew you were all here. We talked about how special it was to talk with all of you today." She looked at each of us purposefully, even Chance, who was now watching his grandmother, and Arinn who had wobbled over to my ankles. Picking her up so that she was between her father and I, I kissed her soft hair and once again listened to my mother-in-law talk about the ending of a life. "We were talking about the song we danced to at our wedding, and then he said it was almost as beautiful as the sound he was hearing right then. When I asked him what he was talking about, he said he could hear all of you laughing and what a good job we did...so good. He told me he loved me and to be happy. And then he said...."

"What mom?" Finn spoke in a hushed tone, respectful of the story his mother was unfolding.

She smiled ever so slightly but peacefully and said, "He said he was just waiting to see Wyatt."

Silence filled that parlor. I curved into Finn a little more. Nola looked at Will who closed his eyes in a serene way on the mention of their deceased son's name. It was sad. But, yet, the image of grandfather and grandson reunited was something I think we all found a little bit of peace in.

After the deserved beat of remembrance, Mrs. Murphy concluded with, "And then he fell asleep. I...I laid there beside him, and then I realized I didn't hear that rough breathing anymore."

***

After all the immediate concerns were taken care of and the important people were notified, it was late. Finn was checking on his hopefully-asleep mom, as Will, Nola, and I sat in a reflective state in the Murphy parlor. He came down the steps, did a quick glance at us, and proceeded straight into the kitchen, where I heard the tell-tale signs of bourbon being poured onto a few cubes. A weary and tired Nola looked over at me and I at her. Before either of us could speak, though, we heard the back door open and close. Finn had escaped to the small, enclosed, private backyard.

"I got him," I spoke softly, while standing up.

Already finishing his drink by the time I took the few

steps outside, he had his back turned, poured another, and downed it just as quickly. I put my palm up to the back of his gray sweater and started a soothing circular motion. It had been the same thing I had done for him when Wyatt passed away years before.

"Maybe you should slow down." I observed his hand once again on the bottle's neck.

He flinched my hand away and turned toward me. "I don't need a police officer."

"I.... Remember, don't drink because you're scared or mad or—" I started reciting the wise words he had previously spoken to me.

"And I don't need to be psychoanalyzed."

"I'm not." I tried to be calm because I knew how much he was hurting. "Finn, I thought I was just being your wife... your girl who loves you."

"I don't need—"

"You're gonna push me away, now?" I practically cried out.

He had done it in the past when Wyatt had died. But that was many years and tears before. We had grown so much stronger and secure as a couple...as one heart. Regardless, I got no response from him.

I couldn't take that. I knew his pain, and I knew where the words, and even the silence that followed, were coming from. But I couldn't take it. Because, as strong as I had to be for my husband, I was hurting, too. And his rejection, on top of my sadness, would break me...or us.

So, I said, very simply and solidly, while resisting adding 'not to sound like a cop,' "Do me at least this much and please don't drive."

It was my past of picking up my dad at the local jail or wondering why his car was parked on the grass instead of the driveway that made me say that. It was my past of my father being killed because of a drunken accident that made me fear that Finn, in his current state, would make the same mistake, too. But the fact was, Finn had never even gotten close to drinking and driving. Besides a controllable bourbon or beer here or there, he didn't even normally drink that much.

I turned and walked back into the kitchen. I didn't want Finn to see me upset. And I couldn't go immediately back into the parlor because I didn't want Nola or Will to see me upset, either. Instead, I just leaned against the counter and breathed in as many strong inhales and exhales as it took before I could face my in-laws.

When I eventually did make my way back into the parlor, I simply said, "I have his keys. If you could, just make sure...." My voice dipped.

Due to his own personal experience and demons with drowning in alcohol, Will took the lead. "He won't go anywhere."

I hugged both of them and went upstairs to the room Finn and I were sharing. As I dressed into my pajamas, my thoughts were entirely on my husband. I knew by the position of our back room, he was practically standing two stories beneath me. I could almost feel him. I ached for him but knew I couldn't help. I wondered if he was thinking of me just a little bit, too.

It was only a matter of minutes, maybe not even, after I had gotten in the bed and turned off the light that Finn entered the room. I didn't see him because my back was turned, but I knew it was him. It was years of knowing his step, his scent, his breath, his presence.

It was a second or two before he climbed into the bed next to me. I felt his arms wrap my body from behind, and I welcomed it. I wasn't mad. I understood his pain. I was more relieved that not only had he found his way back to me...to us, but he had done it rather quickly. And by the feel of his bare chest against my back, I knew he had taken off his sweater and was there to stay.

"You *are* my girl." He was obviously referring to the words I had spoken in that backyard. "And I love you, too, so much. I'm sorry."

I flipped my body so I could see him even in the darkness. "You don't need to be."

"Yes, I do. Pop would have had my hide if he saw how I treated you out there. I didn't mean it, Lar. I'm just so sad."

"I know. It's okay. I swear. I should know by now when to leave you be. I should know that I can't help you." It made me sad, but it was true.

"But you do. You are. You do. Just being here. Because of you, I can get through this. It may not be pretty, but I will. I promise."

"That's all right. You always tell me I'm the pretty one, anyway." I threw in a little sass, wanting him not to have to worry about my feelings on top of everything else.

"Beauty... God..." He dipped his head onto my chest. "Pop was right, you are the best thing that ever happened to me."

"And vice versa." I kissed his bourbon-coated mouth and curled back into his arms.

CHAPTER TWENTY

Finn was much better that next day as both sides of his family began to arrive in Louisville. I think he needed that momentary release the night before, when the reality of death had set in. And, good or bad, he knew he could do it in front of me—that despite the unkind words and alcohol intake, I would understand.

The wake was being held in the Murphy's soaring, old Louisville home. It was just going to be family that evening, and the next day was for anyone else. The funeral director had set up the casket in the living room/parlor area, and neighbors had brought over additional chairs, crockpots, and tea services to help. Just like when Wyatt passed, there was no obituary of any kind because of Finn's connection. The family didn't want to attract people who would only come because of a chance to glimpse celebrity. I know it bothered Finn because he wanted to honor his father as much as he could. But he also understood that, in a way, keeping things private was doing just that. When everything was done, Reese would put out a release.

When the casket was first placed in the living room and before the first guests were set to arrive, Finn and I sat down with our firstborn. Chance was the one we were most concerned about. Because of his tenuous age—just days from turning four—we knew this would be the most confusing for him. Arinn was too young, and Kelsea, at almost ten, unfortunately, completely got it. But for Chance, one moment he had been running into Pop-Pop's room to tell him some earth-shattering preschooler fact and the next moment he was gone. He wasn't even in the house. When he asked the "Where's Pop-Pop?" and "Did he go on the road?" questions, we had been very honest about him dying and making sure to say that, no, he did not go on the road because we wanted Chance to understand that if Finn went on the road he was coming back and Pop-Pop was not.

"Chance?" I nudged when it was just the three of us and our son had his first look at Finn's closed eyed, closed lip father decked out in a full suit inside the casket.

"You say Pop-Pop dead." Chance's little eyes furrowed as if his parents had lied to him. "He sleeping."

"Oh, bud." Finn, who had been standing and holding Chance by the legs so he could see, brought him down to the kneeling stand. "He's not asleep. I know you may think it looks that way," Finn glanced over at me slightly shaking his head. "But he's not."

"It's just his body, Chance." I tried to explain while flanking the other side of our innocent child. "He's in heaven now, remember?" Even though not terribly religious, I thoroughly believed that someone as good and loving as Zak Murphy had a place like heaven to go to.

"He with angels," our son repeated something we had told him earlier.

"Yeah," Finn answered.

When Chance peered into the casket again, as if he needed that second look to believe us, I tried again. "Chance?"

He turned to us and said a little more decisively, "Pop-Pop's dead."

"Yeah. I know." My voice softened with the truth. "Do you want to talk about it? Are you a little scared seeing him in there?" I could only imagine what visions of non-breathing bodies intermixed with an unknown world of cherubs and clouds must be doing to a young, impressionable brain.

"No," he said without hesitation. But that was another way he was like his father. He tried to be brave...until he couldn't.

Finn, possibly recognizing that, piggy-backed on my words, "Tell us what you're feeling then, Little Man."

"Sad." He said the appropriate word, but I think he might have said it because he understood what that emotion was and could clearly see that was what all of the grown-ups were feeling in the house. But, then again, maybe not because he continued with an explanation of why he was sorrowful. "I wish Pop-Pop could get up and play with me. We played the trains."

Finn did one of those halfhearted smiles, which I knew held a mix of kind remembrances and regrets of no more to-bes. "I know," he said. "I wish I could get another bear hug from him."

"I do that for you."

Our sweet little boy had no idea what his offer, so honest and giving, meant to his father. But I did. I could see it by the loving way they embraced and the water-filled eyes of my husband as he looked at me from behind our son's back. It was a father-son bond that would be passed on.

***

And then an overabundance of family, friends, neighbors, and some of Finn's closest posse members came to the celebration of life. It was a lot like a traditional funeral parlor setting, with people shaking hands, giving hugs, saying their condolences, and praying over the casket of my father-in-law. But there were also sandwiches, biscuits, stew, cake, tea, and some alcohol—Mr. Murphy's favorite bourbon. And we all did make a good effort to have more laughter than tears.

Although everyone had tried to make a point of requesting no flowers—instead suggesting donations to St. Jude's research—there were floral deliveries made throughout those couple of days. While keeping the cards, we had the flowers immediately rerouted to the local hospital to cheer up patients. So, when Finn walked up to me with a bouquet mixture of all-white flowers, I looked at him perplexed. He was well aware of my allergy to something so fragrant.

"Why are you—?" I started.

"Your turn," he said.

"My turn for what?" I asked, and he handed me the attached card as an explanation.

I can't tell you how sorry I was to hear about your dad. When Gabrielle called me, I was shocked and saddened. Please pass on my condolences to your mom and sister. – Audrey

I looked up. He was waiting. Finn was waiting for my reaction to his ex-fiancé's gesture. He had reacted civilly to Miller, and now it was "my turn." I bit my tongue on the comment I wanted to say—the flowers were, of course, especially fragrant…and gaudy…and actually looked more like a wedding bouquet than a funeral display.

"She's not attached to them somewhere, is she?" I said instead. It wasn't necessarily a nicer comment, but at least I had amended it slightly.

"No," he said and waited for more because, knowing me and how I detested the woman, he knew there would be.

"Who's Gabrielle?"

"Gabby, appropriately named, is Audrey's gossipy friend from school. Lives in town," he answered, and I silently thanked God that Audrey lived states away.

"Oh." I realized it didn't matter and tried my best to

offer up something kind. "I suppose it was nice of her to send something."

"Pop would have hated it," he said soundly.

Glad to speak honestly, I admitted, "That makes two of us."

"Three of us, Lar." Finn put the arrangement down on the nearby end table and held my hand. "He never said it, but I don't think he liked her from the beginning."

"Hmmm...." I had picked up on that, too.

"He loved *you*, though," he said. "And that also makes two of us."

I smiled. "Why didn't you just send the flowers away like the rest?"

"I thought you might want to do the honors."

"You know me so well." I breathed out a small laugh.

"The delivery person is still in the foyer." He handed me the vase. "I'm gonna go see how Mom's holding up."

I took the flowers and, extending them as far away as I could, I walked toward the entry. Nothing would make me happier than proverbially showing Audrey to the door. Well...maybe drop kicking her out would be even better. I smiled and touched my wood bracelet, imagining my father-in-law belting out his larger than life laugh. He would have enjoyed the sight, too.

***

"Lara?" My husband's voice was tentative which, coming from a usually confident, strong man, made me nervous. "I need to...I need to get out."

I felt my breathing hitch and my body immediately tense. There had been a reason to be nervous. I should have known. His regular meds, coping techniques like meditation, and even little boy's hugs, wouldn't suffice for Finn during such an extreme life changing event. After the bourbon episode, he had done well for two days while meeting and greeting people. I am sure part of his performer persona helped with that. But with the actual funeral coming up the following day, he was going to break. I was afraid by the way he said he needed to get out, that a couple glasses of Kentucky's finest wasn't going to do it this time. And by looking at his tense body, I also knew a visit to a church, like he had done when Arinn was missing, wasn't going to work, either. It worried me. It worried me a lot.

"Fi—" I was bracing for another battle of "don't go."

"Listen," he interrupted calmly. But I had seen him calm before when his disguised body was at its most explosive. His next words, though, were different than I expected...different than I had ever heard before. "Come with me. Just...I can't be here— not with mom and the kids."

"You want me to come with you?" There was no camouflaging the disbelief in my voice.

His immediate reaction to his pain, this time, wasn't to try to protect or reject me by turning away. It was to include me. He was asking me to help him. It was what I had wanted all along. Internally, a little yippee! emoji was dancing around in my head.

He was stressed, though. So, his voice remained serious if not still tentative. "Yes. Can you do that? Do you want to?"

I placed my hands on his cheeks and drew my face close to his. Nodding my head up and down positively, I replied, "Yes." As his cheeks lifted slightly under my hands, I remembered a possible stumbling block to the plan. "The kids."

We had been fortunate over those couple of days to have so much family around that there were always a number of willing and wanting babysitters for Chance and Arinn. Finn's cousin, Summer, and her siblings even took the kids out for most of that second day. It was a true blessing. I didn't think Chance needed to be around the casket any longer than necessary, especially because we were sleeping just upstairs from it. Plus, both he and Arinn needed more attention than we were able to give them right then. My priority was Finn, and his was his mom and sister. And since Summer had babysat for us while we lived in New York, it was an ideal situation. But they were gone for the night.

"I'll watch them." Nola spoke from behind my back. When I swirled around to face my sister-in-law, propped against the wall that separated the foyer from the parlor, she continued, "Besides they're already asleep. Go, Munch." She called her brother by his childhood nickname.

Finn gave Nola an appreciative nod, and I shut my eyes in gratitude. She understood. As Finn's sibling, she had been witness to his PTSD symptoms longer than I had. She was the one he went to when our world had fallen apart and we had separated. She had been the one to get him through—back to his counselor, back to his meds. And she understood now what Finn needed and how she could help.

As Nola walked off, I pulled my gray thermal-lined coat out of the hall closet and threw Finn his warm, camel-hued hoodie. With both of us now more winterized, I asked, "You want me to drive?"

"You want me even more worked up?" He managed to put a half-smile on his face and touch the corner of my cheek with the back of his hand. "No. I need to. Wait here. I'm gonna make a call, and then I'll pull the car up."

Once we were in the car, I understood why Finn needed to drive. It wasn't pure machoism, and it wasn't to continue his everlasting teasing of my driving. It was because he needed the speed, the power, and the assertiveness, even if the dark roads were fairly empty. He needed to control something because he couldn't control his father's passing, and he couldn't control, at that point, his emotions. He was driving fast, but he was driving with precision and caution.

I didn't know our destination, and I didn't ask Finn. He hadn't said a word since the foyer, and I was okay with the silence. I was just glad he asked me along for the ride.

***

When we finally parked, it was at an indoor sports facility. The lot was empty except for a single steel-gray sedan. The light on the main sign was dim, but the lights in the building itself appeared to still be on. I immediately internally approved of what I assumed was the outlet for anger and grief—a workout that did not involve alcohol or distance from me.

As we approached the front door with a sign that said the facility closed fifteen minutes before, an older, balding man met us and welcomed us inside. "Finn, good to see you." He clasped my husband's hand soundly with both of his. "It's been a while."

Finn reciprocated the shake. "It has... too long." He nodded over to me. "Meet my cheerleader."

"Lara." I stuck out my hand to this stranger, who accepted it and offered his condolences to both of us.

"I'm sorry about your father."

"Thanks, Jonathan."

"We spent plenty of Little League days here with you boys." The elder man was obviously referencing Mr. Murphy and the days of Finn's youth.

An image of a young Finn, crooked baseball cap atop his head and a missing tooth smile, floated through my mind. It was one that brought warmth to my chest and a smile to my face. It was one that I imagined seeing of our own son in a few years.

"It helped that you were both coach and owner of this place. How's Nate?" Finn continued, but I could tell he was distracted, anxious, and wanting to be out of the conversation, no matter how old and dear of a friend this man was.

"Still coaching at U.K.," he replied.

"Chip off the old block." Finn was looking toward the artificial turf and sports nets.

With a "yeah," I could tell this Jonathan person recognized Finn's need to get on with his mission, too. "So, I'll let you go," he said. "The place is all yours."

"Thanks. Sorry for the last-minute call. But I think this is exactly what I need. The healthy thing I need." He emphasized the word "healthy" while looking at me.

As I nodded my head in silent agreement, the kind owner said, "No problem, son. You do what you like. The pitching machines are out. There are balls, bats.... Hit a homer for the good ole days. And when you're done, text me. I'll take care of the rest."

I thanked Jonathan as Finn absent-mindedly walked a little more into the facility. As the older gentleman exited, I couldn't help but wonder if it was little Finny Murphy who he had loaned his closed-for-the-night facility out to or the superstar country musician. I hoped that it was both because that was exactly what my husband was— a compilation of all kinds of wonderful things.

Finn set up the equipment, swung a bat around, and then looked at me sitting pretzel style on the sidelines. "You wanta hit or anything?" He was asking legitimately, but I could tell he was still so distracted.

"No, Cowboy," I answered. "I'm just gonna enjoy watching you."

Normally, I'm sure, he would have come up with a creative, sexy remark back to my seductive one. But the solemn reason behind our venture didn't warrant it. He needed to get out some aggression and pain.

Finn spent a good forty minutes or so crushing and slamming the baseballs with the bat. It was a sport that he never seemed interested in watching on television and didn't play as an adult. But it didn't appear that he had forgotten the skills learned in childhood.

When he got through the large bin full of balls, I

collected them for him as he ran some laps. And then he collapsed. Literally…on the ground. His feet seemed to wobble from beneath him as he sank to the turf. He had made it to where I had once again claimed my seat on the floor. So, I knew his crumpling was partially on purpose. I melded myself into his somewhat sweaty torso, and he broke down in rare tears. And I held on tighter.

When he finally let our bodies pull ever so slightly away from one another, he sloppily wiped the tears away from his beautiful gray eyes. "I'm sorry."

"Baby, there is absolutely nothing to be sorry about." His vulnerability made my own eyes teary. "You need to be angry. You need to be sad. You need to let it go. Thanks for asking me to share that with you."

"Thanks for coming with me."

"Always." And, I reiterated. "I always, always want to."

He wiped his eyes once again and then mine. "I know. I want that, too. I do. I get it. With you by my side, no matter how dark the moments get, there is light. It isn't as bad." He paused, partially because he was a natural performer but mostly because he wanted to emphasize something I already knew beyond any doubt. "I love you, Lara."

"You, too."

"Enough so I can have that dance?" I saw the spark start to reignite in his gorgeous eyes. "It helped before."

"I think you might be taking advantage of the situation, Cowboy," I teased but, nonetheless, stood up, taking his hand as he joined me.

We kissed, let tears lightly flow, and swayed more than danced. But it served the same purpose. We were together and our love was strong enough to battle any sadness.

***

We put off having Chance's birthday party until the beginning of February. The reason was two-fold. First, it would separate a little more time between his celebration and his grandfather's passing…a connection we didn't want in our growing boy's mind that year. Second, we could coordinate it, just like we had Arinn's birthday, with another event. Finn was going to be performing at the Grand Ole Opry. He had mixed feelings about keeping that commitment since it would be his first live show since his father's passing. But it was an honor just to play on that stage. Plus, his family would be in town for the birthday party and would be able to attend. And, I had shamelessly pleaded with him. Not being able to turn any of those things down, especially me, he agreed. Little did he know just how big of a night it was going to be.

Finn was going on stage a little after eight p.m. Unfortunately, that was also around the kids' bedtime. They had been in the historic building with us for hours. So, they weren't necessarily the most cooperative of souls as they said good-night to their dad in the large, cozy family area right behind the stage, and I led them back to Finn's dressing room to stay with Shelly.

I knew the Opry was a live radio show. So, timing was everything. But I wanted to see my husband before he stepped onto the stage. It meant something to me, and I believed it did to him, too.

"Hold! Hold! Hold!" Finn called out as I rushed to his side in the wings of the stage.

"Go! Get on stage!" I encouraged, realizing I was holding up the production.

"It's okay. I want that good luck kiss. Can't believe *you* were late. That's a role reversal." Finn, the proverbial nonchalant master of being tardy, laughed.

"Shelly's not used to kids." I ignored the joke and replied with honesty about his older, energetic assistant.

Stocky, silent Hawk, who was kind of standing guard beside both of us, joined in the banter. "Those stilettos certainly don't scream mommy material."

"Hawk…." I shook my head.

But it was true. Shelly was our only option that night. I wanted to be with Finn. But I wasn't ready to trust a babysitter. And everyone we knew was either in the audience or part of the crew.

"You want me to check?" Hawk offered.

"Neh," I replied. "I appreciate it, but it's all good now."

"What happened to that kiss?" Finn interjected with a smile I was glad to see.

Sliding my body up against my husband's, I placed my hands on his behind and tilted up to meet his mouth with mine. "Can't wait to see the show." I straightened his solid black shirt that I picked out for the occasion. "Have fun. I love you."

When Hawk coughed and we could hear the audience begin to murmur, Finn said, "Love you, too." and gave the motion sign for the band to begin.

Although I could have watched the performance from the special family seats located on the stage itself, I didn't want to see the back of the band and him, I wanted to be able to meet his eyes. Therefore, I quickly made my way to where Reese, her husband Roger, Mrs. Murphy, Nola, Will, and Kelsea were seated about four rows back to the left of the stage. There was an open aisle directly in front of us so Finn could easily see all of us.

I had never been to the fairly intimate setting of the Grand Ole Opry. But, of course, Finn had. He had gone first as an audience member and then as a struggling artist. And then he got his break as an opening act and did some volunteer work for them. Whenever it fit into his schedule, he liked to return. With us now living in Nashville permanently, an increase in the frequency of his appearances was much more likely.

I liked watching Finn perform in front of a live audience. It had been a while since I had gotten that chance. I didn't go on tour with him the past summer because Arinn was too young. And since then, our lives had been pretty much turned upside down. I forgot how energized and involved he got with each and every crowd, whether it was a professional sports stadium, a practical corn field in the middle of nowhere, an auditorium, or the Grand Ole Opry. He treated each of them like it was his first time. And I swear, sometimes, despite the ramped-up volume of screaming fans, Finn Murphy was having the most fun of everyone.

But my husband was a perfectionist when it came to his craft. There had been times when he would get completely frustrated because the guitars weren't strung right or someone in the audience was not being appropriate. He was the hardest on himself, though, if he thought his voice was off or when he, on rare occasions, forgot a lyric.

That's why I felt so bad about what I knew was going to happen. Finn, for sure, was going to be initially upset. But then the real reason I had insisted on coming would soon become apparent. It happened in the middle of him performing "Lara's Song" —the song he had written for me before we were even engaged. He was standing on the sacred wood circle in the front of the stage. Behind him was the magnificent all red backdrop with the Grand Ole Opry and WSM radio signs. Besides some soft lights illuminating the band, there was only a single spotlight shining directly on him. Since the first note and lyric of that song, his eyes had not left mine. There had only been one other time I remembered it being so intimate, and that was years before in Baltimore. I hated the attention, but I kept my eyes on my husband's, knowing that everyone else's were on us.

Then his voice started to crackle. He paused, looked to the band, looked to the mic, and tried again. But, once again, his voice was dipping in and out because the microphone was dipping in and out of power. With a swish of his hand, he cut the band off and spoke to the hushed audience without the use of the faulty mic.

"Sorry, folks, for sounding a little Peter Brady 'Time To

Change' here," Finn apologized in good humor.

I laughed right along with most of the audience who caught the *Brady Bunch* reference. At least Finn appeared to be taking it in stride. I tried to catch his eyes to see how the person behind the performer was feeling. But it was to no avail. First of all, he had in his performer green contacts that his label insisted on. And second, he was walking off toward the side of the stage.

"Can somebody see about this mic?" I heard him call out.

Danny Roth, a fellow country artist, came out with his mic. "Here try mine," he said loudly. "Your wife deserves a better serenade than that. In fact, you should do it a cappella." Danny made a point of looking at me.

Finn's head bounced back in astonishment at seeing Danny, who was not on the list to perform that night. "Danny Roth, ladies and gentlemen." Finn acknowledged, not missing a beat.

Danny nonchalantly nodded toward the audience and stepped off to the side. And then Finn, with new mic in hand, reclaimed his spot on the wooden circle. Taking Danny's challenge, Finn motioned for the band to rest. He once again found me in the audience and gave me a look like "here we go again." My stomach actually began to lurch in anticipation.

When Finn went to sing into the microphone, a booming voice came out of the main speakers. "Finn Murphy, the Grand Ole Opry is delighted to invite you to become our newest member."

I think it took Finn a second to a) realize that it wasn't another microphone malfunction, b) figure out where it was coming from, and, most importantly, c) what the message was. The undeniable look of bewilderment was scripted all over his face. It was when Danny once again stepped next to him, that I think things started to register.

"What? What? Really?" We could all hear him now because every mic was working properly.

The audience was on their feet, erupting with applause and a few hoots and hollers. I was on my feet, too. My hands were trying to clap but they also had the task of drying my eyes. Watching him in the midst of having one of his career dreams come true was almost overwhelming.

I remembered back in his college band days telling a bunch of us that he was going to be in the Grand Ole Opry. Of course, most of us laughed. I hadn't even known what it was besides maybe something that seemed like it should be on an old *Hee-Haw* rerun. Finn had laughed right along with us because, even for the best musicians, it was a rare accomplishment. He had also talked about the Opry a few times over the course of our marriage, but it was more out of admiration for those who were on the famous golden plaque wall. I don't believe he ever truly thought his name was going to join theirs.

Once he gained his bearings and accepted Danny's congrats, Finn looked at me. "Did you know about this?" I read his lips more than heard the actual words.

I shrugged my shoulders. Of course I had. And Reese had known. We hadn't known for long, but the powers-that-be wanted our input on how to make it special, and to make sure, of course, that we attended. It had been hard to keep any kind of secret from Finn because I was beaming with excitement for him but also, of course, because of our no-omissions policy.

He hopped off the front of the stage. If all eyes weren't on us before, they definitely were then. He didn't care, though. He beelined directly to our family pew of seats and kissed me sweetly for a good few beats. It was a far cry from the normally intensely private man when it came to his personal life.

"I'm so happy for you." I spoke with honesty and then added some sarcasm. "Even if you did botch up my song."

"I was *not* going to botch up your song," he said solidly before giving his mom and sister a quick hug. "Although..." he turned back to me. "You know, after that trickery, I might just go up there and sing 'Roxanne.'"

"Don't. You. Dare," I warned. I kissed him once again and started pushing him away before the people around us grabbed out for more handshakes. "You have to go say thanks."

After Hawk assisted Finn back up to the stage, the newest inductee accepted congratulatory pats from the band. His family and I were able to watch it all legitimately live because considerate Roger agreed to be photographer and videographer for us that evening. It was much appreciated, as I could have never held a camera or my phone straight, I was so excited for Finn.

"Besides marrying my wife and having my kids, this is the most amazing…oh…" Finn started his speech and then seemed a need to catch his breath. "Oh, my God— The Grand Ole Opry," he said as if it was registering all over again in his brain.

He brought his hands to his knees and paused for a brief second before looking up to the ceiling. Clasping his hands together, he closed his eyes. It wasn't the ceiling he was thinking of. I knew that with the utmost certainty, and I closed my eyes along with him and held my mother-in-law's hand.

"If you know and love country music even in the slightest," he continued, knowing anyone in that audience was beyond "slightest." "If you know country music, you know what an honor this is. It's something as a little boy I dreamed about—the pinnacle of success in this field. Thank you. Thank you all so much. I really don't know what else to say. Thank you."

***

With two slumbering kids now tucked safely in the comforts of their own bedrooms and the rest of our family and friends in a nearby hotel, it was a red wine with hints of bourbon that Finn was pouring in the downstairs great room. The bottle was given to Finn by one his father's friends at the wake. And we knew it was perfect for the occasion.

"He told me, Lara." He spoke of his father as he sat next to me on the sofa. "When we were at their place, he said to me, 'one day when you get in the Grand Ole Opry, I'll be looking down on you. I'll be hollering the most.' It was like he knew—" He stopped mid-sentence and looked at me with sudden clarity. "He did, didn't he?"

"Finn...." I knew this conversation was going to take place. I knew it had to take place. I wanted him to know. I just wasn't sure how he was going to react.

He immediately recognized my hesitation. "I want to know." His voice was calming and reassuring. "I want to know that he knew I made it. That was my biggest regret on that stage."

He didn't need to tell me that. I knew the instant he had paused in the midst of his thank you speech and looked to the ceiling...the sky...heaven. And I hoped that what I would tell him would help bring him resolve.

"Baby, he knew," I confirmed.

His eyes, which were once again void of his performer's contacts, seemed to relax and glisten their unique gray. "You? Did you tell him?"

"The Opry wouldn't let me tell you about the induction. You know that. You know their rules and how they like to make it a surprise."

"Yeah."

"I wanted to tell you, Finn. God, it was eating me up inside. I was so excited for you. You'll forgive me that one omission, right?"

His lips on mine said he did. "Yeah."

"Yes, I told your Pop. He was bursting with pride. He even was in on the whole mic business."

"What?"

"He said you need to loosen up. Music is art, not science." I recalled the exact words my father-in-law had recited.

"Geez." Finn shook his head. "Pop…."

I gently tapped my glass onto Finn's. "To you and your Pop." When both Finn and I took the final sip of wine, I asked, "You ready for bed?"

"How 'bout we just stay here?"

I crinkled my brows at him. It was really late. We needed to get to sleep at some point because, no matter what, the kids would wake us up at the same early hour, and there was also a birthday party to have. Plus, our king-sized bed was much more spacious and comfy than the sofa.

"It all started for us on a sofa," my husband and best friend explained. "Blankies, bed bugs, our first kiss…it was on that sofa in college."

I smiled at his thoughtful remembrance and added my own. "And seven years later, we had a much better kiss on this very sofa. Vavoom," I added.

"There's no place I'd rather end our evening than to be snuggled up right here with you."

"You're right. This is exactly where we both belong."

New roads and memories await in the latest novel by Grea Warner – EVERY MILE, A MEMORY.

Check out a sneak peek of Maya's story – a woman trying to overcome a tragic loss who unexpectedly meets one of Finn Murphy's best friends.

EVERY MILE, A MEMORY

The empty, faux-wood bucket swung loosely in my hand. I was on a mission to find the hotel's ice machine located inconveniently, of course, in an obscure location on an opposing floor. But my real mission wasn't ice. In fact, I rarely put the cold cubes in my beverages. My real reason for the late afternoon search was to have a moment to myself.

We had been in the Keys for a little more than twenty-four hours. Although I loved the warmth and the relaxing, beachy pace, we had been together practically nonstop. But the thing was, I had become used to solitude and realized now I even kind of craved it.

A tall, built man, most likely around my age, was approaching in the otherwise empty hall. He was flanked by two children— a boy, maybe four years old, and a little girl who did more of a waddle than a toddle. I internally cringed, thinking that now I had to acknowledge them with either a generic stranger "hello" or one of those quick, fake smile deals. At least my peace and quiet wouldn't be interrupted that long.

And then it was...in the most violent kind of ways. The popping sound was quite recognizable and one that haunted my dreams on a regular basis. It was loud. It was deadly. And it was definitely near.

Just as startled as I was, the man, still many feet in front of me, grabbed the little girl in one of his well-defined arms and started at a quicker pace in my direction. But the boy didn't follow. He stopped mid-stream and turned toward the obvious gunfire.

See where Finn and Lara's story began in the first book in the Country Roads series.

A young woman content with her solitary life.

A rising country music star.

They were friends once ...until their lives took them down separate roads.

Now, years later, when a child volunteers his uncle to sing for a fundraiser, LARA FAULKNER realizes it is none other than her college pal, FINN MURPHY. As the two get a chance to reconnect, Lara reveals to a compassionate Finn details of her shocking past and the traumatic decision she had to make.

Through trust and love, the bond between Finn and Lara deepens as the country singer manages to get an emotionally scarred Lara to let down her self-proclaimed walls. But will secrets, lies, and tragedy cause a bumpy detour on their road to complete happiness?

ABOUT THE AUTHOR

There really wasn't any other path. Grea Warner knew from a young age that she wanted to write. She was born to write. First it was in diaries with little metal keys and in written tales that she slipped to friends in study hall. School newspapers, a college television drama, and internships in the soap opera world were next. After producing and writing a local show, she decided to delve into the world of the novelist. When her fingers aren't tapping out her latest book filled with angst and romance, Grea can be found hiking the trails or jamming to her favorite country artists on the radio.

Website: http://www.greawarner.com
Facebook: https://www.facebook.com/grea.warner.7
Twitter: @grea_warner
GoodReads:
https://www.goodreads.com/author/show/17230140.Grea_Warner

www.ingramcontent.com/pod-product-compliance
Lightning Source LLC
Chambersburg PA
CBHW022257190626
46812CB00014B/2198